WILDTHORN

Born in Essex, Jane Eagland taught English in secondary schools for some years. After doing an MA in Creative Writing, she now divides her time between writing and tutoring. *Wildthorn* is her first novel, inspired by true stories of women who were incarcerated in asylums in the nineteeth century. Jane lives in Lancashire in a house with a view of the fells.

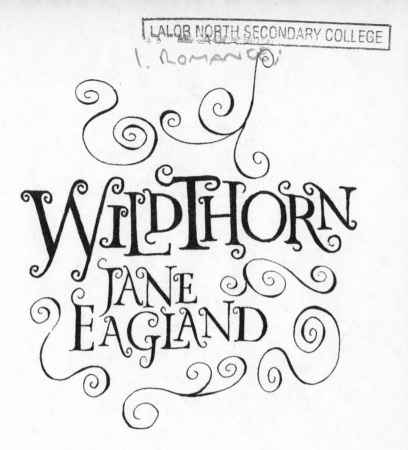

WILDTHORN
JANE EAGLAND

YOUNG PICADOR

First published 2009 by Young Picador
an imprint of Pan Macmillan Limited
20 New Wharf Road, London N1 9RR
Basingstoke and Oxford
Associated companies throughout the world
www.panmacmillan.com

ISBN 978-0-330-45816-0

1 3 5 7 9 8 6 4 2

A CIP catalogue record for this book is available from
the British Library.

Typeset by Intype Libra Limited
Printed and bound in the UK by CPI Mackays, Chatham ME5 8TD

For Sheila

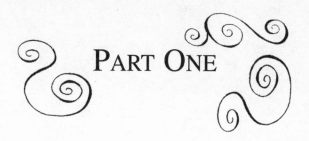

PART ONE

The carriage jolts and splashes along the rutted lanes flooded by the heavy November rains. Through its grimy window, all I can see of the unfamiliar Essex countryside are bare hedgerows, the skeletons of trees, looming out of the morning mist. I shiver and clutch my travelling wrap around me more tightly – the familiar roughness of its wool collar on my neck is comforting.

It smells in here – of damp, rotting straw and something else, like sour milk. Nausea rises in my throat, but I swallow it down and, despite the ache in my bones caused by a night on that lumpy mattress, I sit upright on the hard seat. Even if the bed had been the most comfortable in the world, I doubt I would have slept. But I won't let Mrs Lunt see how apprehensive I am.

Typical of Mamma to insist I have a chaperone. But I'm not a child any longer, I'm seventeen, and I travelled by myself before and came to no harm. I would have managed perfectly well on my own.

It's ironic, really, Mamma's concern – she didn't think twice about packing me off to live with strangers . . .

Perhaps it's because the journey is so long and we had to break it in London. But if I had to have a companion, why couldn't Mary have come with me? Or if she couldn't be spared, why couldn't they have engaged someone friendly? We could have grumbled together about the grubby rooms in the inn, and perhaps I could have confided in her.

I'd never tell this unsmiling woman anything. She makes me uneasy.

Her cloak is worn, her umbrella spotted with mildew, the bag she clasps on her lap shabby, but, in her pinched monkey face, her eyes are bold, inquisitive. And she has hardly spoken a word, not yesterday all the way down in the train from the north, nor this morning on the journey from Liverpool Street by rail and then this carriage. But she has never stopped watching me. Even without looking at her, I know she's watching me now.

Perhaps she's wondering why I've been sent away. It's unlikely that Tom has told her anything, I'm sure, except that she must see that I arrive safely. My brother would not want a stranger knowing our business.

How will these people, the Woodvilles, receive me? I know almost nothing about them, only that they have a charming son, whose mother wants a companion for her eldest daughter. 'Just remember,' Tom said, 'you should be grateful. They're taking you in as a favour to me.'

Taking you in. As if I were a vagrant, a beggar.

How long must I remain there, trying to be agreeable to this girl who will probably despise me? And will I have time for my studies? I wouldn't be surprised if Mrs Woodville really wants an unpaid governess for the younger ones.

It's Mamma's fault. How could she be so unjust?

This isn't what I planned for my life.

When I'm settled in I'll write to Aunt Phyllis and tell

her what's happened. I'm sure she'll have forgiven me for my rudeness by now. She might even invite me to Carr Head. Despite everything, that would be so much better.

As long as she doesn't know. As long as Grace has kept her promise.

We reach a crossroads and turn right. This lane is more deeply pitted, rocking the carriage from side to side. The trees cluster thickly here, deepening the gloom.

'Do you think it's much further?' I ask Mrs Lunt.

'Not far now.' She twists her mouth into a smile, but her eyes slide past mine.

The forest on one side of the lane is replaced by high stone walls stretching into the mist. Before long, the carriage jerks to a halt.

Looking out, I see that we have stopped by some tall iron gates. My pulse beats faster. 'This isn't the place, is it?'

Mrs Lunt nods.

The knot in my stomach tightens. This is far grander than I expected. But I tell myself, Keep your face smooth. Don't betray your feelings to this stranger.

A thickset man slouches out of the lodge, clamping a half-eaten crust between his teeth as he shrugs his shoulders into a crumpled jacket. He unlocks the gates. As the carriage passes he stares in, his jaws moving slowly. I'm surprised the Woodvilles don't have a smarter servant.

The gravel driveway winds through the grounds to an imposing house set on a rise, with an ornate roofline of turrets and cupolas. At the sight of it my heart sinks. Tom was right. The family must be very wealthy.

5

What will they think of me?

When we stop again my companion says, 'Here we are.' She's smiling again, encouraging. She opens the door and descends from the carriage, beckoning me to follow. But I shrink back, feeling a fluttering in my chest like moths trapped behind my breastbone.

I've made a mistake. I should never have agreed to this.

The coachman is unloading my box. Mrs Lunt has climbed the steps and is tugging at the bell. A tall gentleman in a frock coat appears in the doorway and speaks to her in a voice too low for me to hear. She passes him some papers from her bag.

What are those papers?

The gentleman comes to the door of the carriage and looks at me from under dark bushy eyebrows. 'You must get out now.' His voice is polite, but not warm.

He must be Mr Woodville, my new employer. Why is he not greeting me, welcoming me?

Something is wrong.

I hold tight to the seat, my heart bumping in my chest. Over my employer's head I can see, lurking in the doorway, a servant in shirtsleeves and a canvas apron, his arms crossed over his broad chest. Mr Woodville nods and the servant unfolds his arms and takes a step forward. Surely he doesn't mean to –

I will not be dragged from this carriage.

Somehow my feet carry me down to the ground. Next to me is a low railing surrounding the lawn. I could easily step over it, walk away across the grassy space, away from all these staring faces.

But I can't.

For a moment we stand, frozen, then Mr Woodville coughs and Mrs Lunt moves towards the carriage. I go to speak to her as she brushes past me, but without looking at me she gets in. The door slams, the wheels start to turn and she has gone, leaving me behind.

In the misty light a weight of stone looms over me, the house even more forbidding now I can see it properly.

Mr Woodville forms his lips into a bland smile. 'My name is Mr Sneed.'

Mr Sneed? Not my employer then. The butler?

He has a slight cast in one eye and I try not to stare at it, addressing myself to his necktie, neat between the points of his stiff collar.

'Will you take me to Mrs Woodville, please?'

He regards me gravely. 'Mrs Woodville? There is no Mrs Woodville here.'

My mouth dries.

'But isn't this her house?' Despite myself, my voice quavers.

'No, this is Wildthorn Hall.'

'*Wildthorn Hall?* But I'm supposed to be at the Woodvilles' . . . they're expecting me.' I look from Mr Sneed to the servant, then back to Mr Sneed.

He smiles again. '*We* have been expecting you.'

This is a horrible mistake. *But he said they were expecting me. How can that be possible?*

Blood drumming in my ears, darkness slides in at the edge of my vision.

A hand touches my arm and my sight clears.

'Please come with me.' His grip on my arm is firm.

I want to run, but my legs won't obey me.

I glance at my box.

'Don't worry – John will bring that in.'

I walk up the steps, past the stout, heavily studded door. In the porch I stumble on the coarse mat, but Mr Sneed's arm prevents me from falling. My feet carry me through the inner doors past twin suns rising in stained glass.

Inside, I find myself in a wide vestibule tiled in black-and-white diamonds that dazzle my eyes. A vaulted ceiling arches overhead. Directly in front of me is a set of tall double doors. The vestibule is empty apart from a polished table that holds an arrangement of wax flowers under a glass dome. The colours of the flowers have faded; they look pallid and damp, like flesh.

Mr Sneed presses me on. Our footsteps echo on the tiles.

We take a corridor on the right and the tiles give way to a narrow strip of green matting. After passing several shut doors we come to a halt outside another one. Mr Sneed holds up his hand. 'Please wait.' The door closes behind him, leaving me standing outside.

Now – now I must flee. Before it's too late.

But the burly servant, silent as a cat, has come up behind me and leans against the wall, watching me.

I hear a jingling noise and a young woman in a blue dress and an apron appears out of the gloom. A bunch of keys hangs on a chain from her belt. Under her white cap her complexion is sallow, as if she rarely goes out of doors.

Ignoring me, she nods at the servant, then knocks on the door.

Mr Sneed appears. 'Ah, Weeks. Come in.' The door closes behind her.

I can hear voices, but not what they are saying. Then the door opens again and Mr Sneed calls, 'Come in.' I hesitate and the servant shifts his position. I find myself crossing the threshold.

Immediately my eye is drawn to the elegant desk by the window, where Mr Sneed is standing looking at two or three pieces of paper lying on its polished top. He studies them, leaning down and frowning as if the writing is hard to decipher.

The young woman, Weeks, waits, her hands clasped in front of her, eyes cast down. The room is quite large, but it feels airless. I can't breathe. A distant ringing begins in my ears, making my head swim. I sway slightly.

Mr Sneed notices. 'Take a chair.' He gestures to one in front of the desk.

I sink on to it, clutching the arms. Don't faint. Whatever you do, don't faint.

Mr Sneed scrutinizes me for a moment with his one good eye, then feels my brow. His hand is clammy.

'You are very pale, Miss Childs.'

My head reels. 'What did you just call me?' My voice is as thin as tissue paper.

'Miss Childs. That is your name.'

Is this a trick?

And then my blood starts to flow again – they have the

wrong person. That's the explanation. It isn't me they're expecting at all.

'That *isn't* my name. I am Louisa Cosgrove.' I look from Mr Sneed to Weeks, waiting for them to exclaim, to show surprise. But Weeks's expression doesn't change.

Mr Sneed sits down at the desk and leans forward. 'You only think you are Louisa Cosgrove. But we know who you are. You are Lucy Childs.' His manner is kind, as if explaining the situation to a child.

I stare at him bewildered. They are mistaking me for someone else – this other girl. I swallow hard. 'Why would I *think* I'm Louisa?'

'Because you're ill.'

'*Ill?*' I am utterly confused.

'Yes, this is a hospital.' He pauses. 'Or you might prefer to think of it as a refuge – a place of safety, my dear young lady.'

I don't understand what he's talking about. But I do know one thing: I'm not ill. This other girl, this Lucy Childs, she must be ill, and that's why they're expecting her. Her, not me. I explain all this in a loud, clear voice.

Mr Sneed smiles. 'Thinking you are someone else and thinking you are not ill are signs of how sick you are. You are lucky that you are here where we have the skill to cure you.'

He would be looking at me directly if it weren't for the squint. 'You are clearly an unusual young woman. But here you will find we are used to dealing with the unusual. You will soon settle in.'

Unusual? What does he mean?

He turns to Weeks. 'Miss Childs seems quiet enough at the moment, but we need to keep her under close observation. We will try her in the Second Gallery for now.'

He glances at me. 'Fanny Weeks is one of our most able attendants. She will look after you.'

I look at Weeks, wanting some reassuring sign, some hint of pity. But she says, 'Come with me,' in a flat voice, and stands by the door, holding it open.

I look at Mr Sneed. I should say something. 'I . . .' But my voice dies.

Weeks coughs and gestures with her head. Under her neat cap her hair is as dark and shiny as liquorice. I find I have risen from the seat, we are outside the door and Weeks has turned the corner and set off along the long corridor. I want to ask her what illness she thinks I have, but she's moving too fast.

The corridor ends at a door. Weeks selects a key so large it takes both her hands to turn it. The door swings open, we pass through, and Weeks locks it behind us. Another corridor, this one so gloomy the gas jets are lit. Now we're walking on bare flags; the *tap tap* of the attendant's shoes echoes on the stone but I can't hear my footsteps at all.

I try one more time. 'Do stop! This is a mistake. I shouldn't be here.'

But the blue back moves ahead of me relentlessly. Powerless to make her turn, I'm forced to follow her until I'm lost, trapped in a maze of passages and locked doors.

Eleven Years Earlier

Evelina had light brown hair, formed into perfect ringlets. Her cream, lace-trimmed dress, her cream bonnet edged with a frill, her white silk stockings and cream kid boots – all were immaculate. She had a red rosebud smile but her complexion was slightly yellow; her staring black eyes, fringed with stiff lashes, never shut.

She arrived on my sixth birthday, in a parcel addressed to me: *Miss Louisa Cosgrove*.

When I saw it, I was very excited: I'd never had anything in the post before. Inside the brown paper was a box on which someone had written *My name is Evelina*. I opened it and drew out the doll. Everyone was watching me, waiting for a reaction, and all I could do was stare at it.

Papa said, 'You're a lucky girl, Lou. How kind of your Aunt Phyllis to send such a lovely present. She says that Grace helped her choose it.'

I raised my head in time to catch Mamma giving Papa a look I didn't understand. 'Such an extravagance . . .' She turned to me and said, 'It is a lovely doll, but it's too good for every day. I'll put it away safely.'

I was about to protest, but I looked at Evelina again. She was so grand. Not like my old rag doll, Annabel. I could hug *her* soft body without worrying about spoiling her dress. Her homely face was nearly worn away where I'd kissed her and cried on her. I could tell her all my secrets. Evelina's smile was perfect . . . and lifeless.

12

Thinking this, I felt guilty. Although she was somewhat older than me and I hadn't met her often, of my three cousins I liked Grace the best. Her brother William seemed nearly grown-up and her little sister Maud was too young to interest me, but I admired Grace very much. For her sake, I should try to like this new doll.

But then Tom said, 'Evelina! What a soppy name. Still, it suits a soppy useless doll.' He rolled his eyes and simpered in imitation of her expression and Mamma frowned.

But it was Papa who spoke. 'That will do, Tom. It's a very nice doll.'

Papa might say that, but I had an uncomfortable feeling my big brother was right. For his tenth birthday, Aunt Phyllis had sent a folding penknife with a mother-of-pearl handle, two blades, a corkscrew and a pair of scissors. Compared to that, what use was a doll?

Not for the first time, I wished I was a boy. My brother had toy soldiers and a train set, and when we visited our cousins at Carr Head, he was allowed to climb trees and go fishing and swimming in the river. And Mamma expected me to wait on Tom and fetch things for him. It wasn't fair.

It happened one evening a few weeks later. Papa had been called away to a patient, but the rest of us were in the parlour. It was cosy in the light of the oil lamps with the fire flickering: like being in a warm, red cave. It was peaceful too. Mamma was sewing up the hem of one of my frocks. I'd caught my foot in it when I'd been playing at railway-train crashes alone in my room, but Mamma didn't know that. Because she thought I'd been good, she'd brought Evelina down for me, having checked that my hands were clean. But I was itching to join Tom, squatting on the

 13

carpet in front of the brass fender, shooting marbles. I knew Mamma wouldn't approve, though.

The doorbell rang and a minute later Mary appeared to summon Mamma. With a sigh, she put down her mending.

As soon as she left the room, I said, 'Let me play, Tom. I know what to do.' I'd been secretly practising, doing it the right way, with the thumb, just as Tom said.

'Pooh, I doubt it. Girls can't play marbles.'

I glared at him. He was always saying things like that. 'Well, I can. Look, I'll show you.' And I joined him on the floor.

When Mamma returned, Tom and I were in the middle of a fierce argument.

'I hit it, so it's mine,' I said.

'No you didn't,' said Tom.

'I did.'

'Caw, caw, Miss Beaky!'

Tom knew that nickname annoyed me. He always said my nose looked just like a crow's beak.

'That will do!' said Mamma. 'If you can't play without squabbling, the marbles will be put away.' She didn't come back to her seat by the fire, but went over to her writing desk and started sorting through some papers.

She hadn't forbidden me to play marbles so I seized the disputed one, with a triumphant glare at my brother. Tom frowned but, glancing at Mamma, he didn't say anything. I knew he was angry, but I didn't care. At least he wasn't ignoring me.

We played on in silence until at last Mamma closed the bureau lid. 'Time for bed, Louisa. Make sure you pick up all your toys.'

We started gathering up the marbles. I'd given up arguing

14

about the unfairness of having to go to bed before Tom – I knew that Mamma would say: 'When you are ten, like Tom, you can stay up longer.'

'What is your doll doing on the floor, Louisa?' Mamma's tone was sharp.

I started guiltily. I'd forgotten about Evelina. I picked her up. And then I saw it.

'Oh!'

'What's the matter?' Mamma bent to look.

One side of Evelina's face, the side that had been nearest the fire, had melted: from the corner of her eye, her face sagged in folds, her red cheek had slipped and her mouth was distorted into a grimace. Tom pushed in to look and I pressed Evelina to my chest. I didn't want him to see.

There was a horrible silence.

Mamma said, 'Oh, Louisa, how could you be so careless! The doll is ruined. And it was so expensive.'

She prised the doll out of my arms. Studying its face again, she shook her head. Then she said, more to herself than to me, 'What will your aunt say?'

I started to cry. I didn't want Aunt Phyllis to suppose I was ungrateful. And what would Grace think of me?

Through my sobs I watched Mamma, waiting for her to pronounce sentence.

At last she said to me, 'Go to your room and wait for me to come.'

As I went past Tom, unseen by Mamma he stuck his tongue out at me, gloating.

In my bedroom, I waited for Mamma. She came in looking grave, but she didn't mention Evelina. I undressed, washed and put my nightgown on while Mamma watched. I said my prayers and climbed into bed, then waited to hear what my punishment would be.

'Tomorrow you will stay in your room. You can contemplate what your thoughtlessness has led to and resolve to be more careful in future.'

I let out my breath. Not too bad.

Looking at me sadly, Mamma said, 'Goodnight, Louisa.' She didn't kiss me.

As soon as we were alone, I told Annabel what had happened.

'It's that stupid doll's fault. Fancy being made of wax.'

I kissed Annabel's dear cloth face and hugged her until I fell asleep.

I stared at Evelina. Her black eyes, unblinking, stared back at me out of her ruined face. I sighed. What would Grace say if she could see her?

To distract myself from my uncomfortable thoughts, I looked in vain about the room for something to do. Then my eyes came back to the bed where Evelina and Annabel lay side by side.

'Aren't you glad you don't have to wear a lacy dress?' I said to Annabel. 'It would be so hard to keep clean.'

She smiled back at me.

I turned to Evelina, an idea forming in my mind. Papa had told me about scientists, people who asked questions about the world and investigated it to find out what it was like. I could be a scientist and find out what Evelina was like.

Picking the doll up, I untied her bonnet and laid it down. Then I started to examine her dress. It was fastened with tiny

16

hooks and eyes. I undid them and pulled off the dress. She was wearing a pair of cotton drawers. I took those off too. Her body and the tops of her arms and legs were made of cloth, stuffed with something soft.

'She's just like you underneath,' I told Annabel.

The bottom halves of her arms and legs were made of kid leather, like my best shoes. I studied her face. Where the wax had melted I could see something else underneath. I looked round the room. I needed a knife. Tom's penknife. He wasn't allowed to carry it about with him, so it must be in his room.

I opened the door and listened. I couldn't hear anything. As fast as I could, I tiptoed along the landing, into Tom's bedroom, and opened the drawer where he kept his treasures, all jumbled together. The knife was there, half hidden under a magnifying glass and a lump of sealing wax. I seized it and ran back to my room.

My heart was thudding and I had to wait a moment until my hands felt steady. Then I opened the knife carefully. I picked up Evelina and laid her on top of my chest of drawers. I hesitated: it seemed cruel to plunge the knife into her head but I told myself not to be silly.

'I don't love her like I love you,' I said to Annabel. 'And Papa said scientists have to be bold sometimes.'

I put the tip of the blade against her forehead and pushed. It went in easily. I cut along above the eyebrows and down the right side of her face, making a flap which I pulled open. The wax was just a coating. Inside was a lining of papier mâché.

The eyes were glass balls. I pulled one out. It was like a marble. I extracted the other one too.

Having gone this far, I thought I might as well continue. I cut

 17

the arms and legs off at the elbows and knees, where the kid leather covering ended. Next, I split open the body from top to bottom. The stuffing started to come out, stiff and dark: I thought it was horsehair.

There was no more to see.

'Well,' I said to Annabel. 'What shall we do now?'

The door opened.

'It's time to wash your hands for – Oh, Miss Louisa! Whatever have you done?' Mary's shocked face peered down at me, and the remains of what had been Evelina scattered across my chest of drawers. I swallowed. There was going to be trouble.

'What did you think you were doing?' Papa looked at me gravely. He was sitting at his desk in his study, which was also his consulting room. The smell of tobacco smoke and medicines tickled my nose.

I wriggled uncomfortably.

Mamma had been speechless when she saw what I'd done. She'd stared at my handiwork while I waited for her to say something, my heart thumping like a drum. Eventually she'd looked at me and said very quietly, 'I don't understand you, Louisa. I don't understand you at all.' Her voice was like a grey shadow and I felt more frightened than if she'd shouted.

She'd left me sitting on my bed all day until Papa came home.

He was still waiting for an answer.

'I . . .' I faltered. 'I wanted to see . . .' I stopped.

'What?'

'I was being a scientist. I wanted to see how the doll was made.'

Papa had an odd expression on his face, as if he'd swallowed

something too quickly. After a moment he coughed and said, 'But you've ruined a very expensive present.'

'It was spoilt anyway!' For a moment I felt almost cheerful. And then I remembered it was my fault the doll was spoilt in the first place. I hung my head. Papa was hardly ever angry, but this was different. This was very bad.

'Louisa.' Papa's tone was quite unexpected. I looked up at him. 'What are we going to do with you?' He was shaking his head and almost – *smiling*?

I was mystified.

Papa coughed again. Now his face was serious. 'So – for your punishment . . .'

I waited, holding my breath.

'I think you should write a letter to your Aunt Phyllis, telling her what you've done.'

I swallowed. 'All of it?'

Papa nodded. 'Yes, every bit of it. You can write it now.' He stood up.

I thought of sitting at the big table where we did our lessons and trying to write the letter, with Tom watching me and laughing.

'Papa . . .'

'Mmm?'

'May I write it at your desk?'

He looked down at me for a moment, then patted my head. 'Yes, you may.'

I sat down in his chair with the carved wooden back. My feet didn't reach the ground. He pulled the silver inkpot towards me and put a piece of paper in front of me.

'Be sure to use your best handwriting.'

'I will, Papa.'

He went out of the study. I heard Mamma speaking to him in the hall and I tiptoed over to the door and put my ear against it. I heard Papa say, 'But it was just natural curiosity, Amelia, not naughtiness.'

Mamma replied, 'You're too indulgent with her, Edward. It's not good for her to think she can do as she likes.'

The parlour door closed and I couldn't hear any more so I went back to the desk. I stared at the three wooden owls on Papa's pipe-rack. They stared back. I dipped the pen in the inkpot and bent over the paper.

'Dear Aunt Phyllis . . .'

I sighed. This was going to be very hard.

Weeks ushers me into a high-ceilinged, narrow room with a stone floor. It has a row of windows like slits high up in one wall, and along the opposite wall are shelves stacked with linen. A musty smell pricks my nose, a smell of unwashed clothes and damp.

Weeks gestures towards a wooden bench. 'Get undressed.'

I stare at her, too astonished to speak.

'You must have a bath.'

'But I'm quite clean.'

Weeks frowns. 'It's the procedure.' She has a London accent but speaks in a strange, slightly affected way, as if she's trying to sound like a lady.

'But I'm not dirty. I—' I see the look in her eyes. She's not that much older than me – I am at least a head taller – yet she has some power over me.

My hands move of their own accord, taking off my gloves and my hat. I hesitate and Weeks nods at the bench where I lay them down with my wrap. I turn my back on her, unbutton my bodice and step out of my skirts. All the time, a small voice in my head is saying, Why are you doing this? You don't have to do this. But I have the feeling that if I don't do what I'm told, something bad will happen . . .

'All of your clothes, Miss Childs.'

She is not speaking to me.

She is speaking to me.

I undo my corset slowly, hook by hook. I've always hated its whalebone ribs but now I don't want to lose its protection. When the last hook is released, I hold the corset to me for a moment before dropping it on the bench. I take off my petticoats, unlace my boots and pull them off, then roll down my black stockings. When I have nothing on but my drawers and chemise, I stop.

'Those too.' Her voice is expressionless, but her eyes insist.

Naked, I turn at last, trying to cover myself with my hands. There is nowhere to hide.

'Give me your jewellery.' She's looking at my locket and my jet ring. I cover them protectively.

'Come, I must have them.'

'But I never take them off. They mean a lot to me.'

She frowns. 'All the more reason for me to keep them safely for you.'

I hesitate and she takes a step towards me. What is she going to do? Take them from me by force?

Reluctantly, I undo the clasp of the locket and slip the ring from my finger.

'And have you any money? Or a watch?'

I nod.

'I must keep them for you too.'

'What if I need some money?' My voice is too loud. It bounces off the walls.

'You may keep a few shillings. You don't need much money here, for there's nothing to spend it on.' Her mouth twists in a spiteful smile.

I won't be needing much because I won't be here for long.

I fumble at my gown, unpinning my watch. A gift from Papa. *Papa . . .*

Weeks takes the watch and my purse and counts out some coins. She lays them on the bench. 'When you need some more, I will give it to you.'

She doesn't know that sewn into the waistband of my gown are some folded notes, a precaution Mamma insisted on before I ventured out into the dangerous world.

'What about my box?'

'It's quite safe. If you want anything from it, you only have to ask.'

I stare at her. I don't believe her. I open my mouth to say something, but a shiver shakes me.

'You are cold, Miss Childs. Come for your bath.'

Under Weeks's watchful eye, I sit in a few inches of greenish water and soap myself with carbolic. Afterwards I dry myself as best as I can on a thin towel the size of a napkin. Back in the room where I left my clothes I go to put them on but Weeks stops me.

'Your clothes will have to be marked with your name.'

I stare at her. 'But I—'

A flash from her dark eyes and my voice falters.

Don't antagonize her. You don't know what she might do.

She continues as if I haven't spoken. 'You'll get them back. In the meantime, you may borrow some.'

She hands me a set of underclothes then glances at the

watch fastened to her bodice by a chain. Her lips tighten. I try to hurry, my fingers fumbling with tapes and fastenings. With each garment, I feel stranger and stranger. Bit by bit, I am losing more of myself. Soon I won't exist.

At the bottom of the pile, I find a flannel nightdress and one pocket handkerchief.

Weeks goes to the cupboard and takes out a dark dress. Involuntarily my hand goes towards my gown, then I stop myself.

Don't give the game away. The money might still be safe.

The dress Weeks gives me is made of coarse cloth, linsey-woolsey perhaps. I draw it over my head, smell someone's else's perspiration. Whoever it was, she was larger than me; even buttoned up, the bodice hangs on me in folds, the high neck is loose, the sleeves flap at the wrists.

'This is too big.'

'Better that than too small,' says Weeks tartly.

She gives me a cap. I take it reluctantly – I hate having my hair covered, but I can see from her expression that I have no choice. When I've put it on, for the first time she gives a thin smile of approval.

More corridors. Through an open door comes the hiss of hot metal meeting damp cloth and I glimpse women wielding irons amongst piles of linen in a laundry. Next door, in clouds of steam, more women, red-faced and with bare arms, are thumping possers in vast coppers. The smell of carbolic follows us.

Another locked door. When Weeks opens it we are in a different world. A carpeted hallway stretches in front of me with wicker chairs set at intervals, pots of ferns between them. On one side is a row of doors, on the other a long stretch of windows overlooks the grounds. The silence is thick, as if everything is holding its breath. And then a sound shivers the air, a low keening from somewhere close by. The hairs rise on my neck but Weeks takes no notice. She beckons me towards a door. 'This is where you'll sleep.'

In the weak daylight I see five iron beds with neat white covers spaced out on the linoleum. They are all empty. If this is a hospital, where are the patients?

Above each bed is a shelf. Weeks gestures at the nearest bed. 'Yours,' she says coolly.

Mine. But I don't belong here. Now is the moment to speak.

But I don't. What is preventing me? I am caught up in events I can't control; it's like being trapped in a nightmare where you try to cry out but no sound comes out of your mouth.

With a touch on my arm, Weeks signals that we are to move on.

At the end of the hallway she opens another door. In this room, several ladies are sitting in armchairs or perched on wooden settles. It looks like a social gathering of the sort I've often attended with my mother. But something is wrong. These ladies are not talking or laughing – they are silent; their shoulders droop, their heads are bowed. Some gaze at the floor, others rest their cheeks on their hands. A

25

feeble fire sputters in the grate and from above the mantel-piece Queen Victoria's solemn face surveys us.

Weeks beckons me forward but a woman stands in my way. Her eyes are like the glass eyes of stuffed animals. There is nothing behind them.

An icy finger traces down my spine.

Something is terribly wrong.

'This is Lucy Childs, our new resident,' announces Weeks.

My voice spills out. 'I am *not* Lucy Childs, I am Louisa Cosgrove.'

Weeks doesn't react.

'I tell you, I am Louisa Cosgrove!' I grip the coins in my pocket, press their hard edges into my fingers.

Weeks frowns. 'Don't get excited. Otherwise we'll have to calm you down, won't we?'

What does she mean? I look round wildly. Who can I appeal to? No one is taking the slightest notice of us apart from a strapping woman in a blue dress who has risen to her feet. She must be another attendant.

'Where am I? What *is* this place? Why do you insist on calling me by the wrong name?'

Weeks sighs. 'Dr Bull, the visiting physician, will see you tomorrow. He will answer any questions you might have.'

'Tomorrow? Why can't you tell me now?'

As if I haven't spoken, Weeks looks at her watch and announces, 'Time for lunch, ladies. Miss Gorman, accompany Miss Childs and assist her, if necessary.'

With a quick anxious smile, one of the ladies moves to

my side. But I stand my ground. 'Why won't you listen to me? There's been a dreadful mistake—'

The other attendant moves surprisingly swiftly for her bulk. She thrusts her face towards mine. 'I'd be quiet, if I was you, Milady. *If* you know what's good fer you.'

She stares into my eyes, her own unblinking, like a toad's.

On the threshold of the dining room, I stop. I can't take it in.

Miss Gorman tugs at my gown and I sink down on to a bench beside her, staring around.

The cavernous room is packed. A sea of dark cloth, on which white caps float like gulls. Light shines down through the glass roof and the noise is magnified, echoing: the footsteps of the servants passing between the scrubbed tables with trays, the scrape of benches on the flags, the crash of crockery and, above all, voices – muttering, groaning, calling out, even laughing, a hard, wild sound, like the cries of seabirds.

A hand appears before me and slams down a bowl. A basket is placed on the table and the others scrabble for bread, tugging at the basket and squabbling. They cram their mouths, crumbs falling into their laps. I have no bread and now the basket is empty, but I don't want any. My stomach muscles are clenched, my hands are clammy. I'm struggling to keep control.

Stay calm. Don't let them see your fear.

I dip the wooden spoon gingerly into my bowl. Thin, greasy soup with lumps in it. I try a spoonful. The lump

27

turns out to be a piece of gristle. I spit out the gristle discreetly and slip it back into the bowl. I put down my spoon.

My head is starting to ring with the noise. I try to block out my surroundings, shut my ears to the unfamiliar voices I hear all around me, ignore the sucking and gulping noises.

A soft voice in my ear makes me jump. 'Do you feel unwell?'

It's Miss Gorman.

'You're not eating your lunch.' She puts her fingers to her mouth and her eyes widen. 'I hope I haven't offended you by mentioning it.'

'I'm not hungry.'

'You'll feel strange at first. Everyone does. Then you'll get used to it.'

She gazes at me earnestly. Close up, her watery twitching eyes make me want to look away.

'I won't get used to it. I won't be here long.'

She gives me a strange look then but doesn't say anything.

'What kind of hospital is this?'

'Don't you know?'

I think I do know now. But I want to be sure.

'It's an asylum. For the insane.'

My heart seems to stop, even though I think I have known it since the moment the carriage drew up at the door.

Suddenly Miss Gorman grasps my wrist and whispers,

'We are in one of the best wards. Be sure to keep your place.' She nods several times as if to underline her point.

I stare at her, my spine going cold.

'Don't you want your soup, dearie?' The voice comes from my other side. Bright eyes at my elbow, a leering smile, a hand reaching across me. I let her take it, and, guzzling it in a trice, she tries the same trick on someone else. But this patient, a plump woman, holds on to her bowl with both hands.

'Mine! Mine!'

The thief lets go, but the plump woman continues to roar. Others join in, banging their mugs on the table. Two attendants arrive and hurry the plump woman out of the room. Gradually the noise subsides.

My neighbour winks at me. Her hands are filthy, the bitten nails black. Her teeth are yellowed stumps, her breath smells foul.

I shut my eyes. This is a nightmare, it must be. Soon I'll wake up and everything will be all right.

Ten Years Earlier

It was Sunday morning, and Mamma was testing us on our scripture.

Normally I hated being in the parlour in the daytime: it was dark and stuffy, with its heavy velvet curtains and crimson walls. But today we had an audience: our aunt was visiting us. I was sorry that Grace hadn't been able to come – she had a cold – but she had sent me a letter.

While we recited the Commandments, Aunt Phyllis lounged on the sofa, the skirt of her lilac gown spread round her. Even in the gloom, her face was bright: she always seemed on the verge of speaking or laughing. She was such a contrast to Mamma, who sat stiffly on a hard chair, her pale face still and watchful.

I had just repeated the Seventh Commandment, and now it was Tom's turn again.

There was a pause. Tom flushed and shuffled his feet.

I felt a bit sorry for him, but also excited. He didn't know what came next, but I did!

'What *is* adultery, Mamma?' Tom asked.

He was playing for time.

Mamma shifted in her seat and glanced towards the sofa. Aunt Phyllis raised her eyebrows and the corners of her mouth twitched.

Mamma said, 'It's not something you need to worry yourself about now, Tom. When you are older, you may ask your father. Now, the next Commandment?'

I burst in, 'Thou shalt not steal,' and looked at Aunt Phyllis to see if she was impressed. She rewarded me with a smile.

Mamma, however, was frowning at me. 'Yes, that's right,' she said. 'You shouldn't have interrupted Tom though.' She looked at Aunt Phyllis again, almost apologetically.

Tom's elbow dug me in the ribs and I glanced sideways. He was glowering at me, but I shot him a defiant look. It wasn't my fault he hadn't learned his scripture properly . . .

When we had finished, Mamma stood up. 'Have you both got clean pocket handkerchiefs and a penny for the collection?'

With one eye on Aunt Phyllis, I showed Mamma my handkerchief and collection money, proud that I'd remembered to ask Mary for them.

Mamma sighed. 'Oh, Louisa, look at you.'

I put my hand over the dirty smudge on the frill of my best white dress. I'd been trying to teach myself to juggle, using my rolled-up stockings as balls, and they would keep getting under the bed.

But Mamma wasn't looking at my dress; she was frowning at my hair. Several strands were tickling my cheek; they must have escaped my ribbon, as usual. However tightly Mary screwed my hair up in rags at night, it had a will of its own and would never form the perfect ringlets I saw on other little girls at church.

Before Mamma could attack me with the hairbrush, Aunt Phyllis said, 'Come here, darling.'

She pulled me close, in a rustle of silk. 'You're tall for six. You'll be catching up with Grace soon.'

As her hand smoothed my hair, I breathed in her scent. 'You smell nice.'

'Louisa!'

 31

Mamma was shocked, but Aunt Phyllis's eyes crinkled with amusement. 'It's jasmine,' she explained.

She finished retying my ribbon. 'There,' she said, smiling.

I smiled back at her. Her hazel eyes were flecked with gold, just like Grace's.

'She has Edward's hair,' Aunt Phyllis commented to Mamma. 'As a boy, his was always wild.'

I was interested. I'd never thought about my hair in this way before. Mamma's hair was smooth, light brown. I looked at Aunt Phyllis's hair. It was nothing like Papa's mass of dark curls, but a rich colour, like chestnuts, with glinty bits of red in it. It looked as if it always behaved itself.

Now Aunt Phyllis said, 'Speaking of Edward, it's time he came out of his study, isn't it? We don't want to be late.'

We all set off up the hill to the parish church.

Usually I liked to walk with Papa, as Sunday was the one day he had some time to spend with me. He would point out interesting things as we went along and we would talk about important matters, like where the moon went in the day, and how rainbows were made.

But today I chose to accompany Aunt Phyllis. I walked as sedately as I could, my gloved hand in hers, stepping carefully on the cobbles to avoid getting mud on my best Sunday shoes. I couldn't help smiling to myself when Tom stepped in some horse-droppings.

I often found it hard to say awake in church. The vicar's voice droned and he used long words I didn't understand. Today I claimed my place at Aunt Phyllis's side and vowed to stay alert.

Standing so close to her, the fringes of her shawl brushed my

arm. I clutched my hymn book and sang out. During the prayers I bowed my head and shut my eyes tight.

I prayed, 'Dear God, please make me good. Please make Grace's cold better soon. Please let us not have mutton today. Amen.'

For once I didn't peek, even when Tom nudged me.

After lunch (it *was* mutton) we went to the door to say goodbye to Aunt Phyllis and she kissed each of us in turn, even Tom, who squirmed. Just as she was going, she deposited a small paper bag in my hands and another in Tom's.

Mine crackled enticingly; the contents felt knobbly.

'Don't eat them all at once or you'll make yourselves sick,' she said.

As soon as the clatter of the carriage wheels died away, I looked inside the bag. Miniature pear drops, strawberry pink and lemon yellow, with a dusting of sugar crystals.

'What have you got, Tom?'

He showed me his treat: acid drops.

In return I showed him mine, but he pulled a face. 'Pooh, girls' sweets.'

I went to take one from the bag, but Mamma's hand descended and caught hold of mine.

'Not on the Sabbath, children,' she said. 'Remember, it is a holy day.'

I looked up at Papa to appeal, but his eyes were on Mamma; he was shaking his head slightly.

Mamma flushed slightly. 'Yes, I know, it's kind of Phyllis, but I don't know what she's thinking of. It's so bad for the children to indulge themselves with sugar.'

'It won't harm them once in a while.' Papa was brisk.

Mamma pursed her lips, but she turned to us. 'Very well. I shall put the sweets in the sideboard and you may have some after tea, starting tomorrow.'

She took the bags out of our hands and carried them away.

All afternoon we took it in turns to read from *The Pilgrim's Progress*.

My favourite part was where Christian fought Apollyon. The idea of the foul Fiend, with his fishy scales, dragon's wings, bear's feet, and lion's mouth spouting fire and smoke always made my spine prickle delightfully.

But not today. The thought of the sweets burned in me.

That night I lay in bed, clutching Annabel. I was wide awake. I waited and waited until I was sure everyone had gone to bed. Then I tiptoed downstairs, my feet chill on the oilcloth.

At the dining-room door, I hesitated. It was dark inside, and smelt of furniture polish and sprouts.

I was shivering at my own boldness, but the sweets drew me on.

I felt my way along the wall until I reached the sideboard. I ran my fingers over it until I found the lion-shaped handle. Opening the door, I groped inside. Paper rustled under my touch. I plunged my fist inside and grasped a handful of sweets. The gaslight from the hall guided me back to the door and I was away, up the stairs as fast as I could go, my heart racing, one hand holding up the hem of my nightgown, the other clutching my prize.

Under the safety of my quilt, I relaxed a little.

I put one sweet in my mouth. Stowing the rest under my

bolster, I cuddled Annabel to me. The sensation on my tongue was sharp and I stiffened.

Tom's acid drops!

But he wouldn't notice, surely . . . I hadn't taken so many. What a pity. I would much have preferred my pear drops. Cheering myself up with the thought that I still had them all to come, I lay and sucked until the sweet dwindled to a splinter in my mouth.

As soon as I woke up I remembered the sweets. I didn't know what to do. If Tom knew I'd taken them, he'd be cross even if I gave the rest back. Perhaps it would be better to keep them and hope he wouldn't notice. But Mary would find them when she made my bed. I looked round for a better hiding place and finally settled on the doll's house I hardly ever played with.

After tea, Mamma opened the sideboard door. I felt a thrill of anticipation. Because my pear drops were smaller, I was sure I'd be allowed more, but Mamma put the bags in front of us and said, 'Just two.'

I seized two sweets and popped one in my mouth.

Tom was peering into his bag with a puzzled expression. He looked across the table, straight at me. I froze, the pear drop dissolving on my tongue. I could feel myself blushing. But he didn't say anything. Slowly, he put an acid drop in his mouth, his eyes never leaving mine.

When we were sent upstairs, Tom followed me into my bedroom and pounced. 'It was you, wasn't it, Lou? You've taken some of my sweets.'

He was pale with anger, his eyes boring into me.

My heart beat faster, but I stuck my chin out. 'No, I haven't.'

Tom frowned. 'You might as well own up. I know it was you. And it was a rotten thing to do. Didn't I give you a tin whistle just the other day?'

It was an old whistle he didn't want any more, but still, he was right, it was a rotten thing to do even if it was a mistake. And he was bound to find them. 'All right. I didn't mean to take them. I thought they were my pear drops.' I ran to my doll's house, and fetched the sweets. 'See, they're here. I only ate one . . .'

Tom snatched the sweets from me and inspected them. He seemed a little mollified, but he said, 'What would Aunt Phyllis think of you if she knew, Miss Goody-Goody?'

He still hadn't forgiven me for knowing the Eighth Commandment yesterday.

'I suppose you're counting on Papa to let you off, as usual. But I shall tell Mamma.'

'You sneak!' I launched myself at him, my fists raised, but he dodged me and ran from the room.

In the parlour, I stood before Mamma, hanging my head.

'You understand what you've done?'

I studied the pattern on the carpet: dark red and green triangles marching across the floor, converging on the black points of Mamma's shoes, the purple hem of her dress. She sounded more sad than angry.

'Look at me.'

Unwillingly, I raised my head.

Mamma's expression was sombre. 'You know that you've broken three of the Commandments?'

I was puzzled. I knew she thought I'd stolen the sweets,

although I'd only meant to take what was mine. But what else had I done?

In search of inspiration, I looked around the room. The china dogs sitting on the mantelpiece stared back down at me with superior expressions on their faces.

'Thou shalt not steal?' I ventured.

'Yes, and what else?'

I shrugged.

Mamma sighed. 'You've also coveted what was not yours.'

This wasn't true. I'd much rather have had my pear drops.

'And you have disobeyed me, for I made it quite clear when you were allowed to eat those sweets. "Honour thy father and thy mother".'

I could tell from her tone that this was the worst crime.

I shuffled my feet. 'I'm sorry, Mamma.'

Her face softened a little. 'Well, at least you're showing some remorse. But you know you will have to be punished, Louisa. You are old enough to know better now.'

A small worm of anxiety uncurled in my stomach.

She went over to her writing desk, opened the drawer, and took out a thin cane.

Cold fingers ran down my spine. Mamma had never used the cane on me.

'Please, Mamma. I *am* sorry. I'll never do it again, I promise.'

'I am glad to hear you say that, Louisa.' She looked at me sorrowfully and shook her head. 'I don't want to do this, but you must be taught a lesson. Hold out your hand.'

My hand trembled as I held it out to her, keeping my eyes fixed on the lithe thing quivering in her hand.

She raised the cane and brought it swiftly down. My hand

flared with sudden heat. Tears sprang into my eyes, and I bit my lip to stop myself from crying out.

I looked up at Mamma and her face was tight, as if something was hurting her too, but she still raised the cane again.

This stroke stung into the previous one. Instinctively I thrust my hand under my arm to deaden the pain. Through the blur of my tears, I saw Mamma putting the cane away. Furtively, I examined my hand. Two pink weals crossed on my palm.

Mamma took something from her pocket. 'I want you to put these in the kitchen range now.' Her voice sounded funny, not as firm as usual.

She placed a crumpled paper bag in my uninjured hand. My pear drops.

We went to the kitchen together, and Mamma watched while I threw my treasure on to the flames. Then she took me upstairs and helped me to undress, as I couldn't have managed one-handed.

Once I was ready for bed, Mamma produced a brown bottle and my stomach contracted. Rhubarb and soda. She was assuming I'd eaten *all* the missing acid drops, not just one, and needed a dose of purgative!

Tom must have eaten the rest. And I was the one being punished. It wasn't fair. But it was no good telling Mamma – she'd believe Tom, not me.

Mamma made me swallow a large mouthful of the horrid pink stuff. I gagged as it slid down. Then she stood over me while I knelt to say my prayers.

'I want you to say this today, Louisa. "Wash me clean of my guilt, purify me from my sins."'

I bowed my head.

'O Lord, wash me clean of my guilt . . .'

'Purify.'

'Purify me from my sins. Bless dearest Papa and Mamma.'

'You forgot Tom.'

I hesitated. Mamma frowned. '. . . and Tom. Amen.'

When Mamma carried the candle away, I couldn't hold back the tears any longer.

It was all Tom's fault. He needn't have told. Especially when he ate the sweets and I didn't.

And Mamma didn't love me. Would she tell Aunt Phyllis what I had done? Would Grace find out? She would think so badly of me.

I hugged Annabel to me and wept until her cloth face was soaked with my tears.

As soon as lunch is over, I look for Weeks. I won't stay here a minute longer. She must take me to the superintendent immediately.

I find her in the day room, where a few women are already engaged in embroidery or sewing; most are doing nothing, staring into space, withdrawn into themselves.

'What would you like to do? We have embroidery silks, or perhaps you'd prefer water colours?' Weeks is waiting by a tall cabinet, its bottom doors open.

This is absurd. I'm not going to waste time behaving as if I was at some ladies' sewing circle.

'I want to see Mr Sneed. I'd like you to take me to him now.'

'That's not possible.'

'Why not?'

She doesn't answer. Her black eyes glitter, seeming to say: *Just try to defy me.*

I can feel protest stirring inside me. This is so unjust. How can she simply ignore me?

But then it hits me like a blow.

The more I argue, the more they'll be convinced that I'm Lucy Childs, that mad girl. I must try to stay calm and prove to them that I'm rational, that I shouldn't be here.

Weeks continues as if I haven't spoken. 'What occupation would you like?' She's beginning to sound testy.

If I have to stay here a little longer, I might as well do

something to pass the time. But I can't see any harm in telling the truth. 'I'm useless at painting and I can't understand the point of embroidery. It's a waste of time.' Nothing mad about that. I look Weeks in the eye.

Tutting, she snatches up a length of material from a pile. 'Well, in that case, you'd better make yourself useful and mend this sheet.' She shows me the split in the middle, where it's thin. 'You have to cut this in half—'

'I know.'

I don't need to be told what to do. Mamma taught me how to cut a worn sheet in two, put the sides to the middle, and stitch it up again. I had to do this and other tedious tasks while Tom was allowed to play. *Tom.* Perhaps even now Mrs Woodville is writing to ask him why I haven't arrived . . .

Weeks thrusts the sheet into my arms, with a sour expression. 'Oh, well, if you know, you don't need me to tell you, do you?' As she gives me a pair of scissors, her eyes narrow. 'Make sure you hand them back to me when you've finished with them.'

Mechanically I start to divide the sheet.

I've got to get out of here soon. When they hear from the Woodvilles, what will they feel at home? I know we parted on bad terms, but they'll be worried. They'll all think something awful has happened to me. And they'll be right. But it'll never occur to them that I'm somewhere like this.

I look about me, seeing things I didn't notice this morning: heavy drapes at the windows; a piano in the corner, with some tattered sheets of music on it. *A piano* . . .

A face flashes before me, a fall of red-gold hair.

No, don't think about her. Look at the room: china shepherdesses on the mantelpiece, a canary singing in a cage. Homely things.

But this isn't a home. The shadows of bars fall across the carpet.

An asylum. For the insane.

But I'm not insane. So why am I here?

It's a terrible mistake. But as soon as I can speak to Mr Sneed, it'll be cleared up and I can leave.

The door bursts open and a girl wearing the blue attendant's uniform rushes in, breathless and red in the face as if she's been running.

'You're very late, Eliza,' Weeks barks.

The girl goes to speak but Weeks silences her with a wave of her hand. 'No excuses. If it happens again, I shall tell Matron.'

The girl, Eliza, gnaws her lip. She doesn't look very contrite.

She goes over to the table where an old woman, with her grey hair trailing over her shoulders like a child's, is sitting staring vacantly.

Eliza starts encouraging the woman to sort beads into their different colours. The old woman keeps sighing and wringing her hands but she finally achieves this simple task and Eliza claps her hands, saying, 'There now, look how clever you are.'

Weeks glowers across the room. 'Too much noise, Eliza. Come and supervise the sewing. And straighten your collar.'

Eliza frowns, grudgingly adjusting her collar as she changes places with Weeks. She seems about my age and hers is the first cheerful face I've seen here.

But it doesn't matter what the staff are like. I shan't be here much longer.

The shadow of the bars has crept into my lap when Weeks looks at her watch and says, 'It's time for your exercise now.'

We can't go till the other attendant, Eliza, has counted the scissors. She frowns, glances at Weeks, who is putting the beads away, and counts again.

'What's the matter?' Weeks's voice is quiet, chilling.

'There's a pair of scissors missing.'

Weeks is across the room in a second.

'How could you have let this happen? You're so careless.'

A flush creeps up Eliza's neck.

Weeks interrogates each of us in turn. With each denial, her expression hardens.

'Have you taken the scissors, Miss Gorman?'

Miss Gorman's face turns white then pink. Her eyes blink rapidly. She seems unable to speak.

Weeks barks, 'Don't deny it. I see your guilt. Give them to me at once.'

I can't watch this. I look down and there's the glint of the scissors lying half hidden under a chair.

They could be useful, but dare I?

For a second I hold my breath, then I cover them with my foot. No one has seen me; they're all looking at Weeks.

Miss Gorman's mouth is a frozen 'o'. Weeks puts out her hand and Miss Gorman shrieks, a tearing sound that jangles my nerves. She starts darting round the room, bumping into furniture, uttering wild cries, like a trapped bird trying to escape.

Eliza goes after her, catches hold of her and then puts her arms right around her. For a moment they struggle, then Miss Gorman sinks to the ground.

'There now, see what your carelessness has led to,' Weeks hisses at Eliza as she tugs on the bell-pull.

We stand round watching Miss Gorman, who gibbers and jerks like a puppet whose strings have tangled. Eliza chews her finger, looking miserable.

I can't bear it. 'The scissors are here, look. They fell on the floor.'

Weeks swings round. Her black eyes narrow suspiciously. 'You hid them.'

My legs are shaking, but I make myself look her in the eye. 'I didn't. I found them.'

At that moment the door opens and another attendant comes in, diverting Weeks's attention.

She makes Eliza and the other attendant haul Miss Gorman to her feet and they half carry her from the room.

After locking the cabinet, Weeks turns back to me, fixing me with her black eyes. 'Mind yourself, Miss Childs. You think you're so clever, but I shall be watching you from now on.'

'**K**eep your hands relaxed. Don't pull on the reins.' Papa's instructions floated across the paddock from where he sat on Midnight, Uncle Bertram's black hunter.

We were staying at Carr Head again. About once a year Aunt Phyllis managed to persuade Papa to leave his patients in the care of another doctor, and take a brief holiday. To entertain us, she organized various excursions: this time we had enjoyed a boat trip on the river and a picnic on the moors. But today we were staying at home and it was the best day of all.

When Aunt Phyllis had proposed riding for this morning, Mamma had tightened her lips. But she hadn't said anything.

Later I'd heard her arguing with Papa: she thought it was too dangerous and I certainly mustn't ride, it was unladylike.

But Papa had said, 'Lou has as much spirit as her brother, if not more. Why should she be thwarted?' Then he'd said, 'Don't worry, they won't come to any harm.'

Mamma never seemed happy when we stayed at Carr Head and briefly I wondered why. But then I forgot all about Mamma as Lady, the dapple-grey pony, moved easily beneath me, and I relaxed into her walk, breathing in the warmth of her coat, the smell of leather, aware of Grace watching from the fence.

I was always a little shy of her, but this holiday, even more so. She was nearly twelve now, only three years older than me, but in her dark green riding habit my cousin seemed elegant, grown-up. She had a new mysterious way of smiling, as if she knew things I didn't. It made her look beautiful, like the princess in Hans Andersen's story about the wild swans.

I sat up straighter, hoping she would notice me and approve of my seat.

Behind her stretched the park, an expanse of grass dotted with sheep and toffee-coloured cows. It was much nicer than the paddock, churned by hoofs, but it didn't belong to Uncle Bertram.

'Sit up straight, Tom. You look like a sack of coal. See how Lou is sitting beautifully upright.'

I flushed at Papa's praise but Tom scowled. He glanced across at Grace and I couldn't help sympathizing – I'd hate to be shown up in front of my cousin.

Tom was riding Chevalier, who belonged to Grace's brother, William. When I'd referred to the horse as 'brown', Tom had explained, with that new superior manner he had nowadays, that Chevalier was a bay, because he had a black mane and tail. He was rather big for Tom. Grace had warned Tom to keep Chevalier away from the other horses because he could be aggressive and would bite if he got the chance.

Tom seemed to be heeding her: he was keeping Chevalier several feet away from Lady but he hissed across the gap, 'There's no need to look so pleased with yourself, Miss Smug-Boots. Just because you're Papa's pet.'

Mindful of Grace, for once I didn't retaliate, but I wished Tom would be more agreeable. These days he seemed so distant, as if now that he was almost thirteen and going away to school soon, I was beneath his notice.

I sighed, thinking enviously of Tom's new box of mathematical instruments – the shiny compasses and the folding ruler, that

fitted so neatly into their red velvet grooves. They seemed like keys to an exciting world, from which I was shut out.

I sighed again and then put it out of my mind – it was a lovely day and I was determined to enjoy myself.

Still keeping my back straight, I glanced down at the riding habit Grace had lent me. It was her old one, too big for me, but I felt very proud. In my borrowed gloves and hat, I almost looked like a proper horsewoman. I would never look like my cousin though.

Every night before we went to sleep, she let me brush her long tawny hair; it was fine and smooth, unlike my dark tangle. Then we'd curl up together in Grace's big bed – 'snuggling' Grace called it – and talk.

The night before Grace had been telling me about William, who was away at school. He wrote her letters all the time. I couldn't imagine Tom bothering.

William was going to take over Uncle Bertram's business one day.

'Should you like to do that?' I'd asked.

Grace had laughed. 'Of course not. I shall be a lady like Mamma. I'll marry a handsome man like Papa and have a big house with servants to do all the work. We'll have lots of children and horses and dogs. What about you, Lou?'

This was easy.

'I'm going to be a hero.' I had been sneakily reading one of Tom's books, *Every Boy's Book of Heroes*. 'I wouldn't mind being an explorer and discovering a new country no one else has ever seen before. But what I'd really like is to be a scientist and discover a cure for – for typhoid or diphtheria.' These were some of the illnesses I'd discussed with Papa.

 47

Beside me in the dark, Grace had giggled. 'Oh, Lou, you are funny. You can't be a hero.'

'Why not?

'Because only men are heroes.'

I puzzled about this a long time. I was a bit bothered that Grace thought it was a funny idea. Why couldn't ladies be heroes? Perhaps they didn't want to be. In that case it was simple. Just before I fell asleep I made a decision: 'I will be the first lady hero.'

Papa's voice broke into my musings.

'Are you ready to try trotting?'

'Yes, Papa.'

Papa smiled his approval at me. 'Tom?

My brother nodded and we set off at a faster pace.

'Remember to rise with the motion.'

Once I managed to adjust to Lady's rhythm, I loved it. I was riding, really riding.

After a while Papa stopped and said, 'Have you had enough?'

'Oh no, Papa, not yet,' I said.

Tom narrowed his eyes at me. But he said, 'I'd like to carry on, Papa.'

'I'll join you,' said Grace leading her pony, Shadow, forward. Before Papa could help her, she was in Shadow's saddle, laughing. 'Why don't we ride into the park? Squire Chilsey won't mind. And Tom and Lou are more confident now.'

Papa looked dubious, but I said, 'Please, Papa,' and he gave in.

We set off, Grace riding beside Papa, me following, with Tom at the back.

In the park the grass was thick, still shining with dew. Every

now and then we rode into the shade under the chestnut trees spreading their candles above us.

Suddenly Tom's voice was at my ear. 'So, Miss Beaky, I suppose you think very highly of yourself. You're not afraid, eh?'

I pulled a face at him.

Chevalier dashed his head at Lady, who skittered sideways.

'Keep away, Tom. Remember what Grace said.' I patted Lady.

'Oh, I can handle Chevalier. You're not the only one who knows how to ride,' said Tom. He pulled hard on the reins.

Chevalier laid his ears back, rolled his eyes and lunged at Lady, nipping her neck. She shied and I lost my balance. The next minute I couldn't help screaming as Lady took off, galloping across the park.

Bumping up and down in the saddle, I clung to her mane, my teeth rattling. I shut my eyes but that was worse. I opened them again to see a high stone wall looming ahead of me. I hauled on the reins trying to make Lady turn. It was no use. We were at the wall. Lady's neck arched up in front of me, I clutched at her mane, missed, felt myself sliding back then falling, falling, sideways towards the ground that rushed to meet me.

'Louisa, Louisa!'

The voice seemed to come from far away. I opened my eyes. Papa's anxious face was bending over me.

I didn't want to move. Somewhere under me my wrist began to throb. 'It hurts.'

Papa gently raised me into a sitting position. He felt down my legs and arms. When he touched my wrist, I bit my lip hard to stop myself crying out.

 49

Papa said, 'Go back to the house, Tom, and fetch some help. You'd better run. We don't want any more accidents today.'

But Tom didn't seem to hear him. Shifting from one foot to the other, he was staring at me.

'Tom?' Papa spoke again.

Tom came to with a start. 'Is she badly hurt?' he asked anxiously.

'I don't think so,' said Papa. 'But will you hurry?'

With a last glance at me, Tom sped off.

Grace appeared, leading Lady, who was still panting. 'Is she all right?' she called out, tethering Lady to a tree.

She knelt beside me. 'Lou, I'm sorry. Lady has never done that before. Do you know why she bolted?'

I hesitated. It was Tom's fault, but I didn't want to sneak on him.

'No. I don't know what happened.'

A groom arrived and took charge of Chevalier and Midnight. Papa picked me up and carried me back to the house, while Grace and the groom followed behind with the horses.

Mamma ran out to meet us, with Aunt Phyllis following behind, restraining Maud, who was agog with excitement. When she saw me, Mamma went white. 'Oh, Louisa, what have you done?'

She gave Papa an anxious glance and he said, 'She's all right, Amelia. Nothing serious.'

Aunt Phyllis said, 'Well, young lady. I hear you've been practising jumping. Next time you must remember to stay with the pony.'

This made me smile but Mamma wailed, 'Next time! There

will be no next time, it's too dangerous. I've said so all along.'
She seized Papa's arm. 'Edward, I told you—'

'Hush, Amelia.' Papa gently disengaged his arm. 'Louisa is not badly hurt, but she needs attending to.'

'I'll help you then.'

Mamma gave me a wobbly smile, but I said, 'I want Aunt Phyllis, and Grace.'

Mamma's smile vanished, her face crumpling.

I felt a bit guilty, but she'd make too much fuss.

Papa carried me upstairs and sat me on my bed. While he fetched his bag that always travelled with him, and Grace poured some water into the basin, my aunt helped me out of the riding habit. When she took off the jacket, I winced and tears sprang into my eyes.

Aunt Phyllis smoothed my hair. 'There, darling. It will be all right.'

Papa returned. He examined my wrist. It was puffy and swollen. Papa was trying to be gentle but his slightest touch caused me pain.

'I think it's fractured,' he said. Then seeing the puzzled look on my face, he said, 'It means your wrist bone is broken. But because you are young, your bones are pliable. I may be able to push it back into place.'

I blinked at the thought of it.

Papa said, 'It will hurt. Are you ready?'

I could feel my heart thumping but I nodded. Heroes had to be brave.

Grace sat on the bed beside me. 'Here, Lou, hold on to my hand with your other hand. Hold as tight as you like.'

Papa sat on my other side and put his hands on my wrist. I

 51

made myself keep my eyes open because I wanted to see what he did. He pushed hard with both his thumbs. The pain shot, red-hot, up my arm. I shut my eyes and cried out, clutching tight to Grace's hand as if I meant to squeeze it in two.

'It's all right,' Papa said. 'It's done.' I opened my eyes. I couldn't see anything for tears.

'Can you let go now, Lou?'

Grace's face swam into view. I released her hand, which had turned white, and she rubbed the circulation back into it, with a wry smile.

Papa took a bottle of pink lotion from his bag and wiped some on the swelling. It was cool and smelt of peppermint. Then Aunt Phyllis held a splint against my wrist, while Papa wrapped a bandage tightly round it. Finally he made a sling so my wrist was resting against my chest.

'That's my brave girl.' He kissed my forehead. 'Now you must lie down and rest. You've had a bad shock.' He nodded at the others.

I raised my head. 'Papa, will I be able to ride again?'

He exchanged a look with Aunt Phyllis, who laughed. 'I expect so. Although it will take a while for your wrist to mend. Now try to rest.' They went out, Grace going last and giving me a little wave at the door.

I relaxed.

My wrist was very sore but I didn't care. If Papa said I might ride, then Mamma could be ignored.

I thought about Lady with her soft grey nose and sensitive mouth and imagined I was on her back soaring over hedge after hedge, while Grace applauded.

Our exercise takes place in what Weeks calls the 'airing court'. After the stifling atmosphere of the gallery, it's cold – raw – outside and I pull the threadbare cloak I've been given more tightly round me and stand for a moment, breathing in the fresh air.

I feel guilty about Miss Gorman – I should have given up the scissors sooner. But it's no good thinking about it . . . I must think of myself and how I can get out of here. If I don't see Mr Sneed soon, and explain this dreadful mistake, I might have to try something else.

I set off along the gravel path, my eyes darting about, scanning everything, looking for ways to escape. The airing court is square with high walls. Too high to climb over.

I walk on, passing shuffling figures. An old woman comes to a standstill and calls out, 'Oh, help me, do. My legs are turned to glass. They are breaking.'

I feel a pang of pity for her, but what can I do?

Across the court, a commotion breaks out. A gardener has been digging over a flower bed, but now one of the patients is tugging at his elbow. Weeks pulls her away. I hear the patient's high voice protesting, 'But it's Alfred come to visit me. Let me speak to him.'

Weeks says something to the gardener. He scratches his head, shrugs and pulls his fork from the soil. As he goes past me, I smell a whiff of beer and tobacco.

At a barred iron gate in the wall, the gardener takes a key from his pocket and unfastens the padlock. I move closer, but he is already through, locking the gate behind him and walking off into the park. He nods at two attendants hurrying towards the building. They don't come to the gate but pass by, ignoring me.

Without touching it, I examine the padlock. It looks heavy, the clasp as thick as my finger. With a sigh, I stare out through the bars at the khaki-coloured grass, the bare trees. Growing up the wall close by there's an ancient wild briar, its trunk gnarled and twisted. Perhaps it's one of those that gave this house its name. Some of its branches are pressing against the iron bars, as if the thorns themselves are conspiring to hold me in here.

Despite myself, my eyes blur with tears.

A shout makes me look round. A patient with a paper crown on her head is approaching, trailing a shawl from her shoulders. She sweeps me out of her way, waving a piece of paper, and as she passes she calls out, 'A letter from Mamma. Her Majesty is quite well.'

I wipe my eyes and give myself a shake. It's no good giving way: I must be strong. I look round the perimeter, examining the walls carefully; there are no other gates, but the mention of a letter has given me an idea.

A voice at my ear makes me jump. 'You are not walking, Miss Childs.'

It's Weeks, carrying a handbell by its clapper, so that it makes no noise. She's standing close, too close. Her eyes narrow to splinters. She grasps my wrist. 'Be careful, Miss Childs, be very careful. Remember – I'm watching you.'

Her fingers are like claws of steel. Then as if nothing has happened, she releases me. 'It's time to go in now.' She moves away from me and starts ringing the bell.

On the threshold, I stop and take a last breath of air. I can still feel the grip of Weeks's fingers and when I turn my wrist over there are red marks on my skin.

After supper I'm relieved to see that it's Eliza supervising us in the washroom. After I've waited at the end of the queue a long time, she beckons me to a vacant sink, stained with a brown deposit. When I turn on the tap, black hairs float up from the outlet pipe.

What am I doing in a place like this?

Avoiding the hairs, I cup water in my hands and splash my face. A cold shock.

As I'm drying myself, Eliza says quietly, 'Thank you, Miss, for handing over the scissors. Most patients would've kept them. Then I'd have been in trouble all right.'

I look round. Everyone else has gone. 'What would have happened?'

She shrugs. 'Don't know. Weeks would've probably sent me to another gallery.'

'Would you mind that?'

Her eyes go big. 'Of course, Miss. Despite Her Lady-ship, I wouldn't want to be anywhere but here. 'Cept the First, of course, but there's small chance of that.'

'Eliza, do you know what's happened to Miss Gorman?'

She glances towards the door then says in a low voice, 'Solitary.'

'Solitary?' I don't understand.

'Till she calms down.'

'Is she – is she locked in?'

Eliza nods. 'Course.'

I go cold at the thought of it. 'Do you know when she might be back?' I feel uncomfortably responsible for what has happened to her.

Eliza shrugs. 'If she comes back.'

Her words send a shiver down my spine. 'What do you mean?'

She looks round before saying in a low voice, 'Weeks might not have her back.'

'But where will she go?'

'To another gallery.'

Be sure to keep your place.

I've got to get out of here.

'Eliza, I need to see Mr Sneed urgently. Is there a way? Weeks won't listen.'

Eliza snorts. 'You're wasting your time, talking to her. The best thing to do is to ask Dr Bull tomorrow.'

'I see. And there's another thing – can you tell me how I can send a letter?'

'Ask Weeks for paper and an envelope tomorrow. You'll have to pay for it.'

It's all right. The coins are safe in my pocket.

Eliza leans closer to me and says quietly, 'You'd better give me the letter to post.'

We both jump as Weeks's face appears at the door. At

the sight of us, she scowls. 'Hurry up, Eliza. It's time Miss Childs was in the dormitory.'

I'm just about to get into bed when Weeks comes with a glass containing a colourless liquid. Before I drink it, I smell it. 'Chloral!'

Weeks's brows lift in surprise, but her black eyes give nothing away.

It's like recognizing an old friend. Immediately I'm back in Papa's study, hearing his voice: *You need to be careful with this one, Louisa, it's a powerful sedative. Four drachms to half a tumbler of water . . .* My throat constricts . . .

But Weeks is growing impatient. 'Take it, Miss Childs,' she orders.

Obediently I swallow the draught down, and Weeks moves on.

Perhaps it's just as well to have a good night's sleep, ready for my meeting with Dr Bull.

I was overcome by shock today, but it will be different tomorrow. I will insist that Dr Bull arranges for me to see Mr Sneed. And if that doesn't work, there's always the letter. I'm sure Eliza was warning me not to give it to Weeks to post. But if I ask Weeks for paper, she'll expect a letter. I'll have to work this out.

Six Years Earlier

I was on my way from the kitchen, where I'd been to borrow some more things I needed, when I caught my name. I pressed my ear to the dining-room door and I heard Mamma say, 'I'm worried about Louisa, Edward.'

I heard a 'Hmm?' from Papa and I knew he was reading the newspaper.

'She's getting out of hand.'

I suppressed an 'Oh!' of outrage. What had I done? Lately I'd been trying very hard to be good.

'She's untidy, careless, but the worst of it is that she keeps taking things from the kitchen without asking. Cook has been complaining. And I don't know what she does in her room but the result is shocking disorder for poor Mary to clean up. You shouldn't encourage her to do these experiments.'

I held my breath. Would Papa tell me to stop?

'Why shouldn't I encourage her? She's so keen to learn. You know how eagerly she asks questions and she understands my explanations so readily. You've got to admit she shows far more initiative than Tom did at her age. Her incendiary experiments were most enterprising.'

I breathed again. I knew he would understand. These days he made more time for me and he seemed to enjoy our sessions together as much as I did.

'How can you take it so lightly, Edward! It's a miracle she didn't burn the house down.'

Mamma always exaggerated so. The match had only made a small hole in the oilcloth.

I was pressing so hard on the door, my ear was beginning to hurt. Swapping to the other ear I heard Mamma say, with a sigh, 'I thought having a girl would be a pleasure. And easier too . . . but Louisa's turning into such a tomboy. If she doesn't grow out of it, I'm afraid she might . . .' Mamma didn't finish her sentence, and I wondered what it was that 'I might'. But then she said, 'Perhaps if she had another little girl to play with, an example to follow, she might learn more becoming ways.'

I gritted my teeth. I wasn't a little girl, I was nearly eleven, which was very nearly grown-up. And I didn't play any more; I had too many important things to do. Papa had recently given me my very own copy of *Science for Boys* and it was giving me lots of ideas.

'Perhaps she *is* too much on her own, now that Tom's away . . . I'll speak to Mitchell. He has a daughter about the same age as Lou.' Papa's voice was suddenly louder as if he was coming towards the door. I fled upstairs, wondering about this girl. Would she be like Grace? I hoped so.

The first thing I noticed about Charlotte Mitchell was her hat: a perfect miniature replica of the pork-pie hats, made of felt and trimmed with a feather, that I had seen ladies wear in church. The second thing was her hair, which fell to her shoulders in a cascade of perfect blonde ringlets. I couldn't think who she reminded me of and then I remembered the doll Evelina, long since consigned to the dustbin.

I had asked Mary to show Charlotte to my room when she arrived. I knew that ladies received visitors in their best rooms

 59

and as far as I was concerned mine was the best room in the house because it had my own things in it. Mary raised her eyebrows at my request but she complied, even going so far as to announce, 'Miss Charlotte, Miss Louisa.' Then she spoilt it by biting her lip to stop herself smiling and I had to glare at her.

Now Charlotte stood just inside the doorway as if wary of venturing further. I had risen to my feet as I had seen Mamma do when a guest arrived but now I hesitated, not knowing what to do next.

After some moments of mutual silence, I remembered my manners. 'Would you like to take off your hat? And your gloves?'

She looked at me as if I had uttered the most shocking suggestion in the world.

'Mamma says it's the mark of the truly genteel lady that she never removes her hat and gloves in company.'

I stared at her in amazement. I'd never heard anything so silly. And I was already tired of playing at ladies and wanted to do something interesting. A hat and gloves could only get in the way. But I knew one had to make a guest feel comfortable so I didn't say anything.

I thought she would like to see my treasures, and I started with my most precious possession, a gift from Grace, in pride of place on my chest of drawers.

She stared in incomprehension. 'Why did your cousin give you a ship?'

I thought it was obvious. This creation in blue and white glass seemed like a miracle to me. 'Look how delicate it is – the ropes are as fine as hairs. The pennant seems to be flying in the wind and see, there are even tiny sailors in the rigging.'

Charlotte shrugged. 'Ships are for boys.'

I searched about the room for something else to show her. 'This is Annabel.'

She gave poor Annabel one disdainful glance. 'Is she your only doll?'

I frowned. Annabel wasn't a doll – she was my companion, my confidante.

Charlotte tossed her ringlets. 'I have ten dolls and four sets of doll's chairs and tables and five little china tea sets and a doll's house this big.' She raised one gloved hand to shoulder height.

She was obviously proud of these things so I tried to look impressed.

Searching for something to impress her in my turn, I said, 'Would you like to see my collection?'

This seemed to provoke a spark of interest. 'Oh, do you have a collection? I have three drawers of shells my sister gave me.'

I thought the whole point of collecting was that you did it yourself, but it seemed rude to say this. 'My collection isn't one thing – it's more of a variety,' I explained, rummaging under the bed for the box.

Smoothing her skirts, Charlotte sat down on the bed and I proceeded to lay out my collection on the counterpane, beginning with a handful of leaves I had picked up because I liked their colour and shape. The original reds and golds had faded now, but I liked to trace the pattern of veins and to hear their crisp rustle. I had five big shiny conkers from the tree down the street, several feathers from different kinds of birds, and a dead beetle in a matchbox. I couldn't tell what Charlotte was thinking. She regarded everything with a small frown but she shuddered at the beetle.

I had saved the best till last and brought it forth with a flourish. 'And this is my mouse!'

Charlotte's reaction was disappointing. She shrieked and put her hands to her mouth.

'Don't worry, it's dead,' I reassured her. 'And it's not rotting because it's in formalin. Papa showed me how to do it.' I regarded the contents of the glass jar fondly.

'Take it away. It's disgusting. Ugh, I'm going to be sick.'

I was disconcerted. 'But look, you can see everything – the pink lining inside its ears and its little claws.'

Charlotte wailed.

I obviously wasn't going to be able to interest her in the finer points of my specimen so I put it back in the box, together with the rest of my collection, and stowed it under the bed.

Charlotte leaped up as if she'd been stung.

I tried not to let my exasperation show. I knew from observing Mamma that a polite hostess hid her true feelings from her guests, but I was finding it very hard indeed. Charlotte wasn't anything like Grace. The long afternoon stretched before us interminably.

But then I noticed her legs, and I cheered up. Surely this would interest her. 'I see you're wearing green stockings.'

She looked affronted. 'That's a very personal remark. Why do you comment?'

'Would you like me to test them for arsenic?'

'What?'

'Arsenic. Green clothes often contain it. It's quite easy to test for it, Papa showed me how.' I felt under the bed again and pulled out the old case I kept my equipment in.

I took a phial from it and removed the stopper. My eyes

immediately started watering but I pressed on. 'What you do is drop liquid ammonia on the stocking and if they've used arsenite of copper for the green colour, it turns blue. Isn't that exciting! It means your stocking is poisonous.'

I held out the phial towards Charlotte. 'Do you want to have a go?'

She backed away, staring at me with eyes as round as pennies. Then she let out a sigh, as if she had been holding her breath. In a voice as small as a pin she said, 'I think I would like to go home now.'

Glee filled me at her words.

'All right. I'll go and ask Mamma.'

As I went towards the door, Charlotte shrank away from me, pressing herself against the wall. Silly girl – why was she frightened of me?

Well, I didn't care. As long as I could continue with my experiments, which Papa approved of, I didn't care what Charlotte Mitchell or anyone else thought of me.

After breakfast the following morning, Weeks makes us stand by our beds with Eliza stationed at the door to watch over us. As soon as Weeks goes out, the old woman, Miss Coles, collapses on to her bed, weeping.

Eliza has been peeping out of the door.

Suddenly she announces, 'Ladies, Dr Bull is coming.'

Everyone stands to attention. Even Miss Coles, red-eyed, hauls herself up from the bed. A procession enters the room: an imposing woman who must be the matron, followed by the doctor, then Weeks, who is carrying a set of document files. They halt at the bed opposite mine.

This is wrong.

We should be able to talk to the doctor in private.

But I will speak. I *must* speak. The doctor will listen to me and soon I'll be leaving.

Dr Bull is nothing like Papa. He is young with bushy side-whiskers and black hair gleaming with macassar oil; his parting looks as though it has been drawn with a ruler. An expanse of white linen cuff extends beyond his coat sleeve and he carries a large shiny leather bag. His appearance suggests he thinks a lot of himself.

But he is a doctor; it may be all right.

The matron announces the first patient's name. 'Mrs Thorpe.'

Without greeting Mrs Thorpe, the doctor makes a quick check of her tongue and pulse. Then he turns to the matron.

She reports that Mrs Thorpe is eating and sleeping well, is in good health and behaves in a quiet and orderly manner.

How does she know all this?

I suppose she gets her information from Weeks. She doesn't tell him that Mrs Thorpe makes baby clothes all the time for the baby she isn't going to have. I heard Weeks telling Eliza about her. But maybe the doctor knows already. He doesn't ask any questions. Mrs Thorpe doesn't say anything. She clasps her hands in front of her and keeps her eyes on the floor. Only the matron speaks.

'Continue with the treatment?'

Like an echo, Dr Bull agrees. 'Continue with the treatment.'

He moves on. He hasn't asked to look at a file and his bag has stayed shut.

The pattern is the same at the next bed. I can feel myself tensing with annoyance. These poor people deserve better than this.

The routine is disturbed when Miss Coles grips the doctor's hand and won't let go. 'Oh, Doctor, I'm so sad today. You can't think how miserable I am. It's my own fault, I know – I've been so wicked. I deserve to be punished. Don't you think so?'

The doctor doesn't answer. His face reddens.

The matron says sharply, 'Let go of the doctor's hand now.' And when the hand is reluctantly released, she says to Dr Bull, 'Dover's Powder?'

The doctor coughs and says, 'Ah yes, Dover's Powder,

three times a day.' He nods at the matron and they move on.

It's an opiate, a sedative. They must want to quieten her down.

Being nearest the door, I'm last. I brace myself as they approach. At that moment Miss Coles darts across the room and falling on her knees, she seizes the doctor's hand again and cries out piteously, 'Oh, Doctor, help me.'

My heart goes out to her, but I keep my eyes on Dr Bull. This is my chance.

Matron nods at Weeks who pulls Miss Coles away. 'You mustn't bother the doctor.' She jerks Miss Coles to her feet and back to her side of the room.

The doctor tugs at his sleeves, clearly embarrassed by this episode. The matron announces, 'This is our new resident – ah, Miss Childs?' She looks at Weeks for confirmation, and Weeks nods.

Immediately I say, 'Doctor, I am not Miss Childs, I am Louisa Cosgrove. And I shouldn't be here.'

Dr Bull reacts as if a specimen under his microscope had spoken. He looks at the matron for assistance.

She frowns at me and says, 'Miss Childs arrived yesterday. You will need to examine her. Eliza, take Miss Childs to the examination room.'

'But, Doctor, please listen to me, I—'

The matron interjects. 'Dr Bull will speak to you in a minute. Now go along with Eliza.' She nods towards the door.

Out in the hallway, I screw up my face and clench my fists with frustration.

'Why won't anyone *listen*!'

After a moment, something touches my arm. 'You'd better come, Miss.'

Eliza's freckled face is wary but her warm hand lingers as if she wants to reassure me. Her fingers and the back of her hand are red and raw-looking, like Mary's when she has been scrubbing floors.

I take a deep breath and compose myself. 'Sorry. It's just that I *have* to see Mr Sneed. It's very important.'

Eliza nods sympathetically. She points along the hallway to a door next to the entrance. 'If you wait there, the doctor will come when he's finished in the other dormitories.'

'Thank you.'

She gives me a quick, surprised look. She's obviously not used to patients speaking to her with normal politeness.

I nod at her hands. 'They look sore.'

Eliza flushes, putting her hands behind her back.

'Have you tried Fowler's Solution? That might clear it up.'

She looks even more surprised, but her face breaks into a smile. 'Thanks. I'll try it.'

I hear a sound. Someone nearby is crying quietly. I remember the keening I heard yesterday when I arrived. 'Who is that?'

'Miss Hill. That's her room. She's always upset, poor thing.'

'She has her own room?'

'Yes. Her family must have some money cos those

rooms cost more. Mrs Smythe's in one – you know, her that reckons she's related to the Queen.'

I nod, but I'm not thinking of Mrs Smythe. Who is paying for me – or rather, for Lucy Childs? And if I am here in her place, where is she?

Eliza clears her throat. 'I have to get back, Miss, to watch the others.'

Alone in the hallway, I try the handle of the gallery door. It stays shut.

I want to beat it with my fists but I stop myself. You must be calm. They must see that you're not mad. Concentrate. This is your chance to escape.

Dr Bull approaches, followed by Weeks, who is now carrying one file. It must be mine, or rather, Lucy Childs's. I wonder what it says.

Unlocking the door for the doctor, Weeks allows him to enter first. He doesn't look at either of us, which is just as well. I can tell from her expression that Weeks doesn't think much of him. She nods at me to enter.

The room is small, windowless. There's nothing in it apart from an examination couch, a desk and a chair. Putting down his bag, the doctor sits at the desk and turns to me. 'Ah, take a seat on the couch . . .'

He seems nervous. Perhaps he is missing the matron's support. Maybe the imposing bag and cuffs are not to show off but to boost his confidence.

'Now, Miss . . .'

'Childs,' says Weeks. 'Lucy Childs.' She hands him the file.

He is opening it when I say in a loud, firm voice, 'I told you, that isn't my name. I am Louisa Cosgrove. And I'm not meant to be here. There's been a mistake.'

He pauses, glances at Weeks, then turns to read the page of cramped writing I can see inside the folder.

It suddenly occurs to me – perhaps they're pretending they don't know who I am. Perhaps they're *trying* to drive me mad.

I take a deep breath. 'I'm not mad, Doctor. You can see that, so—'

'Just a minute, Miss Childs. I'm reading your notes.'

I glance at Weeks, who's watching me narrowly. Perhaps it's better to play the game for now. Make them see how rational you are.

'Put out your tongue, Miss Childs.'

Obediently I stick my tongue out and the doctor inspects it. Then he feels my forehead. His hands smell of soap and black hairs curl out from under his cuffs. He takes my pulse, then writes.

If he is trying to find out how mad I am, this won't tell him.

He takes a stethoscope from his bag. *A stethoscope*. I catch my breath. It's just like the one I have in my box – my box that they've taken from me. Instantly, I'm back in Papa's study, hearing his voice . . .

Dr Bull misunderstands my reaction. As he unscrews the stethoscope and tips out the contents, he says, 'Don't be alarmed, Miss Childs. With the aid of these, I can check the condition of your heart and lungs.'

'I'm not alarmed. I know what those are.' I point at each item, naming it. 'Stethoscope. Pleximeter. Percussor.'

His mouth drops open. Weeks frowns.

'You seem very familiar with these instruments, Miss Childs.'

'My father taught me how to use them. He shared a lot of his medical knowledge with me.'

'Oh?' He seems surprised, and something else. Disapproving?

After he has listened to my chest, he makes a brief note, then turns to Weeks. 'Have you anything to report?'

She speaks rapidly, mechanically, Dr Bull struggling to keep up with his notes. 'Miss Childs keeps denying her name. She has been argumentative at times.'

'I haven't!'

Weeks ignores me. 'She has not been eating. She attempted to conceal some scissors.'

'Doctor, that isn't true!'

But the doctor is sweeping on. 'I would like a urine specimen. And has Miss Childs opened her bowels today?'

This is for me to answer. But Weeks says, 'No, and not since she arrived.'

My face goes hot. No privacy, not even in this.

The doctor turns to me again. 'You haven't been eating?'

'Would you eat that food? It's not fit for pigs.'

He blinks at that and writes something in his notes. 'And, um, do you menstruate regularly?'

I can feel my face flushing again, but I'd better say. They'll find out. 'No.'

'When was the last occurrence?'

'I can't remember.' This is true. I can't remember exactly. About six months ago?

I suddenly go cold with anxiety. What if Dr Bull gives me a physical examination? His hands are white, like lard.

But he's pulling out his watch, frowning as he writes some more. Time is running out.

I take a deep breath. 'Doctor, I must speak with you. Alone.'

Startled, he looks at Weeks for help. 'I don't think—'

'Please. I am entitled to a private consultation.' I don't know if I am or not, but I say it assertively and I can see him hesitating.

He makes up his mind. 'Very well.' He nods at Weeks who purses her lips, but she goes.

As soon as the door is shut, I drop my voice. 'I have to see Mr Sneed. I have to explain to him that I shouldn't be here. As I told you, I'm not Lucy Childs.'

'Right.' He nods thoughtfully.

Encouraged by his apparent willingness to listen, I press home my advantage. 'Please don't take any notice of Weeks – she's not telling the truth about me.' As I say it, the sense of injustice that I've tried to repress wells up, and I can't help myself. 'Do you know, yesterday afternoon I wanted to read and she said I couldn't. She behaves like a tyrant, making up petty rules—'

Dr Bull interrupts me. 'You're misjudging Weeks, Miss Childs. She's merely carrying out orders.'

'Orders?'

'Yes. Mr Sneed has prescribed a period of rest from reading for you—'

'But that's absurd!'

Ignoring my outburst, the doctor continues, 'And I would support him in that recommendation. Excessive study, especially in one of the fair sex, often leads to insanity.'

I gape at him. I've never heard anything more ridiculous. But he is standing up as if the interview is over.

'Wait! There's something else about Weeks – she terrorizes the patients.'

Instantly his manner changes. 'That's a serious charge, Miss Childs. What evidence have you to support it?'

'She . . .' I falter. What *has* Weeks done? Nothing obvious. But the other women *are* scared of her.

The doctor is waiting. 'Well?'

I look down at the floor.

He makes another note. By leaning closer I can just make out the words 'moral derangement'.

I've made a terrible mistake. I must try to save myself.

I can hear my voice, much too loud. 'I'm not mad. You can see I'm not! Why don't you say so?' I can feel the tears rising.

The doctor looks alarmed. Going to the door, he calls Weeks back in.

She enters with a suspicious glance at me. Did she hear what I said? But that doesn't matter now. What matters is that the interview is over.

In a last desperate attempt I say, 'Doctor, please, I'm

not meant to be here! It's a mistake. Or some plot against me.'

I don't know why I said that but as soon as the words leave my mouth I experience a tremendous jolt.

Why didn't I think of it before?

But I've no time to consider it because, for the first time in the interview, Dr Bull looks interested. 'Tell me, do you hear voices when you are alone?'

'No.'

'Do you see things other people can't see?'

'*No!*'

He writes a final note, puts the paper into his bag. 'Um, Weeks, see that Miss Childs is given daily a dose of castor oil, and some iron tonic. She needs a warm bath for at least two hours. Should she continue to refuse to eat or become over-excited, you know what to do.' He is patently relieved that this is over.

I make a last effort. 'Doctor, I must see Mr Sneed.'

He looks at Weeks, who shrugs slightly. Picking up his bag, he says, 'I will pass the message on.'

Back in the day room, supposedly mending sheets again, I can scarcely push the needle through the cloth, my fingers tremble so.

My own words ring in my ears: *some plot against me . . .*

Has someone contrived to have me shut up here? Who would do such a thing? And why? My mind races feverishly, thinking and thinking.

Suddenly I exclaim aloud. Because I know who's responsible.

'Are you all right, Miss?' Eliza is threading a needle for a patient.

'Yes – I pricked myself, that's all.' To keep up the pretence I suck my finger, inwardly elated by my discovery.

No wonder my travelling companion, Mrs Lunt, behaved so oddly. Lunt probably isn't even her real name. Lucy Childs must be her daughter or a relative, who was meant to come here – and to save her from her awful fate, Mrs Lunt tricked me into coming in her place. She will have contacted the Woodvilles and made up a reason why I'm not coming.

I'm certain this is what has happened; I never liked Mrs Lunt.

Oh, the joyful relief of finding an explanation.

Weeks is frowning over some poor patient's shoulder, pointing out mistakes in her work. No good telling her – she won't believe me. I'd love to tell Eliza, but I can't as long as Weeks is within earshot.

Now it doesn't matter that the interview with Dr Bull was a disaster. They probably won't take much notice of him anyway – he's clearly inexperienced. As long as he tells Mr Sneed I want to see him – he's the one with the power to release me. And he will, as soon as I tell him about Mrs Lunt.

By tomorrow I could be free!

I bend to my sewing again and try to concentrate but inside, beating in time with the thumping of my heart, I'm singing: *I'm going to get out, I'm going to get out!*

One Year Earlier

I eyed the corset with suspicion; with its stiff whalebone ribs and starched white casing, it looked very uncomfortable.

I was right. When Mary tightened the laces, I couldn't breathe. 'You're pulling too tight. It's like a suit of armour.'

'Now, Miss Louisa, stop fussing. You know what your mamma said.'

I sighed – as well as I could with my ribcage imprisoned.

Mary put on her coaxing expression. 'You want to be a lady, don't you?'

I didn't answer.

The dress was Mamma's choice – a green plaid taffeta that made me look washed out. It would have suited Grace, with her red-gold hair and creamy complexion. I remembered I hadn't replied to her last letter. I would do it after tea.

Mamma came in. 'Are you ready yet?'

'No. All this takes an age.'

'You'll get used to it.' She put some hairpins and a small pot on top of the chest.

'I feel like a parcel,' I complained.

'Don't be silly.' My mother looked at me and sighed. 'I'll deal with Louisa's hair, Mary,' she said. 'You'd better see to breakfast.'

'Yes, Ma'am.' Mary slipped out.

'You'll have to sit down,' Mamma said to me. I did so gingerly, aware of the corset digging into me.

The brush kept snagging on tangles. Mamma tugged, jerking my head back.

'Ow!' I pulled my head away.

'Keep still.' The firm strokes continued.

When she was satisfied, Mamma lifted the top off the pot. Digging out a blob of greasy cream, she started smoothing it over my hair. Beneath the fragrance of rose petals, I could detect a whiff of castor oil and something else.

'What's that smell? Like something cooking.'

'Lard.'

'Ugh!' I wrinkled up my nose.

My mother took hold of my hair and twisted it into the nape of my neck, fastening it with pins. She pulled something from her pocket.

'What's that?'

'A hairnet.'

'I don't need that.'

'You certainly do. Otherwise your hair will never stay in place.'

My mother fastened the hairnet with more pins and patted a last stray hair into place. 'Don't slouch, Louisa.'

I straightened up and then looked at myself in the mirror.

I recognized my nose, of course. Tom's childhood taunts were even truer now: my nose was a huge beak with an ugly bump in it. But otherwise the girl who gazed back at me didn't look like me at all. She was a solemn-faced stranger.

I was scanning the headlines of *The Times*, which Papa had left on the table, when Mamma put her cup down and said, 'This afternoon, I want you to come with me when I pay my calls.'

I stared at her. 'I can't, Mamma. I have to study.'

My mother frowned. 'You're spending far too much time with

your books. It isn't healthy. And now that you're sixteen and a young lady, you have other duties, social duties.' She rang the bell for Mary, and left the room.

I scowled at the table, covered with the remains of breakfast. Why couldn't Mamma understand?

When I was twelve and wanted to go to school and Mamma had agreed, I was amazed. But it made sense – she was glad to let someone else teach me and deal with my awkward questions.

I'd been shocked when Papa had said no. But when he'd explained that what girls did at school – spending hours lying on a backboard improving their posture, copying 'Lord Tennyson is a poet' a hundred times, and making wax flowers – was a waste of time it all became clear.

Mamma didn't want me to be educated – she wanted me to acquire what she called 'some graces'. She wanted me to be out of the way at school in the morning and then come home and be patient, cheerful and obedient and do boring ladylike things, instead of shutting myself in my room with my books.

She had hated it when Papa arranged lessons with Mr Fielding, the local schoolmaster, for me. She thought it was totally unsuitable that I should study the same subjects as boys. What did she say to Papa? 'It will spoil her chances of marriage. Do you want her to become *mannish*?'

Her mouth had twisted then, as if she was eating lemons.

But I'd been excited to have a chance to study seriously – I couldn't wait to know all those things. And I thought it was a chance to show Tom that I wasn't 'just a useless girl'. I thought he might even respect me for it. Silly of me. When he was home and deigned to take any notice of me, Tom teased me about my studies, obviously thinking it was a great joke.

 77

The lessons with Mr Fielding – Algebra, Geometry, Latin, Greek and Science – were harder than I'd expected, but really interesting. And I hadn't told Mamma or Papa yet, but Mr Fielding thought I would soon be ready to take some of the Cambridge Local Examinations, and not just the Junior ones but the Senior ones that boys took just before they left school.

The reason I hadn't told them was because I was beginning to form a tentative plan for my future. But I wasn't as clever as Tom, who'd just started his second year at medical school in London. If I was going to pass these exams I'd have to work hard, which was why I couldn't afford to waste any time on pointless things like paying calls with Mamma.

I sighed. For now, I didn't have any choice.

I put my gloved hand to my mouth to stifle a yawn and tried not to stare at the clock. Mrs Piper's drawing room, crammed with outsize chairs, little tables and ugly ornaments, was stuffy. I was warm in my bonnet and cloak, but my mother had warned me not to take them off unless I was invited to. I remembered Charlotte Mitchell. Apparently she had been right.

She would have been at ease in this situation even at the age of ten. She wouldn't have had to search for another pair of gloves because she'd split one cramming hands that were too big into the delicate kid. Her face wouldn't have ached with the effort of smiling.

Mamma and Mrs Piper were discussing some charity or other. This was our fourth call of the afternoon. Mamma had told me it wasn't polite to stay for more than fifteen minutes, which was a relief, but each visit seemed to last an age. I wondered whether

Grace had to put up with this. I couldn't see Aunt Phyllis tolerating such tedious conversation.

My eyes slid to the clock again. Five minutes to go. I suppressed another yawn.

The door opened and the parlourmaid appeared. Unlike Mary, she wore a smart apron and cap. She bobbed a curtsy. 'Mrs Winterton and Miss Winterton, Ma'am.' She withdrew.

Mamma gave me a significant look. What did she mean?

Two women entered the drawing room. The stout mother was squeezed into a dress in garish shades of green and violet. The daughter was older than me. Her grey gown with scarlet trimmings was a perfect fit; she had a handsome but haughty face. My feet suddenly seemed enormous. I tucked them under my chair.

My mother rose and coughed. After a second, I stood up too.

To my surprise, Mamma said, 'Goodbye, Mrs Piper.' She looked at me.

'Oh, goodbye, Mrs Piper,' I echoed.

I followed my mother to the door. As she passed the Wintertons, she bowed her head, receiving a slight nod in return. The daughter looked down her nose at me, making me conscious of the sooty mud on the hem of my gown. I ignored her and left the room with as much dignity as I could manage. In the chilly hall, I retrieved our umbrella from a cast-iron stand decorated with two pelicans. They looked as if they would like to peck me with their vicious beaks.

It was still wet when we got outside, a cold rain turning to sleet. I hurried after Mamma. 'Who was that? What an awful dress the mother was wearing.'

 79

'Don't make personal remarks, Louisa, it's not kind. They're Mr Winterton's wife and daughter. You know – the banker.'

'Oh, that's why they give themselves such airs. And I suppose we had to leave because we aren't good enough for them.'

Mamma tutted. 'Don't be silly. It's the correct thing to do. One always leaves when the next visitor is announced, whoever they are.'

The adult world was certainly mysterious, but I wasn't complaining; at least it had cut our visit short. Now I could go home to my studies with a clear conscience.

The next morning at breakfast Mamma said, 'We'll have to pay some more calls today.'

I gaped at her.

'Close your mouth, Louisa.'

I found my voice. 'But I came with you yesterday.'

My mother sighed. 'Yes, but Mrs Fielding was out and there are some other people I need to see today.'

'But why do *I* have to come?'

My mother looked at me reproachfully. 'I told you why yesterday. You're not a child any more. You need to learn the way these things are done.'

'Why should I learn something I won't ever be doing?'

Mamma stared at me. 'What do you mean? Of course you'll pay calls.'

'I won't. It's such a waste of time.'

Mamma looked at me helplessly. Before she could say anything else, I said, 'And I can't believe you enjoy it either.'

I didn't mean to say this. It just slipped out. Mamma looked away and her mouth trembled. After a pause, she said, 'You're

right, Louisa. I don't enjoy it. But I do it because it's my social duty.'

Those familiar words! I couldn't stop myself. 'Social duty! What does that mean? Only what other people think you ought to do. Who cares what other people think!'

My mother shook her head. 'You don't understand. I don't do it because I care what people think. I do it to help your father.'

It was my turn to stare. 'How can it possibly help Papa?'

'Now that your father has a position at the Dispensary, he has to try and increase the subscriptions. I do what I can by speaking to the wives of influential men. It helps to create the right impression. It isn't a pleasure, I assure you, but it's for a worthwhile cause.'

I hadn't thought of that. A guilty sense of being in the wrong made me blurt out, 'Then it's better if I don't come. I'll just create the wrong impression, slouching and looking common.'

I'd gone too far.

Mamma said 'Oh, Louisa.' She sounded weary. 'You can behave perfectly well when you choose to. Why won't you?'

I heard the appeal in her voice, but I ignored it. I stood up. 'I'm not coming. I've more important things to do.' Turning my back on her, I went out, banging the door behind me.

Once inside my room, I took a deep breath. I was trembling. I'd never opposed Mamma so openly before. She'd tell Papa and what would he say? He'd see that I needed to study, wouldn't he? Picking up the volume of Euclid, I found the page.

Though I tried all morning, I couldn't concentrate. I kept thinking about Mamma. At lunchtime I couldn't face her so I stayed in my room, miserable but defiant.

Eventually Mary came with a plate of bread and butter and slices of cold ham on a tray.

'Where's Mamma, Mary?' I was beginning to think I should go with her.

'Your mother has gone out.' From her tone I could tell she wasn't pleased with me.

'Oh.' I was too late. 'Did she say anything?'

'She asked me to give you this.' Mary fished a parcel out of her apron pocket. 'She meant it for your birthday, but she thought you had enough presents then.'

'Oh.' Prickly with shame, I took the rectangular package. I looked at Mary, hoping for some comfort, but she pursed her lips and went out without another word.

I undid the brown paper. It was a book. Mamma had never given me a book before. I looked at the spine: *Girlhood* by Marianne Farningham. Not a promising title. I opened it at random.

Hoydenism, frolic and exuberant mirth will now become unseemly and therefore will be exchanged for a soberness of manner.

So. Presumably Mamma thought I would be more influenced by something I read in a book than by anything she tried to tell me. I flicked through the pages until my eye was caught by a section headed 'The Dangers of Excessive Learning'. The chief danger, according to the writer, was that a girl who studied too much would become 'dogmatic and presumptuous, self-willed and arrogant, eccentric in dress and disagreeable in manner.'

As I read these words, the pressure inside me that had been

building all day exploded. I flung the book away from me. It hit the wall and landed face down. Hot angry tears ran down my face. How could Mamma do this to me? Why didn't she understand? I put my head on my arms and sobbed.

After a while I sat up and blew my nose. I picked the book up and smoothed its crumpled pages. What could I do with it? I didn't want to see it ever again. Kneeling down, I thrust it under my bed. It could stay there with the chamber pot.

Later that afternoon, when Mary and I returned from my lesson at Mr Fielding's, I went into Papa's study to wait for him. I wanted to get this over with as soon as possible.

I picked up a copy of the *Medical Times and Gazette* and flicked through it, listening for the sound of the front door opening.

After a while I looked at the clock. Papa was late. The committee meeting must have overrun as usual. I turned to the letters. The Dean of St Thomas's Medical College was justifying his refusal to admit women on the grounds that the arrangements of the Medical School were not suited to the reception of female students. In other words, presumably there were no ladies' lavatories and they did not intend to install any.

I threw down the paper in disgust. Then I heard Papa's steps in the hall. He went into the parlour, where Mamma was waiting. I stood up and paced about. Finally he came in. He went and sat at his desk and looked at me over the top of his spectacles, his eyes red with tiredness. I'd been telling myself that Mamma didn't deserve any consideration, but now I felt a pang of remorse. I shifted my position, waiting for him to speak first.

'Sit down, Lou.'

I sat in the chair where his patients sat.

'Now what's all this about? Your mother tells me you were very rude to her this morning.'

This was unfair. I stuck my chin out. 'I wasn't rude. I didn't want to go out with Mamma, that's all. I had studying to do. And Mamma said I had to go, she—'

He held up his hand. 'Whatever you feel, you should do what your mother asks, shouldn't you?'

'But supposing what she asks me to do is unreasonable? Supposing she—'

His look silenced me. I hung my head.

He sighed. 'You're too old for this now, Lou. You must realize that you can't always have what you want.' He gestured at my dress. 'You look like a lady – and very elegant too.'

I blushed but he went on, 'Now you must learn to behave like one.'

This was too much. He was sounding just like Mamma.

'But, Papa, I've got so much to learn. I don't want to waste time listening to a lot of ladies talking about – whatever ladies talk about.'

He smiled at this.

Encouraged, I went on, 'I'd much rather come out with you and help you with your patients, like Tom did.' I'd envied my brother his two years as Papa's assistant before he started his course.

His expression changed. 'Would you, Lou?'

'Yes. Mamma doesn't understand. She wants me to be just like her. But I'm not like her, am I?'

'No, you're not like your mother.' He regarded me thoughtfully without saying anything, and then he cleared his throat.

'There's something I think you should know – and maybe it will help you understand your mother better.'

I was very curious. What was he going to say?

'You know, don't you, that your mamma lost her mother when she was a little girl?'

I sighed. That old story again. It was sad but Mamma had been very young. It wasn't as if she'd known her mother.

'But what you don't know is that Mamma had a brother, Thomas, whom she idolized.'

I stared. This was news.

'He was twelve, two years older than Mamma, when he died of typhoid.'

'Why haven't I heard of him?'

Papa shook his head. 'Your mamma has always found it difficult to speak about. I expect she doesn't want to bring back the sad memories. Think how hard it must have been for her growing up with only Grandpapa and the servants for company.'

I was touched. It must have been horrible. I couldn't remember my grandfather: he'd died when I was three, but there was a painting of him hanging in the dining room: a grim-looking old man with a bushy grey beard, like an Old Testament prophet.

'What was Grandpapa like? Was he as fierce as he looks in his portrait?'

Papa leaned back in his chair. 'He wasn't the easiest of men. Hardly surprising – he'd lost his wife *and* his beloved only son. Luckily, he seemed to like me. And –' he smiled mischievously – 'your mamma was pleased I came to help him.'

This part of the story I did know. Mamma was old when Papa arrived, nearly thirty. She must have been very glad to see him. When I was little, I'd imagined Papa breaking into the house like

 85

the prince come to rescue the princess. He arrived on a white charger and wore a dark green velvet cloak. My imagination had failed when I tried to picture Mamma as the princess . . .

Now it was something else that interested me. 'What was it like working with Grandpapa?'

'By the time I joined the practice, he was ready to retire, so he was mostly happy to let me do things my way.' Papa laughed. 'We did have one or two fallings-out – mainly over the wealthy women who fancied themselves ill when there was nothing wrong with them. I didn't have the time or patience to attend to them. They soon found themselves other doctors.'

I laughed too. I could just imagine it.

Papa went on, 'Your grandfather forgave me eventually. And he was delighted when we had our Tom. He had expected his son to be a doctor so he was glad he had a grandson to carry on the family tradition.'

'Is that why he left Tom a legacy for medical training?' I couldn't help the note of jealousy creeping into my voice.

But Papa didn't seem to notice. 'Yes, I'm sure.'

It was becoming clearer to me why Mamma always favoured Tom. It made sense but it still wasn't right.

Papa's expression was serious now. 'I want you to realize that, until she had Tom, poor Mamma had a difficult life with Grandpapa. I think she felt that, being a girl, whatever she did she would always be a disappointment to him, that she could never make up for the loss of her brother. And your grandpapa had very rigid ideas about girls' behaviour.'

I could see what Papa was implying, that Mamma couldn't help treating me the way she did. But it still didn't seem fair. Just because Grandpapa had been strict with Mamma, I didn't see why I had to suffer.

Papa said, 'Try to see it from her point of view. She's doing her best.'

I gave him a pleading look. 'I can see that. But I still don't understand why I have to go visiting. I don't have to, do I? I'll tell Mamma I'm sorry, but I need to study. She can't make me go, can she?'

He shook his head. 'No, she can't make you. But I'm asking you to do it.'

I stared at him. 'But—'

'No, listen, Lou. You have plenty of time in your day for study. And Mamma's right: it's not good for you to work too hard. It only means giving up an hour or so to please her. And it's not even every day. That's not much to ask, is it?'

I looked at his tired face. 'No, Papa.'

He smiled. 'Good. And as for going out with me on my calls, we'll see. It might be possible for you to assist me when it's appropriate.'

'Appropriate? Oh, Papa, you don't think it's improper for a woman to practise medicine, do you?' I couldn't believe that he did but I wanted to make sure.

Papa laughed. 'I think you are too young for some aspects of the work. And I am certain that some of my patients would think it inappropriate to have you present. But in other cases, you could be of great assistance, certainly handier than Tom, at times.'

I was thrilled. But Papa was taking off his spectacles and rubbing his eyes. He looked pale, drained. Suddenly I felt anxious. 'Are you feeling all right, Papa?'

'Yes. I have a headache, that's all. Now, are you going to speak to your mother?'

'Yes, Papa.' I stood up and kissed his forehead. 'I'm sorry to worry you. I'll try to do better.'

He patted my hand. 'I know you will.'

We haven't been out today: rain has been falling continuously. Looking out of the window at the end of the gallery, all I can see are dark clouds and bare trees whipped by the wind, patches of wet leaves on the muddy ground. It's so gloomy the gas jets have been lit already.

Since Dr Bull's visit this morning, I've been waiting for the summons from Mr Sneed. It hasn't come. Gradually during the endless afternoon, my optimism has evaporated. Now I feel an ache inside.

Normally at home Mary would be drawing the curtains now and pouring the tea. I wonder what they're doing today. They must know by now that I never arrived at the Woodvilles'. Will they have informed the police?

I hope Mamma is blaming herself for sending me away.

Eliza emerges from the day room. 'All right, Miss?'

I want to trust her but I don't know if I can.

'Has there been any message for me from Mr Sneed?'

'No, Miss.' She pulls a face. 'Sorry.'

I can't wait any longer. If Eliza will post the letter for me today, I could be free by the day after tomorrow at the latest – that won't be so bad.

I go in search of Weeks. She's not in any of the dormitories or the washroom.

At the other end of the hallway there's a thin shaft of

light from an open door spilling into the corridor. I hesitate. And then I hear a sound that makes the hairs rise on the back of my neck. A high-pitched wail, as if someone's heart is breaking. It goes on and on and then subsides into choking sobs.

Almost without realizing, I've drawn nearer that finger of light and then I hear Weeks's voice, low and urgent.

I can't help myself, I have to listen.

'You should be ashamed of yourself, lying around in bed all day, expecting me to wait on you. Do you think I'm your servant? If you were physically sick, there might be some excuse, but there's nothing wrong with you, is there?'

The sobbing increases in volume, a hard, hopeless sound.

Moving as silently as a cat, I edge towards the door. Through the narrow gap I can make out the end of a dressing table, part of a rocking chair, but I can't see anyone.

Weeks's voice continues, 'You might as well dry your tears, Miss Hill. You'll get no sympathy from me. And as for these claims of yours, this nonsense about a baby – you're making this up to get attention, aren't you? Admit it. *Admit it*.'

My heart is hammering so loudly, I'm surprised she can't hear it. There's no answer, only those dreadful sobs. Clenching my fists, I shift my position, carefully, carefully, a step at a time.

I glimpse a figure sitting up in bed, a white face, framed by a fall of hair like pale silk. My chest tightens. There's something about Miss Hill, some echo of Grace in the shape of her face . . .

My eyes are drawn to Weeks's hands, raised to strike. For a moment they're poised – I hold my breath – then they swoop and seize the girl's thin arms.

'You will admit it, my lady, before I have done with you.' Weeks's eyes are glittering coals. 'And–I–am–not–your–servant–do–you–hear?'

With each word, Weeks gives Miss Hill a hard shake so that her head flops like a rag doll's, then she flings her back on to her pillows, where Miss Hill goes into a kind of spasm, shuddering and choking, her eyes bulging, her face turning red.

I'm trembling myself. This is outrageous!

Weeks stands, hands on hips. She speaks calmly, as if nothing exceptional is happening. 'Convulsions, is it now? Another of your fine tricks.'

Taking the jug from the washstand, she pours water over the girl's head, then, as her victim splutters, she seizes a towel and slaps her about the face and neck with it.

Perhaps I move without realizing. At any rate a floor-board creaks, and Weeks looks towards the door.

At the sight of me, her face darkens. She launches herself forward and for a moment I think she's going to hit me but, instead, she propels me out of the room. 'What are you doing, Miss Childs? You're not allowed in here.'

My heart's in my throat but I force myself to meet her eye. 'I was looking for you. I want to write a letter.'

From the room I hear a kind of sigh. Abruptly Weeks pulls the door to behind her.

Her eyes bore into me. 'How long have you been here?'

'I've just come from the day room.'

She isn't sure. I hold her gaze. She lets out her breath. 'Well, return there now.'

She turns to go back into the room. I'm still shaking, but I'm determined. I try to keep my voice polite. 'My letter?'

She wheels round, frowning. 'You must ask after supper. That's the time for writing letters.'

'Right, I see.' I make myself sound meek, but I want to shout at her, shake *her* as she shook Miss Hill.

I'm heading back towards the day room when Weeks's voice floats after me.

'Oh, Miss Childs, Dr Bull said you must have a warm bath, didn't he? Go and wait by the washroom.' She goes back into Miss Hill's room and shuts the door.

Standing outside the washroom door, with only the hissing of the gas jets for company, I relive what I've just seen and heard.

That girl, Miss Hill, she's nothing like Grace – not really – and yet . . . my stomach tightens.

No, don't think about it . . . Think about Miss Hill.

She doesn't deserve to be treated like that. How can Weeks be so brutal? How is she allowed to be? If Miss Hill were my patient, I would speak to her calmly and quietly, try to find out what's wrong.

An image comes into my mind of Papa tending to a patient, his big hands gentle, their touch reassuring, healing.

The ache in my chest starts up again, an ache of longing.

Papa . . . Grace . . .

I watch the light fade from the window.

Seven Months Earlier

'**K**eep still. I've nearly finished.'

The itch on my nose desperately needed scratching, but I forced my hands to lie still in my lap.

Grace laughed. 'You look like a rabbit.'

'Itch.' I tried not to open my mouth too far.

'You can talk. As long as you don't move.'

I didn't want to talk. I was quite happy to sit and watch Grace's serious face bent over her sketchbook, her hair striped gold and blue from the spring sunshine glowing through the stained-glass window. But when she looked up at me, I suddenly felt oddly vulnerable – exposed, somehow, under the directness of her gaze.

I told myself it was only that she was seeing me with an artist's eye.

We were in the conservatory, my favourite place at Carr Head, apart from the library. It was peaceful to sit with Grace amongst the ferns, breathing in the scent of the camellias and hearing the musical splash of water from the dolphin fountain.

Grace broke the silence. 'I expect you're sorry we dragged you away from your studies. All this must be an awful bore for you.'

'No, I'm glad you asked me.'

This was only partly true. The thought of being a bridesmaid at Grace's wedding alarmed me, but I was very happy to see my cousin again.

Now that I was old enough to come on my own, I tried to visit at least twice a year. On this occasion, discussions, decisions, preparations for the wedding had occupied nearly every minute since I'd arrived. I missed the evenings we usually had, when Grace played the piano and sang, her light, melodious voice sending shivers down my spine. But there were moments like this when Grace and I were alone together, and then I was truly glad I'd come.

'Finished! You can move now.'

I jumped up and went to look over her shoulder, smelling the soft fragrance of her lily-of-the-valley perfume.

'What do you think?' Grace turned her head to look up at me.

I focused on the sketch. A serious girl with a determined chin and intense eyes stared out at me, but Grace had made my nose look smaller than it really was.

I was distracted by Grace's hand, holding the drawing: on the inside of her wrist, a tracery of blue veins showed through the delicate skin.

With a start I realized she was still waiting for my answer.

'That doesn't look like me. Too flattering.'

'I don't think so.'

Her steady regard embarrassed me. I poked the drawing. 'My nose is bigger than that, and that noble brow you've given me – that's not accurate.'

Grace smiled. 'Maybe I've exaggerated a bit. Artistic licence or ineptitude – I'm not sure which.'

'Not ineptitude. Look at the way you've done the wickerwork of the chair. I hope Charles appreciates you.'

I was only half joking. I hadn't met Grace's fiancé yet, but I'd already decided he couldn't possibly be good enough for her.

Grace blushed. 'Oh yes. Charles is well aware of what an

accomplished wife he'll have.' A faraway look came into her eyes. 'Dear Charles . . .'

Something seemed to flip over behind my ribcage.

The parlourmaid appeared. 'Mrs Hiddlestone is here, Miss Illingworth.'

'Thank you, Susan. Does my sister know?'

'She's already in the sewing room, Miss.' Susan went out.

Grace stood up, making a rueful face at me. 'More fussing. Can you bear it?'

I wasn't going to let Grace know what I really felt. 'Of course.'

'Thank you. You're a love.' And she reached up and kissed my cheek. She'd kissed me many times, but, for some reason, today I felt a sudden heat spread over my face.

Luckily Grace was already on her way out of the room.

We found Maud encased in pink and white satin, looking ecstatic. Aunt Phyllis was watching her younger daughter with a critical frown, while Mrs Hiddlestone, her mouth full of pins, knelt at Maud's feet.

As soon as she saw us, Maud crowed, 'Look at me. Isn't this heavenly? Put yours on, Louisa.'

Aunt Phyllis hushed her. 'Keep still, darling, or you'll have a crooked hem.'

Mrs Hiddlestone spat the pins into her palm. 'Aye, Mrs Illingworth, you're right there. You don't want to look like a merry-go-round, Miss Maud.'

Maud dissolved into giggles.

Aunt Phyllis looked at us in mock-despair. 'Will you try yours on? Give this child a chance to calm down.'

Maud pouted. 'No, finish me first. I'll keep still.'

She posed like a memorial sculpture, causing Mrs Hiddle-stone to shake her head. 'Eeh, Miss Maud, you're a mischief.' But she resumed her pinning, while Aunt Phyllis helped us into our dresses.

I caught sight of myself in the full-length mirror. I was trans-formed into Maud's twin, albeit taller and gawkier. A crow dressed as a bon-bon.

I looked away, looked at Grace.

Her bright face, emerging from a cloud of white satin and floating feathers, was like a flower on her slender neck. And again I had that peculiar flipping sensation . . .

Maud clapped her hands. Aunt Phyllis regarded her elder daughter with an expression of fond pride. Even Mrs Hiddlestone paused in her work. Folding her arms across her broad chest, she surveyed Grace before pronouncing, 'Aye, I reckon you'll do, lass.' Then she looked at me. 'Now then, Miss, your turn next?'

Thinking she meant a wedding, I felt my face go red. Aunt Phyllis must have guessed my thought for she said, 'Why, Lou, have you a secret sweetheart?'

Everyone laughed and Mrs Hiddlestone waved her pin-cushion at me.

I realized my mistake. She only meant it was my turn to have my dress hemmed.

Afterwards we all sat in the morning room. It was so different from our dark, suffocating rooms at home; with its walls papered with a design of pale leaves on a light blue background, it was light and airy. In front of the white marble fireplace stood a screen decorated with irises. Aunt Phyllis's handiwork. She'd even painted violets on the globed shades of the oil lamps.

Grace and my aunt were checking off acceptances against the list of invitations – and a very long list it was. I had a book in my hand, but I wasn't concentrating. I couldn't stop looking at Grace: her small white hands opening and refolding letters, her animated face, her gold-flecked eyes.

It was peculiar, but I felt as if I was seeing her properly for the first time . . . and she was lovely. It gave me a strange, fizzing sensation around my heart; it wasn't unpleasant, but at the same time I felt unaccountably frightened.

Suddenly Maud, who was idling in the window-seat, shrieked, 'Grace, Charles is here.'

Grace coloured. 'Oh no. He mustn't see me like this.' She looked perfect to me, but she said, 'Run down, Maud, and tell him I'll be down in a minute.' They both left the room.

Putting down my book, I hastened to the window. Charles was dismounting. All I could see from this angle was the top of a hat and smart riding clothes. Not enough evidence to prove Grace's claim that he was 'wonderfully handsome'. The next minute Maud had joined him, talking energetically, and waving her arm at the house. Charles looked up and I shrank back.

Grace had said, 'You're sure to like him, Lou.' But I felt shy of meeting him. Apart from Tom and my cousin, William, whom I rarely saw, I didn't know any young men.

Occasionally, in the holidays, Tom would bring his friends to the house, but I kept out of their way. I once met one in the hall-way and afterwards I heard him say, 'Was that your sister, Cosgrove? Didn't you say she was something of a bluestocking?' Tom had made some reply I didn't hear and they both laughed.

I hadn't heard the term 'bluestocking' before, but I guessed it was an uncomplimentary reference to my interest in learning.

Now I watched as Grace ran to meet Charles and he bent to embrace her. From my angle it looked as though she were being smothered in his arms. Then her face emerged as she raised it for a kiss. My stomach lurched and involuntarily I clenched my hands.

Whatever was the matter with me?

I watched them walk off round to the back of the house, Grace's head at his shoulder, her face turned up to his.

Recently, often when I was supposed to be studying, I'd catch myself thinking about Grace. At night, she visited me in my dreams, a smiling mysterious presence, and I woke up and felt strangely bereft when I realized she wasn't with me.

Now it was coming home to me what her marriage meant. Although we only met now and then, in future it just wouldn't be the same. It was as if she was travelling away from me – I was losing her.

I jumped as my aunt put her arm round me. 'Don't fret, Lou. Your turn will come.'

Pulling away, I declared, 'I'm not fretting, Aunt. I don't want to be married.' I blushed. What on earth had made me say that?

But as I thought about it, I realized it was true. In my plans for the future I'd never included a husband.

My aunt smiled indulgently. 'You used to say that when you were a little girl. You're still young, but one day—'

I cut in. 'I'm sixteen. I'm not a child any more. I know what I want and it's not marriage.'

I was sorry immediately. I hadn't meant to be so sharp. My aunt stepped back, obviously disconcerted. She smiled tentatively and said, 'But – how would you be happy without a husband or children to care for?'

I thought about this. I had a sudden vision of Mamma, with a furrowed brow, discussing mutton with Mary; the slow ticking of the clock in the airless parlour as she dusted the heavy, dark furniture; endless afternoons spent visiting . . .

I said, 'I should think it would be boring, spending your day fretting about tradesmen and laundry and meals, looking after small children and waiting for your husband to come home.'

My aunt laughed and relaxed. 'That does sound boring. But if you're lucky in your husband, as I'm sure you will be, you'll have servants to do that for you, and you may please yourself.'

I didn't want to hurt her feelings – it was her own life she was describing – but I knew I wouldn't be satisfied. I wanted more than to fill my house with pretty, useless things, like the ones around us: pictures made from seaweed, boxes covered in shells, flowers made from feathers.

I chose my words carefully. 'I want to be useful.'

Aunt Phyllis nodded. 'There are many opportunities for charity work.'

I blurted out, 'I don't want to do charity work. I want to be a doctor!' I stopped. I hadn't meant to tell anyone yet.

'A doctor?' She half laughed but I saw that I'd shocked her again.

'Yes.' I spoke with more conviction than I felt. Hearing myself say it, it sounded absurd.

My aunt sighed and patted the sofa. 'Come here, my dear.'

I went and sat beside her. She regarded me seriously. 'I know that some women are taking up nursing as a profession—'

I interrupted. 'Yes! Papa has told me all about Florence Nightingale and her work in the Crimea. And I've read about her school for nurses at St Thomas's Hospital. But—'

My aunt held up her hand. 'It's admirable, of course. But those women have few other options, poor things. Whereas you—'

'That's it exactly. I can choose. And this is what I want.'

The more I'd read Papa's books and talked to him about medical matters, the more convinced I was that I wanted to follow in his footsteps. Since I'd found out there was a medical school for women in London, I'd been very excited, but so far I'd kept it to myself. I was sure Papa would like the idea, but I was equally sure Mamma wouldn't, and I didn't know if Papa would let me do something that would upset her.

My aunt was shaking her head. 'I'm sure you could do anything you put your mind to. You're such a clever girl . . . It's just – you don't need to work at all. It doesn't seem right that you should be thinking of it. You will gain such satisfaction from using your gifts to educate your children and support your husband in his career.'

I was shocked. I'd always thought Aunt Phyllis was, like Papa, very open-minded, not stuffy at all. And here she was, sounding just like Mamma!

In an effort to convince her, I said, 'I've been out with Papa on his rounds and watched him. I've helped him sometimes.'

'You haven't!' My aunt's eyebrows shot up.

'Yes. So, you see, I do know – it's what I want to do more than anything else.'

Aunt Phyllis rose and went over to the window. She stared out into the garden. 'Oh, Edward,' she said, half to herself, shaking her head regretfully. Turning back to me she said, 'You've discussed this with your parents, of course?'

'Um – no,' I admitted.

 101

My aunt looked at me gravely. 'But you will?'

I sighed. 'Yes, I'll talk to them about it when I go home.'

The candles in their silver holders threw a flickering pattern of light and shadow over us. In a dreamy rhythm, I moved the ivory-backed brush up and down the bright fall of red-gold hair spread over Grace's shoulders.

It seemed just like the old days when we were children, but it wasn't.

For one thing, the nursery was now a young lady's bedroom. Bead-encrusted boxes full of silver necklaces and bracelets lay on the dressing table before us. Crystal bottles and jars glittered in the candlelight. Before we could climb into bed, Grace had to remove quantities of cushions from the lace counterpane.

But the most important thing that had changed, in a way I didn't understand, was me.

I had always been happy, if a little shy, to share Grace's bed, but tonight, sinking into the feather mattress and breathing in the smell of lavender from the linen sheets, I was painfully aware of her body lying next to mine. If I moved a fraction of an inch, we would be touching. *Touching.*

I couldn't relax. There was a tension in the pit of my stomach, my skin prickled as if an electric current were running through it, and my heart was beating fast.

To distract myself, I said, 'What are you thinking?'

She turned her head towards me. 'Mm?'

I repeated my question.

Grace looked embarrassed. 'You'll think I'm silly, but I was just telling myself, *Soon I'll be Mrs Charles Sedgewick.*'

'Oh.' It was all I could manage.

She smiled. 'I'm so glad Charles has met you. I want you two to become friends.'

I thought this unlikely.

Charles had stayed for tea and I was shocked when I went into the drawing room and saw him: he seemed so old – a middle-aged man, not at all the gallant admirer I had imagined from Grace's description. When we were introduced, he nodded at me rather stiffly across the teacups. Afterwards he came across and said, 'Grace tells me you're quite a reader.'

There was something in his tone I didn't care for. Wanting to make sure he realized I didn't just read novels, I told him what I'd been studying lately. Rather than looking impressed, he frowned and said, 'Hmm.' Then he took his leave of me and went to sit beside Grace, leaving me struggling with painful feelings I couldn't untangle, except for the knowledge that I felt alarmed. Could my cousin really love *him*?

Impulsively I asked, 'Do you think you'll be happy?'

Grace smiled. 'Yes, I think I shall.' A faint pink flush appeared on her cheek.

Unbidden, the diagrams in a section of one of Papa's medical textbooks referring to 'the act of sexual congress' appeared in my mind.

The first time I'd come across them, I'd stared at them, fascinated and yet with a creeping feeling of unease. I couldn't imagine the reality represented by the diagrams. And soon Charles would be occupying my place in bed beside Grace . . . my stomach lurched again and I felt slightly sick.

Pushing the thought from my mind, I made myself say, 'I'm happy for you then.'

Grace leaned over me and I felt her lips brush my cheek.

 103

'Thank you, Lou. You're a dear. And now we must go to sleep. There's so much to do tomorrow.' She turned away from me and blew out the candle. 'Goodnight.'

'Goodnight.'

Soon her breathing deepened into sleep.

I lay still, aware of the warmth of her body beside me, of that strange, sweet feeling in the pit of my stomach. I had the oddest desire to put my arms round her and hold her close. I felt such a longing, a painful, lovely feeling that we might be like this always, that we might never be apart. And suddenly with a hot rush it came to me: *I love Grace, I love her.* In a confused way I knew I didn't just love her as cousins do. This was different, this was . . . I felt . . . *I felt about her in the way that she felt about Charles!*

My heart stopped. Then it sped on, as if I was running a race. I was trembling as if I had a fever and I tried to calm myself, to think, but my thoughts scattered like beads of mercury from a broken thermometer.

I told myself: *It can't be true, it can't.*

But even as I was denying it, I knew I was deceiving myself.

'What do you think, Lou?'

'Sorry?'

'Should we have salmon *and* lobster?'

It was the next morning. We were all sitting in the morning room and Aunt Phyllis and my cousins were discussing the wedding meal.

I shrugged, trying to smile. But I really didn't feel like smiling. I couldn't stop thinking about Grace – and me.

I kept telling myself that I must be mistaken. Of course I loved Grace, that was natural. We were cousins . . .

But this was different. This was . . . I didn't know what else to name it. This was being *in love*. But how could I be in love with her? If it were true, what did it mean? And what would Grace think of me if she knew?

I'd lain awake for hours, not daring to go to sleep in case I accidentally moved too close to her and gave myself away. Now I felt tired and wretched and the questions wouldn't stop chasing each other round and round in my head.

I dragged my attention back to the conversation.

'We must have jellies, blancmange *and* fruit tarts.' Maud had abandoned her efforts to be grown-up for the moment.

Aunt Phyllis laughed. 'You won't be able to eat all those. You'll be sick.'

'And don't forget there'll be the cake,' Grace put in. She glanced at me, smiling, but I couldn't meet her eyes. What if she saw the truth in mine?

'But there'll be so many people,' said Maud. 'And it's very *grand* to have a choice.'

She put her nose in the air as she said this, and everyone laughed. I joined in, but I didn't feel like laughing.

Without warning the door opened and Susan burst in. Her cap was awry and her face was flushed.

'What is it, Susan?' said Aunt Phyllis with unusual sharpness.

'Oh, Ma'am. It's a telegram. For Miss Louisa.'

For a second no one moved or spoke. Then I seized the yellow envelope and with trembling fingers drew out the thin sheet of paper. As I read it, I felt the colour drain from my face.

 105

'What's happened, Lou?' Grace was watching me with concern.

I stood up. 'I have to go home immediately. Papa is ill.'

There was a general exclamation.

'May I?' Taking the telegram from my hand, Aunt Phyllis scanned it. 'Your mother doesn't say what is wrong.' She gave me a lopsided smile. 'Perhaps it's not so serious. You know your mother.'

'Yes. But I must go. I must see how he is.'

She nodded. 'Of course. Whatever it is, he'll feel better for the sight of you. The maid will pack your things and I'll order the carriage.'

I left in a confusion of goodbyes. At the last minute Grace thrust something through the carriage window. It was the sketch she'd made of me. 'If Uncle Edward is all right, you'll come back again, won't you?'

Her beautiful face was creased with concern and I wanted to jump out of the carriage and bury myself in her arms. But I was also frantic to get home.

We set off. I sat staring at the sketch, but I didn't see it. Was Papa seriously ill? Had Mamma sent for Tom too? Or perhaps she was mistaken and it was a false alarm. Oh, if only it was and I could go back to Carr Head . . .

In time with the rhythm of the rolling wheels, my mind spun between two desperate poles: Grace, Papa, Grace, Papa.

The journey had never seemed so long. We had to stop to change horses, but I wouldn't go into the inn, I didn't want to waste a minute. And I couldn't eat. The coachman stood in the

yard to have a bite of bread and a few mouthfuls of ale, then we sped on again.

When I reached home, Mamma met me at the door. She looked pale and the lines on her face were deeper.

'Where's Papa?'

'He's just gone upstairs to fetch something.'

I stared at her. 'He's not in bed then?'

She shook her head. 'He says it's nothing. Just a bilious attack.'

'You sent a telegram for a bilious attack!' My voice echoed in the empty space of the hall. I wanted to shake her for dragging me away from Grace, frightening me for nothing.

Mamma sat down on the hall chair as if she was tired. 'I'm so worried about him.'

'But why? What's the matter?'

Before she could explain Papa appeared on the landing. 'Lou? What are you doing home?'

He started down the stairs but I ran up and met him halfway. I hugged him round the waist. Under his jacket, I could hear his heart, a steady, reassuring beat.

He smiled down at me. 'I didn't expect you for another week.'

'I couldn't stand any more fussing and furbelows.' Angry as I was with Mamma, I didn't want to tell Papa about the telegram. That he was at home in the afternoon was unheard of. Perhaps Mamma had good reason to send it.

To change the subject I said, 'Shouldn't you be in bed?'

'I'm only feeling a little unwell. And I have been taking things easy.'

I shook my head. 'You should be lying down. That's what you would tell your patients.'

He laughed. 'Doctors make the worst patients. It's well known.'

'And what are your symptoms?'

He ticked them off on his fingers. 'A headache, a touch of diarrhoea and I don't care for my pipe. Oh, and a disinclination to work. It's probably something I ate.' He smiled. 'You know how the ladies like to spoil me. Very likely it was Mrs Petty's fruit cake. Months old, I expect. And now, if you'll excuse me, I think I'll read the paper.'

He passed me and continued down the stairs. He was moving slowly and holding on to the banister but he was steady. He disappeared into his study.

I felt reassured. Mamma had caused unnecessary alarm and I was about to say so when something in her stiff posture silenced me. She hadn't moved from her seat and, in the dim light, her eyes looked like bruises in the pale oval of her face.

Steam is rising from the surface of the water in the bath. I hunch into myself, but I can't cover my nakedness.

'Stand up straight, Miss Childs.' Weeks is thin-lipped.

I don't trust her for a moment. But Eliza is here, standing by the taps, and she gives me an encouraging look.

'But I had a bath yesterday when I arrived.'

'This is good for you, Miss.' Eliza glances at Weeks and adds in an undertone, 'You know, for your monthlies.' As if she thinks I might find the subject too indelicate, she mouths the last word. But Weeks has heard.

'Eliza's right – this is the recommended treatment for aymen-oria.' She stumbles over the last word.

I'm puzzled. I've never heard of this before. And then I realize – 'Oh, amenorrhoea'.

Weeks scowls. 'Hold her arms, Eliza.'

It's too late – I should have run. But without my clothes, how could I?

Weeks is holding a canvas strap in her hands. What's it for? My skin crawls. I saw what she did to Miss Hill. What's she going to do to me?

Eliza gives me a rueful look as if she's sorry for what she has to do. I cling to this. Weeks can't do anything bad while Eliza's here.

Swiftly Weeks wraps the strap around my chest, pinning my arms to my sides.

'What are you doing?' My voice wobbles.

109

'Now, Miss Childs, don't make things worse for yourself.' She is efficient. She has already put another strap round my thighs and is bending to fasten my ankles together, giving the strap a painful tug before standing up.

She reaches towards me. I can't help it – I jerk away, lurch, lose my balance and fall. My chin cracks on the stone and hot pain shoots up my jaw. Stunned, I lie still for a moment.

'Miss, are you all right?' Eliza is bending over me.

'Of course she is, Eliza. Don't make a fuss.' Weeks's tone is acid.

I feel foolish, lying naked on the cold floor, unable to get up. I explore my mouth gingerly with my tongue. All my teeth are in place but I can taste the metallic tang of blood.

'Let's get this done.'

The next minute Eliza and Weeks haul me to my feet and before I can say anything, they pick me up and drop me in the bath. Water fills my mouth and nose. I can't breathe. Panicking, spluttering, I scrabble with my feet and manage to push myself up, bring my head into the air. I gasp for breath, inhale hot steam.

Behind my head, I hear a cupboard door opening. Now Eliza is standing beside the bath, her arms clasped round something that is rolled up; in the dim light, it looks like a thick blanket or a rug.

Weeks moves to the other side and between them, they unfold the roll and hang it over the bath. It's a canvas cover, which comes up to my neck and stretches down to the taps.

My spine prickles with apprehension. 'What's this?'

Weeks ignores me. Eliza explains, 'We can't stay and watch you, Miss.' She's busy fastening the cover under the rim of the bath. Rough canvas chafes my neck.

'But I don't need watching. I won't climb out.' How can I, strapped up like this?

'It's the rule,' Weeks snaps, checking the fastening. The cover's too tight. It's choking me. I press my head against the back of the bath. This is mad. They know I'm sane so they're trying to drive me mad.

'Right, Eliza.'

Eliza gives me another rueful look but she has to follow Weeks out. They take the lamp with them.

I daren't move. The darkness presses on my eyes and ears and I listen out for footsteps. Surely they'll be back soon? All I can hear is a muffled *drip drip*.

I realize I'm holding my breath. I let it go, then breathe in just a little through my nose. I'm scared of swallowing the blackness.

Why have they done this to me? I've done nothing wrong.

You've made an enemy of Weeks. And you know what else you've done.

I close my eyes. Then jerk them open.

Don't fall asleep. Think. Think. Find something to focus on. How to amputate a leg? Yes. Apply a tourniquet.

I have to find a way out of here. If I write tonight, Mamma should get my letter tomorrow.

With the knife, cut through the soft tissue to the bone, leaving flaps of muscle.

111

I might hear from her by tomorrow night.

With the saw, cut the bone.

Or perhaps she won't write, but will come immediately.

With the forceps, trim round the edges of the bone.

I might be home in a day or two. Unless Mamma is too anxious to come herself.

With artery forceps, pick up the ends of the major arteries and veins and apply ligatures to stop the bleeding.

She could send Mary.

Fold the flaps of muscle over the cut bone . . .

Oh Mamma, I'm sorry I was so angry with you. Please send Mary . . .

. . . and sew the edges together.

Or perhaps it's Tom I should be writing to. Yes, Tom, he's much nearer. But maybe he can't get away at the moment. Would Aunt Phyllis be better?

Who? Who will come and save me?

The hot steam rises round my face. My sore mouth is throbbing. Mustn't shut my eyes. Mustn't sleep. But I'm so heavy, drowsy in the heat, drifting . . .

I'm in a green, leafy place. Somewhere water is trickling and I can hear laughter.

I go in search of it, brushing aside branches bowed down with white blossoms. It's warm – I'm hot in my heavy gown. And then I hear a familiar lilting voice. It's Grace! She says, 'Why don't you take off your clothes?'

I obey, undressing slowly as I stroll dreamily on, leaving a trail of garments behind me. Grace's voice soothes. 'Isn't it lovely? Feel the cool grass under your feet . . .'

For a moment I'm utterly happy.

But then a different voice hisses in my ear, 'You're a bad girl, a very, very bad girl, and you must be punished . . .'

My feet are clamped to the ground and I can't move. Long white fingers like maggots creep over my body, I'm sinking into the earth, deeper and deeper until I'm lost. The cold creeps up my body and then I know. I'm dead. I'm buried.

I open my eyes.

It's totally dark. I'm numb with cold, and fear beats in my ears. I can't move. A heavy weight is pinning me down. My mouth, my eyes, my ears are blocked with darkness. I've been buried alive. They have dug a pit and put me in it and stamped the earth down on top of me so that I can't cry out . . .

Drip.

I remember. I'm still in the bath. How long have I been here? Why has no one come?

I try to call but only produce a croak.

The door opens, sending a bar of light across the canvas cover.

'Miss? You're still here?'

It's Eliza, with a lamp.

'Oh, Miss, are you all right? I'd have come to top up the hot water, but Weeks sent me on an errand. I thought she'd see to you.'

All the time she's talking, she's unfastening the cover, helping me out. I can hardly stand. My teeth are chattering.

Eliza supports me on one arm, rubbing me vigorously with a towel.

'You're right perished! It's wicked. Can you walk?'

A nod. All I can manage.

Eliza helps me along the hallway to the dormitory, where she unlocks the door.

'You'd best get into bed, Miss. It's the only way to warm up. Here, slip under the covers while I fetch your nightgown.'

She holds back the bedclothes and I climb stiffly into bed. I lie curled up with my arms wrapped round me, trying to get warm. My hands and feet are numb.

Eliza is soon back. She helps me to sit up and puts my nightgown on me, as if I'm a child. My skin is blotchy, wrinkled like a prune. I try to fasten my nightgown, but my shrivelled fingers won't work. Eliza does it for me, patiently tugging at each button with her broad fingers.

She smells of milk and almonds.

When I am tucked in, she pauses by the bed.

'I'm sorry about this, Miss. I'd say something, but it'd cost me my place, you see.'

I manage another nod.

'You have a good sleep.'

Don't take the lamp away. Don't leave me alone.

The light goes from the room. I'm in the dark again. The fear is waiting.

Just once I let myself think, Grace, where are you? Then I roll into a tight ball and tell myself, over and over again, It will be all right, it will be all right . . .

Six Months Earlier

I didn't want any pudding and, strangely, Mamma didn't insist. She was staring out of the window and seemed to have forgotten the food going cold on her plate.

Neither of us spoke. In the silence, the ticking of the clock seemed louder than usual. I wondered if Mamma, like me, was thinking of Papa, lying in bed upstairs.

I looked at her. 'Shall I see how he is?'

'Yes, do.' Another strange thing. Usually I couldn't leave the table until everyone had finished.

Papa was lying back on his pillow. On the tray in front of him, the bowl of soup was half full. Still, he had eaten a few spoonfuls.

He smiled at me. 'Hello, Lou. Had your dinner?' He was trying to speak normally, but his voice sounded hoarse. His face was flushed again, a deep red.

'Papa, I think I should take your temperature.'

'Don't be silly, Lou. It's not necessary.'

'I think it is. Papa, you know it is. Please.'

He gave in as if indulging my whim, and I fetched the thermometer from his study. When I saw the result, I exclaimed, 'It's a hundred and three! We should send for Dr Kneale.'

He lifted his hand in protest. 'No. There's no need to trouble him. I've probably got a touch of influenza, that's all.' He broke off in a fit of coughing. Perhaps he was right about the influenza.

 115

When he'd recovered, he murmured, 'What I need is a good sleep.'

I took the hint and left him in peace.

Alone at my desk, I tried to read, but I had to keep going back over the same sentences. I couldn't stop thinking about Papa.

'Louisa!' It was Mamma's voice, sharp, urgent.

I ran to my parents' bedroom.

Papa had vomited. He was tossing around in a tangle of sheets and he still looked very hot.

Mamma tugged at his soiled nightgown but he was flailing his arms so wildly she couldn't get if off. 'Help me, Louisa.'

We managed to pull the gown over his head but as we were trying to put on a fresh one, he sat up and pushed us away.

'Don't touch me, you blackguards!' he shouted and, seizing his pillow, he thrashed it about as if he was fighting off an unseen enemy.

'Papa, it's me. Louisa!' But he didn't know me.

Mamma cried, 'Edward!' and tried to catch hold of his arm, but he pushed her violently against the chest of drawers.

I went to the door and shouted for Mary. As soon as she appeared, I said, 'You must run for Dr Kneale. Hurry, Mary!'

It seemed like an age until the doctor came. All the while Papa thrashed about and babbled nonsense in a voice I'd never heard before. Mamma and I watched in silent horror. There was nothing we could do.

Dr Kneale arrived. Although he was a colleague of Papa's at the Dispensary, we didn't know him very well. He examined Papa then turned to Mary and said, 'Have you any ice?'

When she nodded, he told her to fetch some, wrapped in a

cloth, and hold it on Papa's forehead. Papa was less agitated now and submitted to this quietly, although he continued to mutter and once said, very distinctly, 'Pecked off her nose!'

Dr Kneale took Mamma out of the room and I followed.

On the landing, Mamma was saying, 'He's been so restless at night, unable to sleep. It's unlike him.'

'And he's had diarrhoea,' I added. 'Not much and not very often, but it's yellow, like pea soup.'

Dr Kneale surveyed me with his mild blue eyes. 'Well, now. That's a very precise observation, young lady. You're quite the nurse, aren't you?'

His tone made me squirm, but before I could say anything, Mamma asked, 'What do you think it is?'

We both stared at him anxiously until he said, 'I don't think there's anything to worry about. I'd say it was a common fever. It shouldn't last more than a week or so.'

A sigh escaped Mamma and her shoulders relaxed. I felt reassured too. The doctor left, saying that he would look in the next day.

Mamma turned to me. 'I was thinking we should send for Tom. But really, there's no need now.'

I agreed. I wasn't surprised she wanted Tom home, but I could just imagine his annoyance at being dragged all the way from London for nothing, especially as he was about to sit his first medical examinations.

Papa opened his eyes. For a moment he looked round in an unfocused way. Then his gaze fell on me and he tried to smile.

'Lou.' His voice was faint.

As always when he was lucid again, I felt weak with relief. If only this time it would last. If only the crisis were over. I concentrated on practicalities. 'It's time for your pill, Papa.'

I put it between his poor, cracked lips and tilted the glass of water. As he drank, a trickle ran from the side of his mouth. I wiped it away. He licked his lips and I saw that his tongue was brown.

I felt his nightgown. It was drenched with sweat so I fetched a clean one. When I took off the soiled one I was shocked again. In the month since I was summoned home from Carr Head, he'd grown so thin his ribs protruded. And the tell-tale spots were clearly visible on his chest and back.

Why had it taken Dr Kneale so long to realize? I'd shivered when he said the word and Mamma gave a little cry and went quite white.

Typhoid.

Although she didn't mention it, I knew Mamma would be thinking of her brother. But after all, there was hope. People recovered from typhoid.

When Papa was settled on his pillow again, I said, 'Would you like anything? Beef tea? Or toast and water?'

He shook his head. 'Not now. Later.'

'I could read to you.'

'No. Thank you. Feel sleepy.'

He shut his eyes. Soon his breathing deepened.

I tiptoed over to the window and looked out, parting the curtains carefully so the light didn't disturb Papa.

Morning had come to the street. Over the way, the maid was scrubbing the step, her back bobbing up and down with her energetic strokes. A delivery boy with a basket slung over his arm

went whistling round the corner. I felt cut off from them by more than a pane of glass.

This had been going on so long.

I wanted it to end. I dreaded it ending.

The door opened and Mamma came in. Her face was even paler than usual, the hollows beneath her eyes darker.

'How is he?'

'Much calmer now.' We kept our voices low and both glanced towards the bed. Papa stirred but didn't wake.

Mamma was still carrying a handkerchief and I wondered if she'd been crying again. She started twisting it as if she'd forgotten she was holding it. 'Do you think we should send for Tom today?'

She'd asked me this every morning since the doctor had pronounced the word. My reply was the same as usual. 'No, Mamma. You know the doctor said it wouldn't be wise because of the danger of infection. And Papa specifically said we were not to send for Tom or Aunt Phyllis. Besides, it may not be necessary.'

Mamma seemed to seize on my words gratefully. 'Yes, of course, you're right. We'll wait.' Then she stood still, as if at a loss as to what to do next.

Mamma, who'd always seemed so firm, so clear, now seemed to be softening and blurring . . . like a melting candle. She even seemed to be smaller than before, as if she were shrinking.

'Why don't you try to rest?' I suggested. 'I can sit with Papa.'

She came to then. Drawing herself upright, she said, 'I must see to my chores.'

 119

She went out of the room leaving me to watch the rise and fall of Papa's breath.

A few days later, after examining Papa, Doctor Kneale touched me on the shoulder and said gently, 'I think you should send for your brother now.'

I looked at him, not understanding. 'But Papa is better, isn't he? He's been so much quieter the last day or two.'

The doctor shook his head. 'I fear he is sinking.'

He went out and I heard him call for Mary. They spoke quietly at the door. All the time I sat there feeling numb.

Then Mary came in. 'The doctor says you want me to send a telegram, Miss Louisa.' Her eyes glistened as if she were holding back tears.

I roused myself. 'Yes, to Tom.'

'What shall I say?'

'Say, *You must come now.*'

Mamma and I sat there through the evening, not speaking. There was nothing to say.

I didn't want this quiet dream to end. Papa was still here, that was the main thing. I held his hand and stroked it. He was breathing rapidly and there was a dusky tinge to his face but otherwise he lay peacefully.

At one point Mamma went out to fetch some fresh water and while she was gone, Papa opened his eyes and seemed to be listening.

'What is it, Papa?'

He spoke but his voice was a croak.

I bent towards him.

'Birds,' he said. 'I can hear birds.'

He turned his head and looked directly at me. 'Lou?'

'Yes, Papa?'

Speaking with great effort he said, 'You'll make a fine doctor. God bless, my darling.' Then his voice sank to a whisper. 'Fetch Mamma.'

Fierce wings beat about my heart.

He mustn't go. He couldn't.

Tears blurring my eyes, I stumbled to the door and opening it, called out, 'Mamma, come quickly.'

My voice seemed insubstantial, as if the dark shadows were swallowing it.

So. He had gone.

In a state of dreary blankness I did what had to be done. Mary and I drew down the blinds, silenced the clocks, covered the mirrors. I helped Mamma order our mourning clothes and write to those who needed to know. All the time I felt cut off, as if I were under a glass dome. Mamma's anguish, Tom's anger because he had come too late and he blamed me – none of it reached me.

Sometimes I sat with the body, watching the shadows cast by the candlelight flicker over the waxen face. This wasn't Papa any more. He had gone. But even so, when they came to make a plaster cast of his face, I couldn't stay but went and sat in his study. I clasped the cushion that still smelt of him. But I didn't cry.

The undertaker's men brought the coffin downstairs to the dining room and laid it on the table. I couldn't help thinking of Papa carving the Sunday joint and my heart missed a beat. But still I didn't cry.

 121

When it was my turn to say goodbye, I looked down at the face, which wasn't Papa's face any more. I knew I should be feeling something. But I was numb.

Sitting with all the other women in the parlour, Grace beside me, I was all right until I heard the death knell. I knew then that the body had been brought to the grave and I imagined Papa being lowered into the cold earth.

He doesn't feel it, I told myself, but still I shivered.

The house was strangely quiet.

When Grace left with her family, I wanted to run after the carriage and get in with her and be carried away. Not be left behind with Mamma and Tom, as if we'd been marooned.

Mamma was inconsolable so I took over the running of the house. I kept expecting to hear Papa arriving home, to see him at breakfast. Every day it came to me, with a fresh jolt, that I would never see him again. But I still couldn't accept it.

The days went by, each as blank and dreary as the one before, and after a while, at the back of my mind a little voice started up, asking: *What will happen to me now?*

It seemed wrong to be thinking about myself at such a time, but I could see my life stretching in front of me, with nothing in it but staying at home and looking after Mamma.

At the thought of it, I felt stifled and a kind of dread filled me.

I had to do something.

Before he became too ill, I'd told Papa about my dream. He said he was proud of me and it made my heart swell. But he'd warned me not to speak of my plans to Mamma until he'd talked to her first. I was sure he hadn't – she hadn't mentioned it. Now it was too late. I knew she'd never agree but I clung to one hope – maybe Tom could persuade her.

He and I had scarcely spoken since he'd come home. He'd spent time with Mamma, but largely ignored me. I didn't want him to leave with things as they were. Surely we'd be able to mend the breach . . .

I found Tom in Papa's study. I was dismayed to see that he was sorting books into piles. 'What are you doing?'

'Mother said I could take anything that would be useful. I'm leaving tomorrow, you know.'

Papa's books . . .

Aside from the fact that I might want to use them, I couldn't bear to see them going. But I swallowed my protest. I didn't want a row now, when I needed him to be on my side.

I'd decided to approach the subject of my future in a round-about way, so I said tentatively, 'Are you enjoying your studies? Are things progressing well?'

He shrugged. 'Well enough.'

'You know Mamma's unhappy about you going back to London. Now you've completed a year, had you thought of transferring to the hospital at Leeds? Then you'd be able to come home more often. Mamma would be pleased, and so would I.'

As I said this, I realized it was true. Perhaps it was something to do with the loss of Papa, but I wanted to feel closer to my brother, to know him better. And not just because we shared the same interest in medicine . . .

Surely, now that we were older, this was possible?

Tom scowled. 'Why would I want to transfer? Everyone

 123

knows the London teaching hospitals are the best. And if I want to get on . . .'

'Get on? What do you mean?'

He rolled his eyes as if he couldn't be bothered to explain it all to me and took another book off the shelf.

'Aren't you coming back here – to the practice?'

He appeared to be studying the title of the book intently. 'To tell you the truth, Lou, I'm not interested in that any more.'

'But I thought Grandpapa intended—'

He cut in. 'Things have changed since Grandpapa's day. I could be a top consultant in the West End, earning thousands of pounds a year.'

I stared at him. 'Did Papa know about this?'

His cheeks reddened and he dropped his eyes. 'No. I was going to tell him . . .'

We both fell silent. I felt sure Papa would have been unhappy about Tom's plan, but I couldn't speak of it. Even to think about Papa made my throat tighten.

I looked around the study – all the other familiar things were still here: Papa's battered old Gladstone bag, his pewter tobacco jar, the owl pipe-rack. It all looked just the same and yet it wasn't.

I swallowed. 'Mamma will be upset, don't you think?'

He put the book down and took another. The silence lengthened.

I noticed that there were dark smudges under his eyes. Perhaps he'd been studying too hard. 'How did your exams go?'

'Oh, well enough,' he said again. He added hastily, 'We haven't had the results yet.' There was something odd about his

tone, but I didn't want to press him. This might be my last chance to talk to him about my future. I had to seize it.

I took a deep breath, then the words came tumbling out. 'Tom, there's something I wanted to ask you. I spoke to Papa about it and he agreed, but I don't think Mamma will, but she might, if you ask her.'

Tom's frowned. 'What are you talking about, Lou?'

'I want to be a doctor too.'

Tom stared at me. I waited, praying that he'd understand. But to my astonishment, he started laughing. 'A doctor! Don't be ridiculous, Lou. How could you be a doctor?' He shook his head and slapped his leg as if this was the funniest joke he'd ever heard.

His mockery stung, but I also felt a burning sensation in my chest, as if someone had lit a fuse. Why was it so ridiculous?

'Why not?'

'It's not something a woman can do.'

'But there are women—'

He snorted. 'Yes, but it's preposterous!'

I began to tremble, but I bit back the retort that rose to my lips. I had to get him on my side.

I looked him straight in the face and said as calmly as I could, 'I'm not joking, Tom. This is what I really want. I've worked hard and I think I nearly know enough for the preliminary exams. And Papa –' I stopped, swallowed, then went on. 'Papa supported me. He said I could, if Mamma agreed. That's why I'd like you to speak to her.'

I think he could tell that I was serious. Abruptly his manner changed. The colour left his face and he just stared at me, shaking his head slowly.

 125

A horrible feeling started to grow inside me. 'Tom—'

He put out his hand to stop me. 'It's out of the question. I am the head of this house now and I won't allow it.'

I couldn't believe it. Papa had warned me that I'd face strong opposition from other doctors but I never thought my own brother would oppose me.

'But Tom—'

'I won't let my sister embark on an improper course that will bring shame on her and all the family.'

It was my turn to stare. Why was he talking in that odd, stiff way? And then the full import of his words hit me and suddenly all thoughts of being grown-up vanished and we were back in the nursery again, all the familiar old frustrations welling up in me.

'But that's not fair. Why should you control what I do?'

Tom looked at me with the old, maddeningly superior expression. 'Because it's my right.'

I felt as if I'd been struck. I clenched my fists and tried to control myself.

He turned back to the books as if the subject was closed. Over his shoulder, he said, 'By the way, have you still got Papa's stethoscope?'

I was immediately suspicious. 'Yes. Why?'

'Can I have it? It's much better than mine.'

A hot flame seared my chest, but I managed to say, 'No, you can't. Papa left it to me.'

'But you won't be needing it, will you?'

My self-control vanished. *I hate you!* I shouted and flew at him, pounding him with my fists.

He caught hold of my hands and calmly held me at arm's

126

length until, my strength exhausted, I stopped struggling and glared at him, panting.

'You see,' Tom said, with another smile, letting go of me. 'What a temper. You'd need more self-control if you were going to be a doctor.'

I had no breath to respond.

He moved towards the door, carrying a pile of books. 'You're not to say anything to Mamma, by the way. I won't have her upset by your silly notions.'

Then he went out, closing the door behind him.

Seizing the cushion from Papa's chair, I flung myself down and buried my face in it.

'Papa – oh, Papa,' I murmured brokenly, and then I couldn't hold back any longer – all the unshed tears poured out, soaking into the fabric, washing away the last remnants of his scent that still clung there.

All night, fear has fluttered under my ribs.

What will Weeks say about yesterday evening? What will she do?

The door opens . . . I hold my breath . . . but she drops a bundle of clothes on to my bed without a word; she doesn't even look at me. I watch her go round the dormitory, her face closed, grim.

My swollen lip throbs, my arm is bruised where I fell. She was punishing me, I'm sure. For telling Dr Bull about her or for eavesdropping on her attack on Miss Hill? Both probably. I could report her about the bath, but she'll say she was carrying out orders and Eliza can't support me. If I describe her cruelty to Miss Hill, she'll deny it. They'll say I'm making it up, that it's a delusion of my madness. And Weeks will punish me again.

I pull a garment from the pile of clothes. *These are mine. My own clothes.*

For a moment, I hug them to me, as if they are old friends. Then I examine my gown, my petticoats, my chemise. 'Lucy Childs'. 'Lucy Childs'. 'Lucy Childs'. The same name in each garment. Not my name.

Say nothing, play the game. It won't be for long now.

If I don't see Mr Sneed today, I'll write the letter. Nothing will stop me.

Looking to see that no one is watching, I surreptitiously

feel the waistband of my gown. The money is still there! That at least is something.

I dress, moving sluggishly into the routine of the day. My mouth is sore, and I have a dull pain behind my eyes; I feel worn out. I find it hard to sew, fumbling at the cloth with my shrivelled fingers, my eyes so tired I can hardly see the stitches.

By evening there's been no message from the superintendent, so after supper I approach Weeks.

My stomach is knotted, but I keep my face neutral and ask politely if I may write a letter. For a moment I think she'll refuse – she eyes me suspiciously – but then she unlocks the cabinet and passes the things to me without a word. A sheet of paper, an envelope, a pen, some ink.

I try to keep my voice level. 'May I have two pieces of paper?'

Weeks frowns.

I look her in the eye, holding my breath. She's going to refuse. But no, she hands over another sheet. 'That will be threepence.'

Five coins in my pocket. I give her one, then go to the table in the far corner. After some hesitation, I write:

Wildthorn Hall

Dear Mamma,
I have arrived safely and I am well, as I hope you are too.

When Weeks circles the room to check what we're doing, this is the letter she sees, this is the letter I'll give her to

129

post. Hidden beneath it is the other piece of paper. As soon as Weeks has passed on, I pull this out and hurriedly write on it:

Dearest Mamma,

Ignore my other letter. If you have heard from the Woodvilles and are wondering where I am, I'm afraid I have some bad news. I am locked up in an asylum called Wildthorn Hall. I don't know where it is exactly, but you should be able to find it. It's somewhere in Essex, in a forest. Please come and rescue me or arrange for someone else to do it.

I pause and glance round.

Weeks is lecturing Mrs Thorpe, who's been shifting from chair to chair, leaving a trail of white threads on the carpet. I'm safe for the moment.

I think it was that woman, Mrs Lunt, who engineered this. I'll explain it all when I see you.

This is a dreadful place. They have locked me up. They spy on us all the time, and I mean <u>all</u> the time, even in the most private moments. Their treatment of the patients is appalling. Yesterday they tried to scald me and they left me in the dark for hours trapped in the bath.

And they're trying to drive me mad by pretending I'm someone else – they want me to be like all the other mad people here, but I know who I am and I know I'm not mad. But if I stay here much longer, I'm afraid I will go insane.

I pause, my hand trembling. I imagine Mamma at her writing desk, reading my letter. My heart twists.

I dip my pen in the ink and write:

Mamma, I'm sorry for how we parted. Please make them let me out. Please come and take me home.

The paper is full. Just enough space to squeeze in:

Your loving daughter
Louisa

If Weeks opens the other letter and wonders why there's only one sheet of paper, I'll tell her my pen leaked on the second sheet and I screwed it up and threw it on the fire. This letter, the real letter, I'll give to Eliza, with some money for an envelope and stamp. Perhaps she'll be able to post it tomorrow.

In spite of everything, Mamma will come to my rescue, I know.

All I have to do is wait.

I let myself drift with the swaying motion of the train that was carrying me to my new life at the London School of Medicine for Women.

Something hard hit my leg and I opened my eyes.

I was squashed between a fat woman and a girl with a wriggling toddler on her lap. The child kicked my knee again, but the girl turned her head, pretending not to see. Someone was smoking a pipe; people were unwrapping greasy brown packages and soon the smell of ripe cheese and sausage filled the carriage, making my insides heave. The toddler grizzled and the heat rose.

My head was beginning to throb so I shut my eyes again, but this time I couldn't escape into my daydream. I had to face reality. I wasn't on my way to begin a new life; I was going to see Tom, to plead with him.

My stomach was tying itself in knots. I'd never been to London before, never even travelled any distance on my own. On top of that I was apprehensive about seeing Tom.

I tried to reassure myself. We hadn't corresponded at all in the three months since Papa died, but as long as I stayed calm, and stated my case clearly, I could get him to agree, couldn't I?

To distract myself, I started writing a letter to Grace in my head.

Dear Grace,
Do you remember how I wanted to be a hero?
Now my days are spent dusting ornaments and deciding

between scrag end of mutton and fatty strips of belly of pork for dinners that Mamma and I push around our plates, each of us pretending to eat . . .

As you know, Mamma has always been thrifty, but now, although Papa left us plenty of money, she has got it into her head that there isn't enough, and she doles out the money for the housekeeping in such small amounts, I have to scrimp to make ends meet.

Mamma has other anxieties too, and whatever I'm doing, she follows me about, because she can't bear to be alone. I try to set her mind at rest about whether Mary has remembered to buy candles and why Tom hasn't written . . .

And I keep thinking I hear the front door open and Papa's step in the hall . . .

Oh, Grace, I know you must be busy planning your new life, but it would be lovely to hear from you . . . I do miss you . . .

I opened my eyes, blinking the tears away.

I would never send this letter, of course. I wouldn't want Grace to be burdened with my troubles. And Mamma wouldn't want anyone, certainly not Aunt Phyllis, to know how her grief had affected her. Only Mary and I really knew.

I sighed. I didn't like leaving Mary with the responsibility of looking after Mamma, but I had to come. I had to *try*.

And if Tom agreed then perhaps we could make some arrangement for Mamma – perhaps hire a companion for her. Someone that she trusted and felt happy with . . .

As the wheels ate up the miles to London, my heart beat a refrain to their rhythm: *Please let Tom understand. Please let him*

133

change his mind. Please let him say that I can train to be a doctor.

I stepped down from the train into a barrage of noise: steam hissing, shrill whistles, doors slamming and voices, voices everywhere. I was carried along in the crush of bodies. High above, birds were flying in and out of veils of smoke and above them, through the double vault of glass, stained with soot, I caught glimpses of yellow sky.

I reached the end of the platform. This, surely, was where Tom would meet me. The crowd was thinning and I scanned every face but there was no sign of him. What if he hadn't received my letter?

I was afraid to move in case he couldn't find me. Fifteen minutes ticked by on the station clock, by which time I'd chewed a hole in the finger of my glove.

A voice made me jump. 'New to London, are you, dearie? Looking for somewhere to stay?'

I stared at the woman's wrinkled face, seamed with beige powder, at her rouged cheeks, her greedy eyes.

'No, no thank you,' I said hastily, and moved off towards the station entrance. There I stopped, overwhelmed.

The broad street was choked with traffic and the noise was deafening: the grinding of iron-shod wheels over the cobbles, the cries and whip-cracks of the drivers. Crowds hurried past on the pavement, amongst them men with placards advertising theatres, patent medicines, Hovis bread, the *Daily News*. The continuous movement of people in the heavy, humid air and the stench of horse manure and drains made my head reel.

I backed against the stone wall. Its cool, gritty surface felt

solid, comforting, but I couldn't stay there: people, especially men, kept looking at me. I looked up at the clock on the tall red tower to my right: two o'clock already. *Where was Tom?*

Stay calm, I told myself. *Think.* I had the address of Tom's lodgings in my bag; I must go there and see if he was at home. If not, someone might know where he was.

I asked a woman with a kind face the way to the Caledonian Road and she told me it was just round the corner. I pushed through the noisy throng, the sultry air fastening itself like a tight band round my head.

Part-way along the Caledonian Road I stopped and looked at the piece of paper with Tom's address on it: 7, Warren Place. He'd said it was near the canal.

As I hesitated on the pavement, a voice said, 'May I help you, Miss?'

I turned, feeling a surge of relief at the sight of the blue uniform. The constable gave me directions, indicating a narrow passageway between two buildings. 'It's only a short step away, but are you sure you'll be all right on your own, Miss?'

'Of course.' But as soon as I turned off the main thoroughfare my pretended confidence vanished.

The passageway smelled dreadful, as if it had been used as a lavatory. Holding my breath I picked up my skirts. I came out in a gloomy square and here the smell was so bad it made my eyes water. Putting my handkerchief to my nose, I crossed the square and turned into a cindery lane, with a high brick wall on one side and a row of ill-assorted buildings on the other.

Here I stopped. It must be a mistake. Tom couldn't possibly be living here.

I was debating whether to turn back when some ragged children with dirty faces appeared from nowhere and started calling out to me, so I walked on swiftly. I soon came to number 7, a tall, grimy house with brown flaking paint on its door and windows. I was sure I was wasting my time.

Taking a deep breath I pushed the bell. Nothing happened. I pushed again and waited. Eventually the door opened.

'Yis?' A scrawny girl glowered at me, her grubby mob-cap slipping over one eye.

'I'm looking for Mr Cosgrove. Does he live here?'

'He's not in.' She made to close the door.

'Wait!' Desperation made my voice sharp and the girl narrowed her eyes. 'Please. Could you tell me when he'll be back?'

'Dunno.' Her hand was still on the door. 'Is he expecting yer?'

'Yes. That is, I sent a letter. But I don't know if he received it this morning.'

'Nah,' she said, 'he didn't. His letters're waitin' for 'im.'

Tom didn't know I was in London.

''Ere,' she said, 'y'ain't gonna faint, are yer?'

The roar in my ears receded. 'No. But I need to sit down. Please let me wait for him. I'm his sister.'

She smirked at that, but she said, 'I s'pose it can't do no 'arm. Mind, you'll have to sit in the 'all. There ain't nowhere else.' She opened the door wider and I went in.

The dim, narrow hallway was brown too: greasy-looking brown panelling, scuffed brown linoleum; there were even dun-coloured stains on the ceiling. Why was Tom living *here*?

'There y'are.' The girl jerked her thumb at a chair squeezed in between the stairs and a rickety table on which some letters lay.

I let myself down gingerly on to the woven seat which had come unravelled in places.

'Gotta get on,' she said and disappeared through a door in the back of the house, letting out a waft of fried onions.

I looked through the letters: mine was there. I wondered how long it would be before Tom returned, and what he would say when he saw me.

I must have fallen into a doze. Jerked awake by the ringing of a bell, I came to, my mouth dry, my head pounding.

I heard a sharp exclamation from Tom, and a girl's voice saying, 'She *sez* she's yer sister.'

Then two faces stared at me, one grinning and one astonished, with brows beginning to knit into a familiar frown.

Tom took my elbow and steered me out into the street. 'What are you playing at, Lou?' His grip on my arm hurt.

'I had to see you, Tom.' After the dim hallway, the light was dazzling, the heat pressed down on me like a gigantic flat iron. 'Can't we talk in your room?'

'No,' said Tom shortly. He nodded back at his door, which wasn't quite shut, and I saw a pair of curious eyes surveying us. 'This is damned inconvenient.'

I was startled. Tom had never sworn in front of me before. 'Is there somewhere we can go? Somewhere that serves refreshments?'

He gave a little *tsk* of impatience. I added hastily, 'I don't want anything to eat . . . but I'm thirsty.' Was it because my mouth was dry that I was finding it hard to swallow, or because of the lump in my throat? Why wasn't he more welcoming?

He let go of my arm and faced me. 'Look, if you must know, I can't afford to take you into a respectable restaurant.'

 137

I couldn't hide my surprise. What had he done with his allowance?

Abruptly he asked, 'Have you any money?'

'Only a little.'

'So what the deuce am I supposed to do with you?'

I felt dismayed but I steeled myself. 'If there's no alternative, let's go somewhere that isn't respectable.'

He laughed derisively. 'Right, but remember – it's your choice.'

We headed back to the Caledonian Road where we passed several shabby looking chop houses, but for some reason Tom wouldn't stop. Finally we reached a place where, having peered through the steamy windows, he said, 'This will do.'

Tom wasn't joking about its lack of respectability. Like his lodgings, this was another brown-panelled, grimy room, dark enough that the gas jets had to be lit even on this summer day. It smelt of stale smoke, ale and rancid cooking fat.

I hesitated on the threshold, but Tom was already making his way to an alcove, so I followed him, stumbling over a stool leg.

A waiter in a greasy apron took our order and when he'd gone I leaned forward to speak, but Tom shook his head. 'Not yet. Wait till we're served.'

I sat back again on the rough settle and surveyed my brother. He looked washed out and he had dark circles under his eyes. His hair was tousled as if he'd forgotten to brush it, his clothes dishevelled.

'You don't look well, Tom. You're working too hard.'

He frowned. 'There's nothing the matter with me. But you look terrible, Lou. And you've a smut on your face.'

I dabbed at my cheek, transferring soot to my glove. 'I'm just tired, that's all.' 'Tired' was an understatement. These days I felt as if I was dragging a huge weight about with me. If only I could convey something of this to Tom . . .

'I haven't been—' I broke off as the waiter thumped a tumbler of ale and a glass of lemonade on to the table.

While I sipped at my drink, Tom gulped down a large quantity of ale. Then, wiping his mouth with his hand, he said in a disapproving tone, 'So, what were you thinking of, Lou? Coming to London on your own! Anything could have happened to you.'

I thought of the old woman at the station, the way people had stared at me in the street. He was right, of course, but . . .

'Coming down without warning me.'

The unfairness stung me. 'I did write. The letter's at your lodgings. I can't understand why you didn't get it.'

'Oh.' For a moment he looked discomfited. Then he frowned. 'Probably some trick of Sally's. You know, the skivvy. She's an unreliable baggage. But never mind that now. Does Mother know you're here?'

I felt wrong-footed. I was hoping he wasn't going to bring that up. 'Um, she will know by now – Mary will have told her.' As his brows darkened, I said hastily, 'I knew she wouldn't let me come so it was the only way. I have to speak to you . . .'

'You could have written to me.'

'Yes, I know, but –' I couldn't tell him the truth: that I was afraid he'd just ignore a letter – 'this is important, Tom.'

His expression changed to one of alarm. 'Is it Mother? Is she ill?'

'No, not exactly . . .' I took a breath. 'It's partly about Mamma, but mainly it's about me.'

At once a guarded look came into his eyes.

I pressed on, despite it. 'Mamma isn't ill but – she's not herself. I have to do everything. And she doesn't like being left alone – she follows me about, worrying all the time. I feel so trapped, Tom, and the thought that this is to be my life now . . .' I broke off, making a great effort to gain control of myself. I couldn't stop myself appealing to him. 'It would help, you know, if you came back more often.'

As soon as I said it, I knew I'd made a mistake.

Tom snorted with exasperation. 'You've no idea, have you? I can't just drop everything and run home when I feel like it. I have terms to keep, reading to be done . . . those blasted exams!'

I stared at him, puzzled. 'But you've done the first set, haven't you? Aren't the others are a long way off?'

Looking wretched, he leaned closer. 'You're not to say anything at home, but I've been plucked.'

'Plucked? You mean, you failed?'

'I scraped a pass in Chemistry but didn't make it in Anatomy.'

'Oh, Tom. I'm sorry. And you worked so hard.'

He shifted uneasily. 'Yes, well . . .'

'What happens now?'

'I'll have to resit – it's set me back at least a year. And I don't know how I'm going to find the fees.' He ran his fingers through his hair, and then lapsed into a gloomy silence, staring off across the room.

Again I thought, What *has* he done with all his money?

Looking at his face, thinner, older, for the first time I could see a resemblance to Papa. Suddenly moved, I thought, Go on, ask him now. He won't refuse. Not when he understands . . .

'Tom, I've tried to keep on with my studies, but it's been very difficult—'

His gaze spun back to me and he thumped his tumbler down, making me jump. 'What *is* the point, Lou? If you're still harbouring that foolish idea about being a doctor, then you might as well forget it. I told you it was out of the question.'

'But, Tom, it was Papa's wish—'

'Oh, you and Papa!'

'What do you mean?'

'Nothing.'

But I persisted. 'No, tell me, Tom. What about me and Papa?'

'Well, didn't it ever occur to you that I might have liked to join in your cosy chats?'

I stared at him, open-mouthed. 'But you were Papa's assistant for two years – you had lots of chances to talk to him.'

'I'm talking about before that . . .' Putting his elbow on the table and shutting his eyes, he rested his head on his hand.

I was silenced. It had never occurred to me that Tom might be jealous of *me*. I'd thought the appeal to Papa's memory would move him, but I could see now that every time I mentioned Papa's name I was only making things worse.

He lifted his head. 'Let me tell you something, Lou – all that learning – besides being a waste of time, it puts fellows off, you know.' He leaned back in his chair. 'I can see that things are difficult for you at the moment, but if you forget this nonsense and concentrate on getting yourself a husband—'

'Tom!'

He ignored my outburst. 'That would be better for you, wouldn't it? Mistress of your own home and so forth . . .' For the first time, he smiled at me. He looked just like a kind uncle offering sweetmeats.

Whatever made me think he was anything like Papa? He would never understand. My quest was hopeless.

I sat back, defeated.

Another silence descended. Then Tom cleared his throat. 'Have you heard from Aunt Phyllis lately?'

'Yes.'

'What did she say?'

'She asked if we were all right. She wanted to come and see us. But Mamma has turned against her.' My voice trembled. The thought that I might not see my aunt again was sad – but not to see Grace . . .

Tom looked disturbed at my words. 'Do you know why?'

'She feels that Aunt Phyllis didn't do enough to help when Papa was ill. But that's unfair – I know Aunt wanted to come but Papa wouldn't hear of it.'

'Like he wouldn't hear of my being sent for?' Tom's tone was bitter and I knew he still blamed me.

I quickly went on, 'There's something else. Grace's wedding.'

'Oh?'

'Yes, they've arranged it for next month now, which seems a reasonable length of time – you know, since Papa . . . but Mamma thinks it's too soon.' I paused. 'Aunt Phyllis did invite me to stay, but of course Mamma said no.' I toyed with the button on my glove. 'It would be lovely to go.' I spoke lightly as if it was scarcely important. Tom was staring across the room again and I wondered if he'd heard me. 'Aunt Phyllis said William has returned from Europe. He'll be joining Uncle Bertram at the works soon.'

'William?'

'Yes.'

'That's it! You must go to Carr Head and you must set your cap at William.'

I'd just taken another sip of lemonade and I almost spat it out. '*William?*'

'Yes. Don't you see? If you were to marry William, you'd have a fine life, Lou.'

I stared at my brother as if he were mad. 'But that's ridiculous. I hardly know William.' Being so much older than me and usually away when I visited Carr Head, my cousin was virtually a stranger to me. 'Besides,' I added, 'he wouldn't look at *me*.'

Tom regarded me judiciously. 'You're right. You'd have to smarten yourself up a bit.' He stared at the hole in my glove. I put my hands under the table. 'And make yourself agreeable. Don't keep going on about all that reading you do. But if you play your cards right – it would solve everything.'

'Solve everything? What do you mean?'

'Oh, I mean, make things better for you. And – and heal the breach between Mother and Aunt Phyllis, of course.'

He wasn't joking. He meant it. He was carrying on as if the whole thing were settled.

'I'll write to Mother and persuade her to let you go.'

He *was* mad. But still – a visit to Carr Head. A chance to see Grace . . .

Concealing my glee, I said, 'I wouldn't count on anything coming of it.'

'You don't know till you try. But Lou, you'll have to stop

moping about. Fellows like a girl who smiles. And can't you brighten your clothes up a bit now?'

I stared at him. 'But, Tom, it's only been three months since Papa . . .' I couldn't believe it. And I was puzzled too at his inconsistency – he disapproved of my travelling without a chaperone, but he seemed to care nothing for observing the propriety of mourning. Mamma would be so shocked if I started to wear colours again.

Mamma. Abruptly the delightful vision of Carr Head vanished. 'Tom, I can't go away. I can't leave Mamma.'

'You left her today.'

I flushed. 'Yes, but it's only for one day.'

'Well, Mary must see to Mother while you're at Carr Head. She'll manage.' He took out his watch. My heart contracted painfully. *Papa's watch.* 'Sorry, Lou, I've got to go.'

I blinked with surprise.

'Don't look like that. I can't help it. You know the way to the station? And you've got your ticket?'

'Yes.' I found it in my bag and showed him.

'Third class! What on earth were you thinking of?'

'I – I didn't have enough money for anything else.'

'Oh, Lou. You're impossible.' He stood up, feeling in his pocket. 'I say, you haven't any change, have you?'

We were saying goodbye in the street when a young man came up to us.

'Cosgrove, you rascal! How's your head? Recovered, has it? I hadn't the heart to wake you – you were spark out on the sofa.'

'Hello, Taylor,' said Tom stiffly. 'May I introduce my sister?'

Taylor tipped his hat to me. 'I beg your pardon, Miss Cosgrove. I didn't see you there. Come down to see the sights?'

I didn't know what to say but luckily Taylor rattled on, 'Your brother's a wag, isn't he? A regular scamp. But I'll give him this, he's a good sport. He doesn't give up, even when he's losing, does he?' He hit Tom on the shoulder. 'Will we see you tonight, old chap?'

Tom's reply was chilly. 'I don't think so. I have some reading to catch up on.'

Taylor raised his eyebrows, but glancing from Tom to me he said, 'Right. Some reading. Of course. Well, I'll say cheerio then. Miss Cosgrove.' He tipped his hat again and disappeared into the crowd.

I looked at Tom and made to speak but he said hastily, 'I've got to dash, Lou.' He bent and brushed his face against mine in an awkward embrace. 'You'll be all right, won't you? And I'll write to Mother about Carr Head. Goodbye.' He walked swiftly away and soon disappeared in the crowds.

I headed for the station, lost in my thoughts. I had failed to persuade Tom to change his mind. Why had I given up so easily? But then Tom was so unyielding . . .

His worn face came back to me. *He's a good sport*, Taylor had said. *Even when he's losing . . .*

I stopped, nearly causing an elderly gentleman to fall over me. I apologized distractedly.

I suddenly understood why my brother was short of money – *he'd been gambling.*

A great tiredness came over me.

How could he? Wasting his time, throwing away an opportunity that I longed for . . . I smiled bitterly. The London School of

 145

Medicine for Women was somewhere close by. Well, I could forget my hope of ever going there.

I set my face towards the station and trudged on.

Now all I had was Carr Head, and Grace . . . a brief joy before her marriage took her away from me.

Drops of rain cling to the windowpane. They gather weight, shift, catch, then slide in a trail down the glass, like tears. I stare beyond the drops. Nothing moves in the desolate park.

Five days I've been here now – it seems like an eternity.

No summons from Mr Sneed yet and no news of Mamma. But Eliza posted my letter yesterday, so one might come from Mamma today – or she could be on her way. At any moment, I might be sent for . . .

Someone giggles, an unexpected sound in this place. Sitting by the fire, their feet on the fender, Roberts and Eliza are gossiping.

Roberts, a short, red-faced attendant with a bulbous nose, appeared in the dormitory this morning and I wondered, with a surge of hope, if Weeks was ill. But it seems it's her day off. At least that's something to be thankful for – a day without her close scrutiny, her spiteful remarks.

The atmosphere's noticeably different. If Weeks were here, Eliza, cheerful as she usually is, would never sit in the carefree way she's doing now. Her collar's askew and her cap's pushed back, revealing hair the colour of ripe corn. For once we can please ourselves. Some patients are still doing fancy work or embroidery, but others are dozing. It could be a Sunday afternoon in any parlour.

Roberts glances round the room, checking the patients.

Seeing me at the window, she shouts across, 'Now then, Miss What's-Your-Name, it's no good mopin' about. Why don't yer read a nice book?'

Already she's turned back to Eliza. She obviously doesn't know I'm banned from reading, or doesn't care.

Idly I wander over to the cabinet and run my hand along the row of shabby volumes. My old friend, *The Pilgrim's Progress* . . . Not today, not the Giant Despair . . . I let my hand drop.

The attendants are talking in an undertone now, their heads close together, but I distinctly hear Eliza say, 'Miss Gorman.' Taking a book at random, I drift to a chair near them and pretend to read.

Roberts is in full flow. By straining my ears I can just catch what she's saying.

'. . . nothin' the matter with Miss Gorman, sane as you and me, then. After her mother died, she din't have nowhere to go so she went 'n' lived with her married brother. But his wife didn't care to have her in the house. So she made her husband send her here. Fancy, his own sister!'

'How do you know all this?' Eliza is sitting forward, interested.

'She told me – in the early days when she was all right. Course that's not what it says in her papers.'

'You've seen them?'

'Me? No, bless you.' Roberts laughs. 'It wouldn't do me no good if I had seen 'em, fer I can't make out nuthin' that's wrote but me own name. No, it was Alice wot had a peek, when she was cleaning the office. She can read like anythin'.'

The papers. What do mine – or rather Lucy Childs's – say? There might be a clue, a name, an address . . .

Roberts pours a heap of coal on to the fire. Then, settling down again, she puts her head close to Eliza's and whispers. Whatever she's saying, Eliza is drinking it in.

Roberts's voice rises. 'She was out of here and in the Fifth before she knew what'd hit 'er.'

'The Fifth, eh?' Eliza whistles.

'Yeah. But Weeks won't let it trouble her conscience. Bitch.' Roberts spits into the fire.

The hiss makes me shiver. What is 'the Fifth'?

Eliza stands up. 'Time to go for Miss Hill's tray.'

'So it is. When you come back we'll 'ave a game of cards.'

The room is very quiet after Eliza has gone and suddenly I can't bear to sit still. I ask Roberts, 'May I walk in the hallway?'

Weeks doesn't allow this: she likes to keep us under her eye.

Roberts shrugs. 'If yer like. But don't go gettin' up to any mischief.'

I walk up and down the hallway, thinking about what I've just heard. Miss Gorman . . . Weeks . . . the Fifth . . . What does it all mean? I don't know. But one thing is certain. I have to get out of here, before anything worse happens to me.

As I reach the main door, it opens, and Eliza comes in.

Seeing me, she gives a friendly nod and indicates the tray she's carrying. 'All right for some, isn't it, being waited on?'

At that moment, Roberts calls from the doorway, 'Eliza, Mrs Thorpe needs the closet.'

'Right, I'll be with you in a minute.'

'Shall I take the tray in for you?' The words are out of my mouth before I have time to think about them. Ever since I saw Weeks attack her, I've been wondering about Miss Hill. I'd like to speak to her, but she never seems to leave her room.

Eliza smiles gratefully. 'Oh, would you, Miss? That'd be ever so kind. It's the door behind you.' She goes off down the gallery.

I listen at the door.

There's no sound at first and then I hear a quiet sob and a long, despairing sigh. 'My baby.' Pause. And again, 'My baby.'

What can she mean?

I tap on the door, holding the tray carefully, so as not to tilt it.

'Yes? Who is it?'

Miss Hill's lying back, a paisley shawl wrapped round her shoulders. I almost drop the tray. The shawl, with its vivid swirls of blue and green, is very similar to one Grace sent me. I hung it over the foot of my bed, so it was the first thing I saw when I woke. Every morning, Grace was my first thought . . .

With an effort I focus on the girl before me: her face is white against the white pillow, her hair dishevelled. Now I can see her properly, her resemblance to Grace is slight. Miss Hill's face is thinner, her hair fairer. And she's much younger – she can't be more than fourteen, fifteen at the most.

'Do I know you?' Her voice is faint.

'No. That is, you may have seen me the other day . . .' I stop, feeling foolish. I'm still holding the tray. 'Are you ready for this yet?' I take a step forward.

'You're not supposed to come in here.' Large, wary eyes, dark blue, almost violet in their intensity.

'Eliza asked me to; it's Weeks's day off.'

At the mention of the name, a spasm crosses her face. Pain? Fear? I can't tell. Her expression shuts down.

I put the tray down on the table next to the bed.

She looks at me curiously. 'Who are you?'

I swallow. 'Louisa.' It's such a long time since I've heard my own name it sounds strange to me. 'I'm Louisa.'

'Beatrice.'

Something shifts, as if exchanging names has drawn us closer. I lift the cover from the bowl and sniff. 'It's soup. Will you eat some?'

She sighs, but she struggles to sit up.

'Can I help?'

She gives a tiny nod. I plump up the pillow to form a support for her back. Under the scent of rose-water, I can detect other smells: Condy's Fluid, that common disinfectant; camphor; the stale whiff of a body that's been lying too long in bed in a stuffy atmosphere. The familiar smell of the sickroom. My chest tightens. But I mustn't think of Papa, not here, not now.

I place the tray on her lap. She stares at the soup, then she picks up the spoon. Her thin fingers are bloodless, almost transparent. I take a step towards the door.

'Must you go?' That violet gaze . . . entreating. What does she want from me? What can I give? *Be careful.*

I shake my head.

She lowers the spoon into the soup and lifts it towards her lips, but her hand is shaking; the soup splashes over the tray. She stares at the spill and a tear runs down her face.

'Weeks says if I don't eat, they'll force-feed me again.' She shudders, putting her hand to her mouth.

'Here, I'll help you.' I take the spoon from her and dip it into the bowl. She opens her mouth obediently like a child.

She swallows a few more spoonfuls, then turns her head away. 'No more. Thank you.'

Time to go . . . but her tears are welling again and I hesitate. 'What's upsetting you? Is it . . . your baby?'

A look of terror leaps into her eyes. 'What baby? What are you talking about?'

I blink. 'I'm sorry.'

She stares at me, her face a mask, and then the mask crumples and she starts sobbing, racking sobs that shake her thin frame. As she hides her face in her hands, the tears drip down her fingers.

I can't bear it; her misery wrenches my insides. Awkwardly I pat her back, feeling her thin, sharp shoulder blades, like wings.

'Shhh, shhhh, it's all right, it's all right.'

Gradually her sobs subside. She whispers something.

'I beg your pardon?'

'Three months.' She lifts her face from her hands and looks at me. 'It's been three months since my baby died.'

She sounds utterly sincere. But how could she have had a baby? She's so young. 'I'm sorry.' It sounds horribly inadequate. I fumble in my pocket and offer her my handkerchief. She takes it and wipes her face.

I go to stand up, but she grips my arm. 'Weeks is the worst – if I cry for my baby, I make her cross and she hurts me. They all say I'm making it up, that it's just a foolish fancy, a trick of the imagination. But it's not, it's not.' She sinks back on to the pillow and closes her eyes. Her face is bleached with exhaustion.

Of course. She's mad. I'd almost forgotten. Gently I extricate my arm from her grasp and back away from the bed.

She opens her eyes. 'They say, think of bright, happy things. Think of your home, your loving mother. And your generous stepfather.' Her mouth twists into a bitter line. 'Especially your generous stepfather.'

A noise behind me makes me jump. Eliza has come into the room.

'You're still here, Miss? I wondered where you'd got to.' Loud, cheerful normality.

She inspects the soup bowl. 'Is this all you've managed to eat? This won't do, will it?' Like a mother hen, clucking at a chick. 'You have a nice rest now.' She picks up the tray and ushers me out.

Pulling the door shut, Eliza gives me a conspiratorial look. 'I suppose she's been telling you those stories. I don't think she knows what she's saying half the time. And she's not well, poor thing. She's too weak to walk and she's always fainting.'

What can I say? What should I believe?

'You'd better go to the day room now, Miss. I've got to take this tray back to the kitchen.'

Obediently I turn away and walk down the hallway, only half aware of Eliza leaving the gallery.

I'm still inside that room. Hearing that voice. Seeing those troubled eyes.

One Week Earlier

We'd had a letter from Tom. He was coming home in a fortnight's time and bringing a friend called Woodville, who wanted to see our part of Yorkshire.

Why was he coming? And who was this stranger, Woodville? If this was another of Tom's schemes . . . But he didn't yet know of my failure with William. Thinking of William led on to Grace, of course . . .

A hollow space opened inside me, a hot feeling of shame. *Don't think about it.*

I rubbed steadily at the brass candlestick until I could see a distorted reflection of myself in the polished surface. Focusing on the job stopped me thinking, stopped me feeling. I started on its twin.

A knock at the front door made me jump. Who could that be? Mary was out on some errands so I went to see.

'Oh, Dr Kneale!' Flustered, I pushed back a stray lock of hair. Because of the cleaning, I hadn't put it up properly but had borrowed a cap from Mary. I was wearing my oldest dress and a grubby apron.

If he was surprised at my appearance, Dr Kneale didn't show it. He raised his hat to me. 'Miss Cosgrove.'

What did he want? I hadn't sent for him; I hadn't seen him since he attended Papa. Seeing him now brought back painful memories.

He cleared his throat. 'May I come in?'

'Oh. Yes.' I stood aside to let him pass. Pulling off the cap and

155

apron, I rolled my sleeves down. Where should I take him? The parlour was all at sixes and sevens; it would have to be Papa's study. Taking a deep breath, I pushed open the door.

I hardly ever went into this room now. I couldn't bear to see it – the empty shelves, the absences.

The same thought must have been in Dr Kneale's mind as he looked about, shaking his head. 'Your poor father. A sorry business, indeed.'

He shifted from one foot to the other. 'I have heard from your brother, Miss Cosgrove. He asked me to call.'

Tom? Why would he write to the doctor? Unless it was about Mamma. But he'd said nothing about Dr Kneale in his letter. Perhaps he didn't want Mamma to know.

'I'm afraid my mother isn't expecting you. She's resting at the moment.'

The doctor looked surprised. 'Your mother requires my services?'

I was disconcerted. 'Yes . . . that is . . .'

'But it was *you* your brother asked me to visit.'

Me? The doctor must have misread Tom's writing. 'Are you not mistaken, Doctor Kneale? Didn't my brother say *Mrs* Cosgrove?'

The doctor smiled indulgently. 'Now, my dear young lady, if you'll allow me . . .' He put out his hand.

I was puzzled, but followed suit. Why did he want to shake my hand?

He held it tightly and drew out his watch. *He was taking my pulse.* Silly old fool, couldn't he see that he'd made a mistake?

I tried to pull back but his grip was firm.

'Mmm, a little high,' he commented.

I found my voice. 'Doctor Kneale, I'm not ill.'

Again that smile. Humouring a child. 'Let me be the judge of that.' He opened his bag and taking out a thermometer, he put it in my mouth. Affronted, I pulled it out. It dropped to the floor but didn't break.

Dr Kneale stepped back. 'Miss Cosgrove! There's no need for that! Calm yourself.'

'How can I be calm when you won't listen to me? I tell you, I'm not ill!'

The doctor didn't respond. Instead he retrieved the thermometer and slipped it into his bag. Then he studied me, a faint frown between his eyebrows. 'Tell me, Miss Cosgrove. You look thinner. Are you eating well?'

'Yes.' That wasn't quite true – since Papa had gone I'd lost interest in food. And I'd hardly eaten since the visit to Carr Head.

'And are you sleeping well?'

'Not very well,' I admitted.

'It's understandable, given your sad loss and the greater responsibilities you've had to take on.'

At the mention of Papa, my eyes filled with tears; I couldn't help it. I dabbed at my eyes with the apron I discovered I'd been holding all this time. What would the doctor say if he knew all the troubling thoughts that kept me awake . . . Tom's gambling, what Grace thought of me now . . .

The doctor pursed his lips as if considering. 'You say your mother is indisposed?'

'She's . . .' How could I put it? 'Since my father's death, she's not been herself. She experiences great anxiety, even about small things.'

'I will look in on her next time I call –'

 157

Next time?

'– in about a week. Good day, Miss Cosgrove.' Picking up his bag, he left the study and I heard the front door open and close.

I flung the bundled apron and cap on the floor. How dare he! How *dare* he come in patronizing me and insinuating that I was ill! Tom would be annoyed when he found out that Dr Kneale hadn't seen Mamma.

Tom and his friend arrived in time for dinner. To my amazement, Mr Woodville, a dark young man with intense brown eyes, proceeded to charm Mamma. He even persuaded her to take a thimbleful of wine. After one sip her cheeks flushed pink and she responded to Mr Woodville's stories with a girlish giggle I'd never heard before.

I could see he was enjoying his success. But even while he was engaging Mamma's attention, from time to time he looked at me with such interest I went hot and had to look away.

I studied Tom covertly across the table. He was looking sprucer than when I'd seen him last, and in better humour, but his conviviality seemed forced; he was less talkative than usual and seemed rather weary. I noticed he was drinking a great deal.

Catching my eye, he said, 'You'll be interested in this, Lou. Woodville's a doctor already. Qualified this summer.' He smirked at his friend as if sharing a private joke.

I wasn't smiling. How could Tom be so spiteful?

Woodville wasn't amused either. He gave Tom a look I couldn't interpret and then his dark eyes turned to me.

A response seemed called for. 'Congratulations, Dr Woodville. What are your plans?'

Despite my chilly politeness, his manner was friendly. 'I'm off to Vienna soon to further my studies—'

'Vienna!' I couldn't help my envious interjection.

He smiled. 'And when I return I will take up a position as a house physician at Guy's.'

Tom butted in. 'Watch out, Woodville. My sister will pester you to death with questions if you let her.'

I shot him a bitter look. Beyond what was necessary for good manners, I had no intention of talking to Dr Woodville about medicine or anything else. It would be too painful to discuss the world I was barred from, and besides, his apparent interest in me was making me feel uncomfortable.

Luckily Tom stood up and said, 'Come along, old chap, let's have a smoke in the study.'

After they'd gone, Mamma was quiet, lost in her own thoughts.

'Mamma?'

She continued to gaze at the salt cellar. 'Such a nice young man, Dr Woodville, don't you think?'

I shrugged. 'He seems pleasant enough.'

'He reminds me of your father when he was younger.' She fixed her eyes on me. 'You could make yourself agreeable to him.'

'Mamma! Dr Woodville isn't interested in me.' But maybe he was . . . 'Do you want to go to bed?' I asked abruptly.

As usual I helped her to undress and tucked her in, before scrambling into my own truckle bed in the corner. I had taken to sleeping in Mamma's room as, troubled by anxious thoughts, she often woke in the night. But as so often, I couldn't sleep. I felt stirred up: Woodville's gaze, Mamma's ridiculous suggestion – *No, don't think about that.* But other thoughts were worse:

medicine, Vienna . . . all the old longing reawakened. It was no good – I had to put it from my mind.

Mamma was breathing deeply and I tried to relax and follow her into sleep. As I drifted off, the bitter-sweet image that kept haunting me visited me again – Grace smiling in her mysterious way, then her eyes meeting mine and her face changing as she turned away . . .

The next morning Tom took Dr Woodville out after breakfast but before long he returned alone.

'What have you done with your friend?' Mamma asked.

'I showed him where the livery stables are. He wanted a ride out into the country.'

'He's not chosen the best day for it.'

Mamma was right – it was overcast and every now and then a fine rain spotted the windows.

'Oh, Woodville won't mind – he's keen to blow away the city smog.'

'Didn't you want to go?'

Tom smiled. 'I wanted to see you, Mamma.' He pulled up a chair beside her and sat down. She turned to him with that fond look I remembered so well. No matter how long the intervals between his visits, she was always glad to see him. No matter how much care I took of her, she never looked at me like that.

Tom coughed and looked at me over Mamma's head – a significant look. What did he mean?

'Lou, could you ask Mary to bring me some barley water? You'd like some, wouldn't you, Mamma?'

Why didn't he ring the bell? Then I realized – he wanted to talk to Mamma alone. What was it that I couldn't hear? I was

160

annoyed at being excluded. But at least Mamma was occupied and I seized my chance to read in peace.

After speaking to Mary, I fetched one of Papa's medical books – one that Tom hadn't wanted – and, taking it into the dining room, I stoked up the fire. Forcing thoughts of my visit to Carr Head out of my mind, I tried to concentrate on what I was reading.

A little later the door opened and Tom came in. I didn't try to hide my book, but he didn't comment. Pulling out another chair at the table, he sat down next to me and said abruptly, 'I need to talk to you.'

'If it's about William, you'll be disappointed.'

He looked surprised, as if he'd forgotten his grand plan for uniting the family. 'No, it's not about William.'

'And Dr Woodville – if he's another of your schemes . . .'

'Woodville? Well, yes, in a way it is about Woodville.'

I regarded him suspiciously.

'The thing is, Lou, I've been thinking about what you said – about not being happy here and so on, and it's bothered me.'

The turn of the conversation surprised me. It wasn't like Tom to be concerned for my welfare. I kept silent, wondering where all this was leading.

'It isn't fair that you have the burden of caring for Mamma . . .' I suddenly felt light-headed. Tom had changed his mind. He was going to let me be a doctor. My insides fizzed with elation. 'So I've arranged something for you.'

My elation faltered. 'Arranged something?'

'Yes. Woodville has a sister, a little older than you, and their

 161

mother is keen to find a companion for her. I thought it would be just the thing for you.'

I was speechless, incapable of movement.

Tom went on blithely, 'They're pretty wealthy, you know – splendid house and grounds in the Essex countryside. Your duties won't be too arduous – you're bound to have more time to yourself than you do here.'

Still I could say nothing.

'You've seen what a capital fellow Woodville is, and his sister's a jolly nice girl. I'm sure you'll like her.' He paused. 'Lou?'

I managed to find my voice. I tried to speak calmly, although inwardly I was shaking. 'I thought you meant – I thought you were letting me to go to London – to study medicine . . .'

Abruptly Tom stood up and loomed over me. 'Don't start all that again. This is a good chance for you, Lou. You'd better accept it.'

I pushed my chair back and went over to the window. It was raining heavily now. Dr Woodville would be getting wet. Now I could see why he was so interested in me. He was sizing me up. But I didn't want to go and live with strangers far away. I didn't want to be at the beck and call of some wealthy young lady who'd look down on me because our family wasn't as grand as hers.

'Look!' Tom was sounding exasperated. 'It's all been arranged – you have to go and that's that.'

I spun round. 'I won't go. You can't make me.' I jutted my chin out. 'Besides, you've forgotten something. Mamma needs me here.'

Tom shook his head. 'I'm sorry, Lou. I was trying to spare you

this, but you're not helping Mother – in fact you're making her worse!'

'What! What are you talking about?'

'She didn't want to tell me, but I got it out of her. You've been neglecting her, haven't you? Sneaking off to read, instead of spending time with her.'

I stared at him. The accusation was so unfair. I'd hardly spent any time on my own. 'But, Tom, that's not true! I'm always with her.'

'That's not what she says. You let her sit alone, worrying herself half to death. It's too bad of you, Lou!'

How could she say such things? It was so unjust! One thing was clear. She didn't appreciate anything I'd done for her. Very well. I *would* go away and then she'd see what a mistake she'd made. She'd soon be begging me to come back.

Tom was regarding me expectantly as if he was waiting for a storm to erupt. Well, for once he would be disappointed. I drew myself up to my full height. 'I see. In that case, I'll go where I'm wanted. When is Mrs Woodville expecting me?' I spoke as coolly as I could, but inside I was trembling. How could Mamma do this to me!

Tom looked taken aback by my sudden acquiescence. 'Oh, next Wednesday. I thought that would give you enough time to get ready.'

Next Wednesday. So soon? I swallowed. When would I see my home again? I'd been so desperate to escape from it, but not like this . . .

Tom broke into my thoughts. 'I've engaged a companion for Mamma, a Mrs Grey, and she'll be arriving on Wednesday afternoon.'

A companion? Mamma preferred a *companion* to me?

All my sentimental thoughts vanished. If I really wasn't wanted here, it wasn't my home any more. I'd be glad to leave! And I'd ignore Mamma as much as possible in the few days that remained to me.

Sticking out my chin, I said to Tom, 'Please tell Mamma that I've agreed to go. And now if you'll excuse me, I have to think about what I need to take with me.' I swept from the room with as much dignity as I could muster.

Mary was just letting Dr Woodville in at the front door and seeing me, he inclined his head and smiled. 'Not a very pleasant day, Miss Cosgrove.'

'No indeed, Dr Woodville, it is not.'

At that moment Mamma came out of the parlour. She looked red-eyed, as if she'd been weeping. I steeled my heart. She glanced at Dr Woodville. I guessed she wanted to say something to me, but I turned away from them both and walked up the stairs.

I managed to contain myself until I reached the turn of the landing, but, once out of sight, I rushed towards the sanctuary of my old room.

Its emptiness hit me. It was as if I'd already ceased to live there.

Shutting the door, I flung myself down on the bare mattress and seized hold of Annabel, who lay abandoned there. Just as in the old days, I hugged her to me.

She was the only friend I had left.

Mr Sneed has sent for me! At last.

Mamma must have written to him. Perhaps she has come to take me home, is in his office at this very moment, waiting for me. Trust Mamma to wait until Monday; even for this she wouldn't travel on the Sabbath.

Eliza told me just now in the day room. She delivered her message as if it were the dullest news in the world, as if she didn't know how much it meant to me. But then Weeks was in the room, so perhaps she was being careful.

As soon as we're out of the gallery, I say, 'Oh, Eliza, what do you think? I told you I should be going home!'

In a flat voice, she says, 'I couldn't say, Miss.'

What's the matter with her?

I start to speak, but she says, 'We mustn't keep Mr Sneed waiting, Miss.' She sets off at a brisk pace and I have to hurry to keep up with her.

Oh, well, I can't think about Eliza. My heart is jumping too much and in my head I'm singing *I'm going home, I'm going home*, over and over, in time with my boots marching on the stone flags.

Along the grey corridors we go, under the low arched ceilings.

At last we reach Mr Sneed's office and Eliza turns to me. 'Here we are, Miss.'

She meets my eyes for the first time and there is something not right . . . But what does she mean by her look? Is she warning me? Or asking for something from me?

'Eliza—' I begin, but she knocks, a voice calls, 'Come in,' and she opens the door.

'Miss Childs, Sir,' she announces with a bob. Then she's off, the *tap tap* of her footsteps soon dying away.

For a moment I feel strangely bereft, abandoned. How silly. Because this is the moment I've been waiting for. Everything will be all right now.

I stick out my chin and step into the room.

Mamma is not here. My hope dies, like a snuffed candle flame.

Steady, steady, I tell myself. She may not have been able to come yet. But she'll have written.

The superintendent's back is towards me as he stands at the window staring out at the rain. It drums insistently against the glass, cutting off the view. The room feels claustrophobic. Mr Sneed spins round, the eye with the cast, which I'd forgotten, leering at me.

'Have a seat, Miss Childs.'

Still that name. Mamma hasn't written. Perhaps Eliza never sent that letter. The fluttering in my chest intensifies.

Steady, steady, I tell myself again. I must make my case calmly, clearly. He *must* listen.

He sits at his desk and, gesturing to the seat before it, starts to rummage in a drawer. Without warning I'm taken back to all the times I sat by Papa's desk and talked to him. I see him with his tired red-rimmed eyes and his rumpled hair and my throat closes, blocked by sudden tears. *No, not now.*

To distract myself I stare at the desk-top. Each object – silver ink stand, pen-pot, pen-wiper, blotter, silver letter opener – is arranged with precision on the polished surface, which is otherwise bare, except for a document file and two sheets of paper.

At the sight of these, my pulse races. 'Mr Sneed, I asked to see you because—' He shuts the drawer with a thud.

I rush on. 'Because I shouldn't be here. It's either a mistake or a conspiracy. I'd like to see my papers. Once I know what they say, I'm sure I can explain how this has happened.'

His bushy eyebrows rise. Without speaking, he picks up one of the pieces of paper and thrusts it under my nose. A chasm opens inside me. My letter, the one I gave Eliza to post. *She has betrayed me.*

No wonder she was acting so strangely.

Mr Sneed is speaking but I can't hear him for the ringing in my ears. Gradually I register what he's saying: '. . . causing your family great concern, which I share. From the evidence of this letter, in addition to your other problems, you seem to be developing acute paranoia.' He taps the paper. 'These ill-founded claims only serve to worry your family and—'

I break in. '*Claims!* Every word in that letter is true.'

Mr Sneed smiles at me. 'Come, Miss Childs.'

'That is not my name.' I keep my chin up and stare at him.

He brushes this aside and waves the letter. '"They have locked me up." How can you say you are locked up when you have the freedom of the gallery?'

'I can't leave it.'

'That is true but it's for your own good. Your safety is of paramount importance to us. We couldn't have our residents wandering at will, could we? Supposing someone got hurt?' He sits back in his chair and steeples his fingers.

I regard him stonily. Whatever I say, he'll have the answer to it.

Mr Sneed refers to the letter again. 'As for your complaint about the bath, you obviously don't realize that this is the standard treatment for your condition. Dr Bull is a qualified physician and knows what he is doing. And then your suspicion of the lady, Mrs Lunt, who brought you here – plots, conspiracies . . . classic symptoms.'

'But she could have —'

He shakes his head sadly. 'This just goes to show how ill you are. If you were rational, you would see that it was extremely unlikely. So you see, Miss Childs, in future I would rather you followed our procedures with regard to letters.'

He suddenly leans towards me, his voice steel. 'Now tell me, who did you give your letter to?'

Mute, I stare past his ear. The silence thickens. With a sigh, Mr Sneed sits back. 'Miss Childs – your poor mother is not to be bothered with your foolish fancies again, you understand? She was most upset.'

Upset? I suddenly see that it's not Eliza who has

168

betrayed me. She *did* post the letter, but it has been returned. Who by? Surely not Mamma?

'I don't understand. Who sent my letter back to you?'

He shakes his head, sighing, then with an air of great indulgence he takes the other sheet of paper from his desk and holds it out to me, not so close that I can read the words but close enough for me to see the handwriting.

My heart contracts.

It is unmistakable – I recognize the loops and curls, the distinctive ink.

My eye falls on the signature. And a white light bursts in my brain.

The walls of the room are closing in on me, blurring. My blood roars in my ears. I dig my nails into my palm. *Breathe, breathe.*

I am vaguely aware of Mr Sneed saying something, but I can't hear him. I want to cry out, but I clench my teeth. With a tremendous effort of will, I manage to control myself. I even manage to say, 'May I see my papers?' My voice sounds as thin as tissue.

Now a black pillar rises in front of me, and overhead, far away, a voice says, 'Your papers are in order, Miss Childs. Trust me.'

The pillar wavers, and turns into Mr Sneed, tugging on the bell-pull. He says, 'I think it's time you returned to the gallery.'

I have been betrayed and I can't utter a word.

Eliza is hurrying me back to the gallery. My legs don't seem to belong to me, but they are carrying me along. My breath rasps, my ears ring, my heart hammers to the beat of one question: Why? *Why?*

Suddenly Eliza stops and I cannon into her. She thrusts her face close to mine. 'Did you tell him?'

I blink at her, dazed. What's she talking about?

'Did you tell him it were me that posted your letter?'

With a struggle I focus on her question. 'No. He asked but I didn't tell.'

She lets out a great breath. 'Thank the blazing heavens.'

With a stab I realize. 'You knew Mr Sneed wanted to see me about the letter?'

Eliza shrugs. 'I guessed. Matron told us it'd come back and she's been on at us – asking if we took it for you.'

I look at her. Her guileless blue eyes, the pink of her cheeks under their dusting of freckles. I've begun to think of her as a friend. And yet . . .

'You didn't tell me. About the letter coming back.'

She looks away. 'I didn't know how you'd take it, Miss. Thought you might have thrown a fit.'

Of course. As far as Eliza knows I'm a mad girl who doesn't even know her own name. Every time I've objected to their calling me Lucy Childs, the madder I've seemed. Clever. Was this part of the plan?

She moves on and I follow automatically, the march of

170

questions across my brain beginning again. Why has this been done to me? Why? Why?

Beneath the questions, a dark thought is forming. I try to squash it down but it persists until I can't think of anything else.

I stop dead.

Dread has seized hold of me, is spreading through my body. I start to tremble and the thought flies out in a whisper. 'I'm not going to be able to get out of here.'

Eliza has stopped too. 'Miss?'

I can't help moaning.

'Miss, are you all right?'

I try to stop it but it won't be stopped. A wail that starts from the bottom of my stomach and rips its way out of my throat. 'I'm not going to be able to get out of here! I'm not going to get out!'

My legs give way and I sink to my knees on the flags, burying my face in my hands.

All I can see, as if it's still in front of me, is that signature in bold black ink: *Thomas Childs*.

PART TWO

The thumping of the out-of-tune piano and the scraping of the fiddle are giving me a headache. I don't want to be here. But we all have to attend the Christmas dance, whether we want to or not.

Christmas. That means I've been here over six weeks . . .

Eliza's looking forward to the dance. 'It makes a change, Miss, don't it?'

I don't want a change. I prefer routine, the same mind-numbing activities, minute by minute, hour by hour, day by day. So I don't have to think. Or feel.

Otherwise it's too painful.

Tom knows that I'm shut in a madhouse and he wants to keep me here. Why? And why is he pretending I'm someone else?

Does Mamma know?

Has *she* done this?

I try not to ask these questions any more; it's easier to let the chloral dull the edge of my pain, to go on not thinking, not feeling.

Someone has tried to create a festive atmosphere in this dark panelled room: sprigs of holly tacked to the portraits of the asylum founders, a sparsely decorated Christmas tree leaning sideways.

Watched over by Mr Sneed and the matron, both of them with fixed smiles on their faces, the dancers, patients from the First and Second Galleries, appear to be enjoying themselves, despite having their toes trodden on by their partners, male patients with whom they are allowed to fraternize on this occasion. Mrs Smythe's partner is so short his head is almost buried in her ample bosom but she seems satisfied with her beau. There aren't enough men to go round so some attendants are joining in. Every now and then Eliza swings into view, bright-eyed and smiling.

I glance at Weeks. She's not dancing but standing with a sour expression on her face, keeping an eye on us wall-flowers who are drooping on benches at the side. I see, with a start, Beatrice Hill beside her, watching the dancers from an invalid chair. That time I talked to her – it seems an age ago now. Again I see that faint resemblance to my cousin in her profile.

Grace . . . Do *you* know I'm here?

The polka ends and Eliza comes over to me, out of breath and laughing. 'Why don't you have a dance, Miss? It's fun.'

'I can't. I don't know how.'

'It's easy. You just have to follow the music.'

The pianist is starting up again, the fiddler joining in, and suddenly Eliza seizes my hand and pulls me from the bench.

'Eliza, no!'

But she's too strong and I find myself out on the dance floor with her arm firmly round my waist, as she shouts instructions in my ear. 'Put your hand on my shoulder. That's it. And your feet go back, side, side, back, side,

side. Don't look down. That's it. One, two, three, one two, three . . .'

And I'm waltzing for the first time in my life. Stiffly, awkwardly, catching Eliza's foot with mine now and then, but nevertheless waltzing.

We're an ill-suited couple. I'm more than half a head taller and I'm conscious of my big feet, my elbows sticking out. But a reckless spirit seems to have entered Eliza; she clasps me close and whirls me round, her cheeks flushed and strands of hair coming loose from her cap. She grins up at me and I find myself relaxing, listening to the music, letting myself drift away with it. None of the other couples are paying any attention to us as we swoop and swerve between them, coming close but never colliding.

I shut my eyes for a moment, enjoying this unusual sensation.

When I open my eyes, I see Weeks frowning at us. Losing the rhythm, I come down hard on Eliza's foot, causing her to stumble and let go of me.

'I'm sorry.'

Rubbing her foot, Eliza says, 'It's all right, Miss. Luckily you don't weigh much more than a pail of peas.' We both laugh.

'See, Miss, it's done you good. I knew it would.'

'It's been . . . fun.'

I'm surprised. It has. And I feel different. Shaken up. More alive.

The final chords of the waltz die away and Eliza walks me back to my seat.

'See, I told you it were easy!'

'It seems so with you leading. How did you come to learn the man's steps?'

'I teach my little sisters and it works best that way.'

Now Weeks is urging us to stand up and Mr Sneed leads us in the National Anthem, which he sings strongly, accompanied by a ragged off-key chorus. I glance over to Beatrice but Weeks is wheeling her towards the door.

Eliza says, 'I'd better go, Miss. There's supper to be sorted.'

Watching her hurry across the floor, I have a sudden vision of her dancing in a cottage with her sisters.

It gives me a strange ache in my heart. But something else, too. I feel as if I've woken up from a long sleep. For the first time in a long time I feel more like my old self.

What have I been thinking of? Letting the days, the weeks drift by instead of acting sooner? I've been depressed, I have to admit it. And the chloral. That's been partly to blame, drugging me into a semi-stupor, an acceptance of my fate. But I am not Lucy Childs, a poor, mad girl. I am Louisa Cosgrove.

And I must *do* something, try to get out of here . . .

Today, when I enter the day room with the others, a stranger, a man with a shock of ginger hair, is standing by the fireplace talking to Mr Sneed. The superintendent turns towards us with an insincere smile. 'Come in, ladies, come in. Don't be shy.'

We're huddling in the doorway, some stupefied, others suspicious. Weeks pushes her way through from the rear, saying sharply, 'Come along now. Don't keep Mr Sneed waiting.'

We shuffle into the room.

'Ladies, allow me to introduce Mr Allen.' The superintendent gestures towards the ginger-haired man, who gives us a weak smile, his eyes nervously darting round.

With the air of a magician pulling a rabbit from a hat, Mr Sneed announces, 'I have a surprise for you, something to celebrate the New Year. Mr Allen has come to take your *photographs*.'

His eyebrows shoot up expectantly but the response of his audience is disappointing: Miss Coles utters a moan and wrings her hands. Others stare uncomprehending.

Only Mrs Smythe rises to the occasion, sailing forward and taking a chair near the window. 'I believe this is my best side. The light catches my face to advantage here.' As the nonplussed photographer fails to move, she gives him an imperious look. 'I am *ready*, young man.'

This is a change from sewing shirts and sheets.

I can't help watching with interest as the photographer opens a large box on the table. It's no ordinary box. Its lid opens on to the table to form a tray and an inner flap folds out to form a kind of roof. Inside I glimpse some small brown bottles, just like the medicine bottles I used to fetch for Papa. It must be a kind of travelling darkroom.

A hand falls on my arm. 'Miss Childs, give the gentleman room.'

Without realizing it, I've come closer to the table. Weeks ushers me away, but not before I've seen gutta-percha dishes, a spirit lamp, a funnel . . . What exciting experiments I could have carried out, if I'd had such a box of tricks.

The photographer proceeds to set up his camera near to the window. Mrs Smythe bares her teeth in what I suppose is a smile and holds still. But Mr Allen isn't ready yet. He sits down at the table and drapes a black cloth over the box and his head and shoulders. There's a sound of clinking glass and a strong smell of ether fills the room.

Mrs Smythe is growing restive. 'Young man, are you going to be much longer? I have a very important appointment with the Ambassador and I don't want to be late.'

The black cloth convulses and the photographer emerges from his darkroom, red-faced, with tears streaming from his eyes from the chemicals. 'Not long now,' he gasps and plunges under the cloth again. He appears holding a plate of glass by its edges, which he slides into the camera.

He is ready at last. But his sitter isn't. Bored with waiting, Mrs Smythe has tipped the contents of her purse into her lap and is busy sorting through them.

'Um . . .' Mr Allen looks round helplessly.

Mr Sneed is talking to Weeks by the door. Eliza has been going round persuading everyone to take off their caps and doing her best to smooth our hair with a comb. Seeing the photographer's discomfort, she comes forward.

'Um . . . can you tell the – er – lady to hold still. It'll only take ten seconds or so.'

Her eyes dance. 'You could tell her yourself, you know.' But she relents, gets Mrs Smythe arranged, and the photograph is taken.

More activity under the black cloth of the box follows and finally Mr Allen emerges with the plate and places it on the table.

'Is that the photograph?' Eliza seizes the plate.

'Well, yes – but—'

'She's got a black face!'

I press forward with some of the other patients to see. A hubbub of comment breaks out, above which Mrs Smythe is strident. 'Disgraceful. He has made a mockery of me. A treasonable offence, I shouldn't wonder.'

Mr Allen snatches the plate from Eliza, clutching it protectively to his chest. 'This is the negative. I haven't finished processing it yet.' Sweat has broken out on his brow and he mops at it with a large spotted handkerchief.

Weeks comes to his rescue, shooing us back, and the process of capturing our images proceeds.

I wish I could see what he was doing in his box. I would like to know how it works. We never had our photographs

181

taken at home. Perhaps Mamma thought it was frivolous or a waste of money.

One Christmas – it seems a long time ago but it can't have been – Aunt Phyllis sent us a leather case that opened like a concertina, containing six photographs: single portraits of herself, Uncle Bertram, William, Grace and Maud and one of the whole family, sitting in the garden. In this, Maud was blurred – she must have moved – and Grace's face was in shadow. But in the single portrait, Grace was herself, so vivid and alive, my pulse raced every time I looked at it. I wanted to take out the photograph and keep it for myself, but Mamma would have noticed it was missing.

Remembering it now, my heart aches.

Grace, Grace . . . what are you doing? Do you know where I am? Do you ever think of me?

I shake my head at my own foolishness. Of course she won't be thinking of me. Her life is full. No room for thoughts of me in it. And perhaps it's best that she doesn't think of me at all, rather than think of me and shudder.

'Miss!' Eliza is calling me. It's my turn.

The photographer has grown bolder. He comes up to me and tilts my head slightly. His fingers are stained yellow and smell of chemicals. 'Keep looking straight ahead. Hold still.'

I stare at the eye of the camera, keeping still. But the next moment there's a commotion over on the other side of the room and I turn my head to look. It's Beatrice Hill. Weeks must have just wheeled her in. She's staring at the photographer, her body rigid, her face chalk-white, and she's uttering a high-pitched wail that sends shivers down my spine.

For a moment everyone in the room is frozen into stillness, staring.

Then Weeks bends over Beatrice and speaks to her, but the wailing doesn't stop. Mr Sneed says something to Weeks, who seizes the chair and wheels it from the room. The sound echoes down the corridor, grows fainter, ceases.

In the day room the silence is broken by Mr Sneed, who clears his throat and assuming a jovial smile says to the photographer, 'Nothing to worry about. Carry on, my good man.'

For a moment it appears Mr Allen will not be able to carry on, his hands are shaking so much as he carries the plate with my image on it over to the table. He dives under his tent and there is a crash of bottles falling.

I haven't moved from the seat. What was it that made Beatrice so distressed? I haven't had a chance to see her again. I must try, even if I only manage to see her once before I go. She seems so vulnerable, I want to help her. I can't do anything for her, but perhaps talking to me would comfort her.

Eliza's hand is on my elbow. 'Come on, Miss, it's Mrs Thorpe's turn.' As if she can read my mind, she says quietly in my ear, 'Weeks has this afternoon off. And Roberts is on duty.'

After lunch, the room still smells of chemicals, but the photographer has departed. Roberts is poring over our photographs, laid out on the table, and she looks up as we enter.

'Come and see, Eliza,' she squawks. 'Frights, ain't they!'

Jostling with some of the other patients, I look for the one of me.

At first I can't see it, can't distinguish anyone in this collection of dingy, grey images. Then I catch sight of my nose, caught in unflattering profile as I turned my head at the last minute; it can't be anyone else. But if it weren't for that, I wouldn't recognize myself. The girl in the photograph has unkempt hair, a gaunt face and, startled by Beatrice's cry, her eyes stare wildly. She looks quite, quite mad.

With a small cry, I toss the photograph face down on the table. This is what my brother has done to me. Was this his intention?

'Careful, Miss, you'll break it.' Eliza picks up my image and studies it.

'Does it – is that what I look like?'

She doesn't hesitate. 'No, it's rubbish, that.'

I'm sure she's not telling the truth, but I feel better.

She turns to Roberts. 'Mr Sneed's going to put these on the walls?'

She sounds doubtful and I'm not surprised. Who'd want these dismal ghosts haunting them?

Roberts laughs, a short snorting laugh. 'Garn! I dunno what the Chief Loony wants 'em for but trust me, it'll be for somethin' that lines 'is own pockets.' She claps her hands. 'Now then, me beauties, put yer pitchers down, and find yerselves somethin' to do.'

Mrs Smythe is parted with difficulty from her photograph, which she insists on showing everyone. 'It's not such a good portrait as the one taken with the Archduke, but it's not a bad likeness.'

I approach Roberts. 'Is it all right if I walk in the hallway?'

Out of the corner of my eye I see Eliza's head lift.

Roberts exaggerates her surprise. 'Oh, you want some exercise, do yer? Go on then. Don't wear yerself out.'

I tap on the door. No answer. I turn the handle slowly so it doesn't make a noise and peer inside. The curtains are drawn; in the gloom I make out the figure on the bed. No movement. I should go . . . I hesitate. Then I draw closer.

She is curled up on her side, like a child. Her face is partly obscured by her hair, but in the line of her cheek, I see that resemblance again. Without thinking, I put out my hand, about to touch her, when she opens her eyes and looks directly at me. Instantly I draw my hand back. This isn't Grace, this is Beatrice, a stranger.

'Sorry,' I whisper. 'Sorry to wake you.'

Her eyes focus. 'Louisa?'

'Yes.'

In a quiet voice she says, 'I was dreaming. I was walk-ing down a lane picking primroses from under the hedge.'

I've never seen her smile before. It lights up her face. She seems totally relaxed. Maybe it's the after-effects of a sedative.

She starts to sit up but then stops suddenly, her body stiff, her eyes wide. She stares past me. Involuntarily, I glance over my shoulder, but there's no one there.

She starts to shake, making small whimpering sounds.

Drawing a chair to the bedside, I take her hand in mine. She is trembling, staring off into the distance. I should leave her in peace.

'Were you a good child?' she asks suddenly.

I'm so surprised at the question I laugh, and Beatrice's eyes widen. *Was* I a good child? Papa was proud of me, but as for Mamma . . . I never meant to be bad, but I was always upsetting her. Has she put me here as a punish-ment? No, I can't believe it.

Beatrice is still waiting for an answer. 'I tried to be, but Mamma was always in despair over me. I don't think I was the sort of little girl she expected so she didn't think I was very good. Why do you ask?'

She regards me seriously for a moment, then turns her head away. 'Mamma said I was a good child.' Tears run down her face.

'What is it? What's the matter?'

She turns her violet eyes towards me. 'My stepfather – he's a photographer.'

'Oh.' I don't like seeing her so upset, but I have to

admit I'm curious. I don't have to pry though – Beatrice seems ready to talk.

Her words spill out. 'His studio is a glass house on the roof. It makes a great noise when it rains. But when the sun comes out, it's like a house of light. I used to like it then. But my stepfather –' she breaks off and swallows – 'he said it was better when it was cloudy – too much light spoilt the photographs.'

She looks away again and adds, 'It's yellow, the dark-room, yellow, with yellow-shaded lamps.' A tremor goes through her.

With an intake of breath, I remember the photographer this morning – his yellow fingers straightening my head.

Her hand in mine begins to tremble again. 'We'd only just gone to live with him, Mamma and I. We were so poor after Papa died, my little brothers and sisters were sent away to live with various relatives, but Mamma let me stay, because she said I was good and helped her.

'My stepfather said I was a pretty child and he wanted to take photographs of me. At first it was easy – just standing still. And he gave me sixpence.' A pause. 'But then –' she swallows again – 'then he wanted me take off my clothes.'

I gasp, I can't help it. 'Did you?'

Shamefaced, she nods. 'I didn't want to, truly I didn't, but I thought he might complain to Mamma about me. Afterwards he gave me a pretty glass paperweight and said, "Don't tell Mamma."' Tears spill down her face. She brushes them away.

'How old were you?'

'Eleven, when it started.'

'You mean, it went on?' I can't imagine it.

She nods. 'He took lots of photographs. Lots and lots of photographs. He said I was a good girl to make so much money for him.'

I don't understand. 'Money? What did he mean?'

In a voice like a ghost's, she says, 'He sold the photographs.'

'Sold them? To whom?'

She shrugs. 'To the gentlemen who came when the shop was closed.'

A horrible cold sensation slides down my back.

I don't think I want to hear any more, but her thin voice continues, 'I carried on posing for him, even though I didn't want to, because he said if I didn't Mamma would send me away like the others. At first I felt hot . . . as if his eyes could look right into me. But he'd say, "Don't fidget, Bella" – that was his name for me – and I learned the trick of keeping my body quite still while my mind went away far away to somewhere else.'

She's far away now, lost in the moment she is reliving, her hand trembling like a frightened bird.

'Don't talk about it if it upsets you.'

She lifts her head and looks at me through her tears. 'It's all right. I'm glad to speak of these things to you because I think you believe me. You do, don't you?' Her violet eyes are tunnels.

'Yes, yes I do.' I respond instantly. And it's true.

The look she gives me is wretched. 'Louisa, my baby—'

At that moment the door opens, making us both jump. My heartbeat steadies when I see that it's Eliza.

She looks at us holding hands and frowns. 'Time you were back in the day room, Miss.' Her voice seems louder than usual, dispelling the hush that has filled the room.

Beatrice is looking at me, a question in her eyes. I don't want to leave her in this state but Eliza is waiting, hands on hips.

On impulse I say, 'Eliza, when do you think Weeks will be off again?'

'I couldn't say.' There's an edge to her tone, but then she looks from Beatrice to me and her expression relents. 'I'll tell you when I know, Miss.'

Every day I watch the careful unlocking and locking of doors, on the lookout for someone to slip up, waiting for my chance.

So far it hasn't come.

But in the meantime, there's Beatrice: thinking of her helps me to bear the frustration of still being here, gives me something to focus on.

I haunt the corridor, loitering by the window, watching Weeks going in and out of Beatrice's room. Mulling over what she told me, I think I know what happened to her. If I'm right, it's monstrous. I wish I could do something to help.

Today at last Eliza tips me the wink. And sure enough, it's Roberts who comes to lead us back from the dining room after lunch. But it's not Eliza who's with her, but Alice, the sharp-featured servant girl, the one who can read.

This might be more risky. Still, I have to take a chance. But instead of getting out the sewing things, Roberts says, 'Nah then, ladies. A special treat this afternoon. Extra time in the airing court. So off we go fer some luverly fresh air.'

I must do something. *Think*.

I have it. Sinking into a chair, I clutch my stomach and when Roberts says, 'Off with yer outside, now,' I say, 'I don't feel at all well today. Can I stay inside?'

Roberts shrugs. 'Suit yerself.'

Alice doesn't like this, I can tell. She whispers in

Roberts's ear. But Roberts gives her a push. 'Garn – stop frettin'. When you come in to check on Miss Hill, you can check on Madam here 'n' all.'

The others shuffle from the room, their voices die away and I am alone.

I take a great breath and let it out.

I'm tempted to stay where I am, enjoying the peace, but the thought of Beatrice's troubled face sends me hurrying along the hallway.

What a curious feeling it is to know that the gallery is empty, that no one else is here. Even so, I knock gently at the door.

There's no answer so I go straight in.

She's in the rocking chair today, wrapped in her shawl; her face, turned towards the door, is full of fear. When she sees it's me, she sighs. 'I thought you were Weeks.'

A fleeting smile transforms her face, and taking it as an invitation, I settle myself on the bed. She looks at me expectantly, but I feel awkward; I don't know how to say what I've been thinking.

I notice she's cradling something under her shawl. 'What have you got there?'

She looks embarrassed, but she shifts her arm slightly to show me.

It's a rag doll. Different clothes and hair from my old doll Annabel, but the same loved shabbiness.

'I have one – at home.' As I say the word, my throat closes. I swallow. 'She's called Annabel.'

'This is Rosalie.' She darts me a glance. 'I hide her – sometimes in the drawer and sometimes in the bed.' Her

191

tone is gleeful like a naughty child's. 'Dr Bull said I shouldn't have her – that she encourages my fancies – and Weeks threw her away.' She pulls the doll closer to her, cradling it in her thin arms. 'But Eliza rescued her for me. She says it's our secret.' A look of alarm crosses her face. 'I've told you now.'

'Don't worry. I won't tell anyone.'

This seems to reassure her. 'Eliza is kind, isn't she? Very kind.'

'Yes, she is.'

'Not like Weeks.' She squeezes Rosalie. 'She's always doing nasty things to me. And saying nasty things. She says I could walk if I wanted to and I'm just pretending that I can't. And she says I tell lies to get attention.' She starts to rock back and forth.

'Beatrice – the things that Weeks says are lies . . . are they about your stepfather?'

The chair stills. Then she turns on me a look of such anguish I feel it myself.

'Did your stepfather . . .' I pause, not knowing how to put this delicately, then plunge on. 'Did he . . .' I stop again, swallow and then ask quickly, 'Is that how you came to have a baby?'

She starts rocking again, her grip on her doll tightening, turning her knuckles white. She gives a small, almost imperceptible nod.

We both seem to have stopped breathing. I don't know what to say.

After what seems a long silence, Beatrice looks at me. 'You believe me, don't you?'

'Yes.' It's true – I do believe her. Papa always said, 'Listening to the patient, that's the secret, Lou, not rushing in thinking you know best, but listening to what they have to tell you.'

She sighs and her shoulders relax. She starts smoothing Rosalie's hair.

As gently as I can, I ask, 'Do you want to tell me what happened?'

Another long pause. Then her face crumples and she starts to weep.

I put my hand on hers. 'I'm sorry.'

In a voice choked with tears she says, 'It's all right. I can speak of it, to you.'

Her trust in me makes me feel lighter, as if I've been given a present.

She looks at me confidingly. 'I didn't know I was going to have a baby, truly I didn't.'

Although this is surprising, I have read of this in one of Papa's medical journals.

She shudders. 'It was awful – that night. I started to have pains in my stomach, like cramp. After a while the pain was terrible, as if I was being pulled apart. It would stop for a few minutes and then come again. I didn't know what to do.'

'Didn't you tell someone? Didn't they hear you crying out?'

She shakes her head. 'I walked about with my pillow and when the pain was too bad, I buried my face in it. Mamma was away visiting my aunt, so there was only him and the servants in the house. I didn't want *him* to come.'

193

She pauses and then continues. 'It felt as if my insides were being pushed out. I thought I was going to die.' A spasm shakes her at the memory. 'And then – and then . . .' The thud of the rocking chair speeds up.

'Your baby was born.'

The chair is suddenly still.

'Yes.' It is a whisper.

She turns to look at me, her irises blue-black, her face contorted. 'Only she wasn't right. She was *deformed*.' With the word a sob breaks from her.

'What do you mean?

She can scarcely manage to get the words out but I hear them. 'She was quite still, and a dreadful blue-grey colour . . . and there was a thing – a rubbery thing like rope – growing out of her tummy and into me. It was horrible, horrible.' She puts her hands to her face.

'Beatrice . . . listen to me.'

She doesn't respond but keeps her face buried in her hands.

'Beatrice, the baby wasn't deformed. That rope – the rubbery thing – all babies have them.'

She lowers her hands and looks at me through her hair. 'They do?'

'Yes.'

'But she was such a funny colour . . . all wrong . . . and she never cried.'

I take both her hands in mine. 'That's because she'd died already, I think. Before she was born.'

She lets out a little cry. 'So I was right. I killed her.'

194

I squeeze her hands tight. 'You didn't. It was an accident. These things sometimes happen. *It wasn't your fault*.'

She looks directly at me. 'Are you sure?'

'Yes. *Yes*.'

She turns her head away. 'But I'd been bad. It must have been my fault.'

I shake her hands, wanting her to believe me. 'You hadn't been bad. You couldn't help what happened. It was *him*.'

A pause, then a great shudder passes through her and she lets out her breath. I realize that I'm gripping her hands fiercely and I let them go. 'What happened after that?'

Beatrice gazes over my head, into the distance. 'I didn't know what to do . . . I knew Mamma would be so cross with me if she found out.' Her bottom lip quivers. 'I think I must have fainted. When I came to . . . oh, it was horrible . . . I knew the baby was dead then. I cleaned up the mess as best I could and wrapped her and everything in my nightdress. It was very early morning by now, just getting light, so I crept out of the house and down to the river.'

She stops. Her voice, when it comes, is as soft as dust. 'I found a heavy stone . . . I tied it to the bundle . . . and dropped it from the middle of the bridge.'

I have a lump in my throat, imagining what it must have been like.

After a while I ask quietly, 'What brought you here, Beatrice? To the asylum?'

'I couldn't stop crying. Mamma kept asking me why I was crying but I didn't tell her. *I didn't*. She would think I was so wicked . . . The doctor said I should come here to be made better. I tried to keep it a secret here too, but they heard me crying for my baby. But they say it's all in my mind, my imagination, that I couldn't have had a baby that no one knew about.'

Beatrice sighs. 'I often think of Rosalie lying at the bottom of the river and how cold she must be and lonely . . .' She looks straight at me. 'You won't tell anyone what I did, will you? Especially not Weeks.'

'Don't worry. I won't tell anyone. They wouldn't believe me, anyway. I'm a patient, like you, Beatrice.' My voice cracks. I meant only to reassure her but my words have ambushed me.

Silently, she offers her doll. Once, cotton filled with rags could comfort me. Not now. Not here. I shake my head and wipe my face with my hand.

She is looking at me wonderingly. 'The same happened to you?'

'The same? No. *No*.'

'Only I thought, because you're crying . . . You're very kind. I don't believe you can have done anything bad. I expect they'll let you go home soon.'

Home. Can I go home? Will I be safe?

Beatrice interrupts my thoughts. 'Who will sign for you?'

I stare at her. 'What do you mean?'

'The person who signed for you to be admitted has to sign for you to be released.'

I feel as if all the breath has been knocked out of me. 'Are you sure?'

Beatrice nods. 'Eliza explained it to me. When I am better, Mamma will sign for me to go home. Who will sign for you?'

The old question. Who has done this? Those papers would tell me . . .

Part of me still wants to think it was Mrs Lunt. But really I think it was Tom, for reasons I can't begin to imagine. After all, he returned my letter to Mamma and pretended to be Thomas Childs . . . it must be him . . . I don't think Mamma would have done this to me . . .

Is that a noise in the gallery? I must be back in the day room before Roberts returns.

'Beatrice, I have to go now, I'm sorry.'

Her face falls. 'You will come again, won't you?' For the first time she puts her hand on mine.

'Yes, I will. I promise.'

When Roberts and Alice come into the day room, I'm collapsed in a chair, pretending to look weary and ill. But inside I'm not feeling at all weary – my mind is working furiously. Beatrice's story has shaken me. How can they not believe her? Instead of helping, they are making her worse. And if I stay here, the same thing will happen to me.

I do want to see my papers. I want to know the truth.

But whoever admitted me, it's no good waiting for them to sign my release. If I am going to get out of here, I will have to do it myself. And if I can, I'll take Beatrice with me. She has suffered enough.

From now on I must be alert. No more chloral.

And no more waiting. It's time to take action.

I've decided our only chance is at night. During the day we are watched too closely. Tonight I'll watch carefully – I will find a way.

It's the night attendant we often have, the one with eyes like currants. I haven't paid attention to her before – now, covertly, I watch every move. First she lights the lamp on the small table and, as if making herself at home, takes from her basket a pack of cards and a large brown bottle. Then she comes round with the chloral. I'm the last to receive the dose. She doesn't bother to wait and see that we've swallowed it, so I hold it in my mouth, wondering what to do.

To my relief, she starts gathering up our clothes from the beds and as soon as her back's turned, I pull out my chamber pot and spit some of the chloral into it. I know that I mustn't give it up all at once – I might have hallucinations or become delirious. Luckily it's colourless, but its pungent smell might give me away so I use the pot.

When the attendant sees me, she looks disgruntled. 'Pissin' already?' she grumbles.

I climb into bed, but after she's carried the armful of dresses, petticoats and boots from the room, I tiptoe to the door and, peeping out, I watch where she takes them. She goes to the room at the end of the hallway, near the door to the airing court, where our cloaks and galoshes are kept.

I'm back in bed before she returns. She settles into her

chair and, taking a swig from her bottle, begins playing patience.

Gradually the others stop shifting and murmuring as the chloral takes effect. The attendant plays on, drinking at intervals, but her yawns become more frequent, and eventually she lays aside the cards and rests her head on the table. Once she's snoring, I slip from my bed and approach her cautiously.

Like all the other attendants, her keys hang from her belt, but I can only see three. Why does she have so few? Several locked doors stand between here and the front door to the asylum. And then I remember – on my very first day, looking from the gate in the airing court and noticing the attendants who spoke to the gardener. Perhaps there's a side door that the staff use. If so, it can't be far away.

The attendant stirs, muttering, and I dart back to bed. If I could take her keys . . . But she's bound to wake up. And then there's Beatrice. She can't walk. How will I get her out? And if we succeed, what will we do then?

I lie awake for hours, turning these questions over in my mind.

Gradually a plan forms – a risky plan, but one that might be possible. For Beatrice's sake, I have to try it. But how am I going to get to see her? I must tell her about the plan, but, like a cat, Weeks watches my every move. Perhaps Eliza can help.

Two days pass before I get a chance to speak to Eliza. I can barely contain my impatience. But on the third day I have

199

a stroke of luck. Eliza's on lavatory duty before breakfast, so I make sure I'm at the end of the queue.

'All right, Miss?' she asks, as I come out.

Checking that Weeks isn't about, I say in a low voice, 'Eliza, I have to see Beatrice, Miss Hill, again. Soon.'

She frowns. 'It's tricky, Miss.'

'I know, but it's important. Can you help me?'

'I don't know.' She looks away.

'Please, Eliza.' I put my hand on her arm.

She regards my hand then raises her eyes to my face. 'I'll see what I can do.'

'There's something else. I need to know what my admission papers say. Especially who signed them. Can you find out for me?'

Her face falls. 'I can't. Sorry, Miss.'

She looks so miserable I wish I hadn't asked. 'Of course. You mustn't risk losing your place.'

'It's not just that.' Eliza's cheeks are red. 'I'm not a right good reader, Miss.'

I'd been counting on Eliza. I'll just have to go ahead without knowing what the papers say.

In the day room, I bend my head to my work, appearing to be a model patient. But, hidden beneath my skirt, my feet tap. Intoxicated by the thought of freedom, they're ready to run.

L unch is over and it's raining too hard for us to go out. The long afternoon stretches ahead. Eliza has just returned from some errand Weeks sent her on. They're standing behind me and I can hear every word.

'You took your time.' Weeks, sharp as ever.

'Matron stopped me.'

'For untidiness, as usual, I suppose.'

'No.' Eliza's tone is injured and I can imagine her expression. 'She wants to see you. Now.'

My heart jumps.

'Now?' Weeks is clearly surprised. 'Are you sure?'

'Yes.'

The minute the door closes, I whirl round.

But before I can say anything, Eliza clutches my arm and draws me to the door away from the others. 'Hang on. Wait till she's out of the gallery. Then you must be quick. You've got about ten minutes, I reckon.'

'What?' I don't understand.

Eliza shakes her hand impatiently. 'Matron doesn't want to see her – I made it up.'

'Oh, Eliza! You'll be in such trouble—'

'Shh! Don't waste time.' She sticks her head out of the door, then bundles me through it.

I race along the hallway and burst into Beatrice's room. She starts up in bed, eyes wide with shock.

'Don't worry, it's only me. But I haven't got long. I've

something to tell you.' I can see I'm alarming her and I try to slow down.

'Beatrice, it's all right. How are you?'

'I – I've not been well. Weeks . . .' She raises her shoulders as if to ward off an imaginary blow.

'What? What's she done? Has she hurt you?'

'No, but – she keeps saying I'm lying. And she found Rosalie . . . and took her away. She said she was going to burn her . . .' She starts to weep.

I seize her hands. 'Beatrice, listen to me. I can get you out of here.'

She frowns. She doesn't understand what I'm saying and I'm running out of time and this might be my only chance. 'I'll come for you tonight.'

'Come for me?'

'Yes, and we'll escape. I've worked it all out. We can do it, I'm sure.' Instead of looking joyful, her face creases up.

'What is it?'

'I can't go.'

'You can. We'll take the invalid chair. Don't worry about anything. I'll look after you, I promise.'

My words don't seem to be having any effect. She's still looking distressed.

'Beatrice, trust me. I won't let you down.'

How many minutes have passed? I don't know. I don't want to leave her but I must. If Weeks catches me here, Eliza will be in terrible trouble. 'I've got to go now, but I'll come tonight, all right? Tonight.' I give her hands a squeeze.

*

Before Weeks returns, I'm back in my place, hemming industriously. Without turning my head, I see her storm in, scowling. My face feels flushed, and I hope she doesn't notice.

'Eliza!' She snaps the name so abruptly nearly everyone jumps. 'What were you thinking of? Matron didn't want to see me today.'

'I thought that's what she said.'

'Stupid girl! She said she'd told you she wanted to continue our discussions some time, but she didn't say when.'

'Oh! I must have got it wrong.' Eliza opens her blue eyes wide, the picture of innocence.

Weeks frowns. I can tell she's suspicious. Her eyes rake the room, checking if all is as it should be. Then her gaze comes back to me.

I look down, hold my breath.

The next moment, someone cries out, 'No!' and I look up to see Weeks wresting a baby garment from Mrs Thorpe. 'Give me that! It's time you stopped this nonsense. There is no baby, you understand? No baby!'

Mrs Thorpe starts wailing, a thin sad sound, and it sets off some of the others. With a tut of exasperation, Weeks stuffs the offending garment into the cupboard.

Behind her back, I send Eliza a grateful smile and she winks. I'm glad she's not in trouble. She's the only person I'll be sorry to leave. I wish I could say goodbye, but of course, that's impossible.

Tomorrow Beatrice and I will be safe. Tomorrow we won't be here.

I'm poised, waiting for my moment.

For the past few nights I've watched the night attendant and her routine hasn't varied. Now, the instant she's gone from the room with the clothes, I spit the chloral into my chamber pot. I look round. My room-mates are huddled in their beds, twitching and sighing. No one's watching.

Quietly I go over to the table. I uncork the chloral bottle and pour some into the beer. The necks of the bottles chink together and I freeze. A quick glance over my shoulder reassures me – no one's looking my way, so I pour a little more, my hand trembling, and a few drops splash on to the table. It's hard to judge the dose. It must be enough to make the attendant sleep, but not too much. I don't want to kill her.

I push back both corks, mop up the spillage with my nightgown and scurry back to bed.

I shut my eyes, pretending to be asleep, but I listen out for the attendant's movements: her footsteps in the hallway growing louder, the swish of her skirts past my bed, her heavy breathing. When I hear the creak as she settles in the chair, I peer at her through my lashes, my heart beating faster. Will she smell the chloral?

I wait on tenterhooks, but, for once, she doesn't immediately take a drink.

Instead she rummages in her bag, and taking out a

greasy package, proceeds to unwrap it. A savoury smell reaches my nostrils – some kind of meat pie perhaps.

She tucks into this, while turning the pages of what looks like an illustrated newspaper. She seems to be looking at the pictures mainly although every now and then she pauses to read, running her finger across the page and mouthing the words to herself. *Come on, come on, drink!* I silently entreat her. At last she reaches for the bottle and downs a big draught, her attention still on the newspaper. I breathe again.

I don't know how long I'll have to wait – a regular dose would take effect within the hour, but this isn't a regular dose. Peering out from my bedclothes, I keep watching.

Tonight of all nights she seems unusually alert. She starts to play patience, drinks, belches, scratches, lays out the cards again.

What if the dose was too small?

Hours seem to pass, but perhaps it's my agitated state that makes it seem so long. I think of Beatrice, awake and waiting for me, wondering where I am, thinking I've let her down. Once, my own eyelids close and I jerk awake, alarmed. *I* mustn't fall asleep. That would ruin everything.

Just when I'm about to give up, the attendant's head drops and the cards slip from her hand on to the floor. I wait until her breathing deepens, and then I wait some more. I have to be sure the chloral has taken effect, that she won't wake up.

At last I think it might be safe to move. I slide out of bed, trying not make a sound. Holding my breath I tiptoe to her and reach towards her belt. The keys aren't there!

205

I feel paralysed. I could cry with frustration. Then I pull myself together. Think! She must have the keys somewhere – she needs them to get into the gallery. I look in her basket – a purse and another bottle of beer, that's all. No keys.

I scan the table, and then I spot them, half hidden by the newspaper. It would be so easy to take them, but her arm is lying across the page. Gingerly I stretch out my hand, catch hold of the end of one of the keys and pull. Surely she'll feel the disturbance under her arm . . . There's resistance and then the keys come sliding towards me, and with the slightest clink, I have them in my hand! I feel so gleeful I could laugh. I can't believe how easy it was. It's a good omen, I'm sure.

Now hurry, hurry, out of the door, down the hallway, feet stepping as lightly as leaves, so that none of the other night attendants hear. A tiny click and the cloakroom door opens and then I search quickly for my dress – and here it is, on top of the pile! What luck!

I struggle into it, feeling at the waistband for the lump of money – still there – pull on the petticoat and look about for shoes – no time for stockings. These are much too small, try another pair – these will do – in fact I think they are mine – another stroke of good fortune!

I pick up the nearest bundle of clothes for Beatrice. Anything will do for now. I seize a cloak from a peg and put it on, take a couple for Beatrice and I'm ready.

Now I pause, and take a breath. I have to open the main door to the gallery and this could be our downfall. If someone hears – the key turning, the door opening, then closing behind me . . .

Another breath, and then to the door. I try the biggest key and it slides in as if the lock has just been oiled and it turns smoothly without a sound. I turn the handle and, like a dream, the door opens. My heart dances. We're going to do it!

Now to find the side door, the one the attendants and servants use. I've looked for it on my way to and from the dining room but not found it, so I go in the other direction, where I've never been before. At the end of the corridor I turn right into another passageway. And here it is – the side door! I'm sure it will be locked but just in case, before I try the keys, I press the handle and it opens. Someone must have forgotten to lock it. And it's so close to the gallery. I'll be able to wheel Beatrice here quickly.

There's no time to lose, but just for a moment I step outside. It's stopped raining and overhead, stars glitter in the night sky. I breathe in the cold air, its sharpness, the taste of freedom, stinging my throat.

My plan is to make for the side gate into the park – I'm sure there must be one for the attendants and tradesmen – then wheel Beatrice some way away and leave her hidden by the edge of the forest, while I walk to the nearest town. Luckily, it's not too cold. We'll take all the blankets from Beatrice's bed.

From my memory of the journey here, it's quite a distance to the town, but I should be able to manage it. As soon as it's light, I'll hire a carriage and come back for Beatrice and then we'll take the train to the north. I daren't go home. Mamma will tell Tom and there's no knowing what he'll do. So that only leaves Carr Head. Aunt Phyllis will take us in, I know it.

I'm not sure what will happen next, but Aunt Phyllis will sort everything out. She'll make Tom account for himself and decide how we can help Beatrice.

A fleeting doubt about Grace rises in my mind. Instantly I quell it. She'll be in London now, settled into her new home, her new life. She won't have said anything. She won't have broken her promise.

Once we get to Carr Head everything will be all right.

I take one last breath of air before turning back inside.

Hurry now – Beatrice will be waiting. Back along the corridor, round the corner, into the gallery. Pause here to check. Nothing stirring in the long dark hallway, no lights, no voices. No one knows I'm not where I should be.

Along to Beatrice's room, swiftly, silently, and here I am, at the door, and I have my hand on the handle and I'm turning it, but something's wrong. The door won't open. It's locked.

I tap on the door, calling quietly, 'Beatrice, open the door,' but there's no answer.

I don't understand. The door's never been locked before. I look at the keys in my hand. Perhaps one of them will open it.

And then a voice behind me, a voice I know so well, says, 'You're wasting your time, Miss Childs. Miss Hill has gone.'

I spin round. There's a sound of a match striking and

then the steady glow of an oil lamp and in its light I see Weeks's face, mocking, triumphant.

I stare at her, not comprehending. What does she mean, 'Miss Hill has gone'? She can't have gone. She's meant to be here, waiting for me, so we can escape, so we can be free. What is Weeks doing here? This is all wrong. This isn't how it was meant to happen . . .

And then what Weeks said filters through to me, begins to make sense. Beatrice has gone. *Beatrice has gone*.

Rage flares through my whole body and the words fly out of my mouth: 'You bitch, you damn bitch, you've killed her.'

Weeks just stands there, smiling.

I want to hurt her like she's hurt Beatrice.

I seize hold of the nearest object, a heavy pot of ferns, and I hurl it at her head. It misses and hits the window behind her and glass falls in a glittering shower, glass everywhere. I curl my hand into a fist and *crack*, I punch her hard in the face. She gives a cry and one hand flies up to her nose.

Setting the lamp down, she catches hold of my arm, twisting it up round my back. She forces me down, down on to the matting, my face in the glass, and she's shouting now and I'm shouting and kicking and struggling and hands seize my arms and ankles and I'm held so tight I can't move and something's pressing into my back, I can't breathe, I'm gasping for air and then my head's wrenched sideways and I just have time to close my fist before a cloth looms in front of my eyes, a cloth that smells sweet and engulfs me in blackness.

PART THREE

Dark. A dank smell.

I open my eyes. Fog, in my head, in front of my eyes. I blink to clear them.

Dark still.

I listen, my ears straining for clues.

Silence.

Silence and cold.

Such cold.

My thoughts come slowly. I tell myself to move, curl up, wrap myself in my arms.

I can't. My wrists, ankles are fastened down. *I can't move.*

And now I hear it. Rustling. My mouth dries. A mouse? A rat? I'm not afraid of mice, but rats? In the dark, when I can't see where they are? When I can't move and they can? When they can run over me and bite me with their sharp yellow teeth? I try to shout *Help!* but only a feeble croak comes out.

No one answers.

The rustle continues but there aren't tiny feet running over me, or teeth gnawing at me. *Relax. Breathe.* Tell yourself it isn't a mouse, it isn't a rat.

Breathe.

Drip.

My mouth's dry and I can't swallow.

Drip.

213

Somewhere moisture's gathering and falling, but I can't reach it.

What am I doing here?

My mind is a pocket with a hole in the bottom – everything I used to know has fallen out.

I struggle to concentrate. And then I remember . . . Weeks . . . the window breaking . . . the cloth.

They've tied me down in the dark because I attacked Weeks.

I remember everything – how it was all going so well, until Beatrice's locked door – and Weeks. How did she come to be there just then? Only Beatrice and I knew what I was planning. Someone must have overheard me. Alice passing in the hall? Someone must have told Weeks and she waited for me. But before that, what did she do?

Beatrice, what has she done to you?

G rey now. A faint light.

I'm more awake. Slowly I look round. A narrow room like a cell. Walls streaked with grime. A grating high up near the ceiling. In the door, about a third of the way down, a dark hole, like an eye.

I'm stiff with cold. Now I can see why. I'm lying on a mattress which crackles as if it's stuffed with straw, but there are no bedcovers – all I'm wearing is a grubby gown. They've taken everything – all my clothes, even my under-wear. They must have taken my hairpins too – my hair's straggling round my face.

I go to turn over, but I can't. Then I see the metal bolts in the floor, the canvas straps fastening my wrists and ankles. I try to pull loose, clench my fists, and there's a searing pain in my right palm. I remember now – the sliver of glass I clutched at as Weeks held me down on the floor. But I can't reach the strap with it. I tug hard, hoping to loosen the bindings, but it's no good.

My heart flutters, panic rising. To keep it at bay, I look round again. There must be something here, something that will help me. But there's nothing else in the room, except a chamber pot in the corner, a chamber pot I can't reach, and even as I think this, I'm aware of the pressure in my bladder. I grit my teeth.

Hang on. Surely someone will come. Hang on.

I try to think about something else, anything . . . and

then its hits me. Today, now, I would have been free, waiting to fetch Beatrice in a carriage, looking forward to our arrival at Carr Head, Aunt Phyllis's welcome . . .

Stop it, I tell myself, blinking back my tears. At least you're alive. My heart contracts. Please let Beatrice be safe somewhere, even if she thinks I've let her down . . .

With a grating sound, the door opens and I squint at the light spilling in from the corridor outside, at the two women who fill the doorway.

One of them addresses me in a loud voice, as if I'm deaf. 'Well, Milady, got yerself into a fine pickle, ain't yer? This'll teach you to attack the folks what looks after you. There's gratitude. Mind, you, Sal,' she nudges her companion, 'I'd 'ave liked to see it.'

Sal, who is tall with a long face like a horse's, chuckles like a simpleton. 'They say Weeks 'as got a real shiner.'

Her partner purses her lips. 'Serves 'er Ladyship right, I say. Now then, you, time for breakfast.'

They advance into the room and Sal deposits a tin mug and plate on the floor some distance away from me, all the while observing me warily.

'Untie 'er, Sal,' says the shorter one.

The other hesitates. 'I don't want a punch or a kick, Hannah.'

'I won't,' I manage to croak.

'Damn right, you won't. For if you do, you'll feel my fist quick enough. Go on, Sal, 'urry up.' Hannah looms over me with her fist clenched, while Sal fumbles with the fastenings.

216

I try to sit up, but my head swims and I fall back on to the mattress with a groan.

Hannah gives me a shove in the ribs with her boot. 'Come on, we ain't got all day. Use the pisspot if yer going to.'

I haul myself up again and, keeping my hand closed tight on the piece of glass, totter across to the chamber pot on legs that feel like rubber.

I'd like to wash my hands and face, to brush my tangled hair, to rinse out my furred-up mouth, but there's no means to do those things here.

Hannah jerks her head at my breakfast so I perch on the edge of the mattress, whose coarse ticking, I now see, is grimy and stained. The mug contains cold water and I gulp it down gratefully, even though it tastes bitter. I pick up a broken crust from the plate, but, at the first bite, my throat closes.

I can't help it, I can't eat it.

'Right then, get yerself laid down.'

I feel so dizzy, I'm glad to lie down again. But then Sal gingerly takes hold of my ankles and I know she's going to fasten them. 'Please . . .'

'*Please*,' Hannah mocks. 'Polite, ain't we? But orders is orders, and ours are to see yer tied tight as a tick, Milady.'

It's no use struggling – they'd easily overpower me.

Hannah watches while Sal ties the canvas straps that fasten my ankles to the bolts, then she checks them. Satisfied, she nods, and Sal moves to my wrists. I can't help clutching the glass more tightly and a drop of blood falls and stains the floor. It's all over in a second – Hannah

217

darting at me, prising open my hand and wresting the sliver from me. With an exclamation, she brandishes it in front of my face.

'So! Not do us no harm, would yer? What's this for, if not to put our eyes out?'

'No,' I protest. 'It's not for that.'

The expression on Hannah's face changes. 'Hear that, Sal? We'll have to report this to Matron. This one wants watchin' or she'll do 'erself in.'

Sal's mouth is hanging open and Hannah nudges her. 'Stop gawping, will yer! Get 'er fastened.'

When Sal has done, Hannah checks her work and pulls the straps a notch or two tighter. Sal picks up the mug and plate, and they're moving towards the door.

They've gone, leaving me alone in the dark.

I don't know how long I've been in here. The light fades . . . returns . . . they come with the mug and the plate.

At least I think they do. Sometimes I'm not sure if I'm awake or dreaming. I sleep a lot. They must be putting a sedative in the water. When I do wake, I feel very drowsy and my mind's . . . blurry.

Perhaps it's for the best. Better not to think.

Sometimes I hear that rustling and I tell myself it's a tree in full leaf, rustling in the wind. I like to think of this tree, my tree, with its sturdy trunk and roots deep in the ground. I imagine myself perching on its high branches, like a bird . . . and then I spread my wings and fly . . .

It's peaceful here, with no one to bother me and everything slipped away from my mind except for my tree. So when they come one day and I've used the pot and drunk some water and someone, I think it's Hannah, says, 'It's time to go,' I don't want to go anywhere.

'It ain't no use clinging to the mattress. Get 'er hands, Sal.'

Between them they manhandle me to my feet.

I'm so weak I can hardly stand but this doesn't bother them. One on each side, with a firm grip on my arms, they drag me along corridors, my feet trailing. Where are we going? I must have spoken this aloud without realizing it, because Hannah says shortly, 'You'll see, soon enough.'

When we stop in front of a door, Hannah takes a key from her pocket and inserts it in the lock. She winks at Sal and then says to me, 'We hope yer like yer new home, Milady. You'll find it very comfortable.' Hannah turns the key, and opens the door. 'Welcome to the Fifth Gallery.'

I stare at her, numb. Before I can gather my wits, I'm pushed into the room.

A stomach-churning stench makes me catch my breath. And the noise! After the silence of my cell, it's magnified to a painful pitch – and it sounds inhuman, more like the baying and howling of wild animals. There are bodies, bodies everywhere, in a turmoil of restless motion that makes my head spin.

Hannah prods me forward.

A blue uniform emerges from the confusion. 'This her, then, what had a go at Weeks? She don't look like a goer.'

This one has a deep voice, like a man's. She's big too with broad shoulders.

'Oh, yes, she's a vixen, all right,' says Hannah. 'And watch her – she might try to do herself in.'

'One less for us to worry about then, eh?' The attendant laughs, a deep throaty laugh. 'Righto then, Hannah, leave her with us. She'll soon settle in.'

She grips my arm and steers me between the bodies. Those that don't move aside fast enough are knocked out of the way.

I look back over my shoulder at Hannah and Sal, faces that I know. But they've already disappeared.

'This is yours.' The attendant points at a bed covered with a grimy blanket. I look around. The room is full of beds. No other furniture, just beds with a shelf above them. Most of the shelves are empty.

I swallow. 'Where's the day room?'

'Day room! La! We don't have such fancies as day rooms here. This is where you are and this is where you'll stay.' With a push that propels me forward on to the bed, she stalks off.

I scramble to the bedhead and crouch there, my back against the wall. I want to shut my eyes, to make all this disappear, but I feel too vulnerable. My stomach is clenched and my heart is beating so fast I think it will burst out of my chest, but I keep my eyes open, trying to be ready for whatever comes next.

We must be somewhere in the basement of the building; what light there is, filtering through high gratings, creates a muddy, underwater atmosphere.

Everywhere I look I see filthy, scrawny figures.

Some are inert – they stand like stones or crouch, whimpering, under their beds or lie, like bundles of rags that have been flung down. Others, driven by a restless energy, rage up and down the passage between the beds like tottering scarecrows, their thin stick arms gesticulating wildly. Some carry out the same sequence of actions over and over again, like machines. One stands at the door rattling the handle and calling for help. One keeps trying to eat coal out of the bucket until an exasperated attendant tethers her to her bed. My nearest neighbour is shredding her blanket, all the while staring at me and muttering under her breath.

No wonder Miss Gorman was terrified of Weeks,

221

terrified of being sent here again. I look more carefully, but I don't recognize her in any of these creatures. I don't recognize anyone.

'You friggin' bitch!' The sudden shout, so close, makes me jump and my heart hammers. But it's all right – they're not shouting at me. At the foot of my bed, two scarecrows are at each other's throats, scratching, tearing each other's hair and shouting obscenities.

Rather than stopping them, the attendants gather round as if it's an entertainment. But as quickly as it flared it dies down; the combatants lose interest and wander off. My heartbeat slows a little. It wasn't me. But it might have been.

Now a bell rings and the patients are herded towards the door. An attendant approaches and frowns at my gown. 'What have you done with your dress?'

'They took it.' My voice is a wisp.

'Took it! More like you tore it up, you nuisance.'

She goes off grumbling, returning shortly with a mud-coloured bundle that she thrusts over my head. I'm struggling to find the armholes when she yanks and twists my arms into the sleeves. I fumble with the fastenings but before I've done them up she seizes my arm and hauls me from the bed. The dress hangs like a sack to just below my knees. She jerks her head at the pair of shoes she has brought. I squeeze my bare feet into them.

'Come on, you great dollop, move.' I stumble and she punches me on the back with her fist.

Patients under the beds are dragged out and we're

hustled through the doorway and along the corridor. All the time, the attendants chivvy us with blows.

We scramble through a door into a bleak courtyard overshadowed by high walls. I stagger a few paces, using a wall as a support, but I haven't the strength to stand. I collapse on to the hard ground and it takes me a while to get my breath back, for the shuddering in my body to subside.

This must be our exercise yard. There are a few snowdrops in one corner, but they're lying on top of the soil, their blooms crushed. The light hurts my eyes – above our heads is a square of blue sky, so bright I can't look at it. The air is fresh and sharp and I breathe in great lungfuls. How long since I've been outside? Not since the night I tried to escape . . .

No one is walking. They carry on as they did inside while the attendants stand round gossiping. Some patients squat in the dirt. One piles stones up in a heap, another is eating a snowdrop. Out here the rampaging ones have more room to fling themselves about and I hunch up close to the wall, trying to keep out of their way. Some are amusing themselves by throwing things over the boundary. One has a crust in her hand, which she launches with a whoop, while another tips out her shoes. A brown lump falls out – and I suddenly realize, with a little shiver of revulsion, that it's excrement. This is hurled over with a scream of glee and the shoes follow after.

Something sharp strikes my head.

'Come on, you booby. Time to go in.'

The attendant moves off, her keys dangling from her hand, leaving me stunned, but not from the blow.

What roots me to the spot is the realization that to her, I'm no different from the others. I'm one of these lost, abandoned souls.

I've entered the lowest circle of hell and there is no escape.

I still feel weak and lethargic, even though I've been trying to eat a little. But I don't feel as light-headed or confused and my hands aren't shaking as much now.

I'm even getting used to the violence. The attendants are worse than the patients, especially the big one with the deep voice – Scratton, I think she's called. She likes to taunt patients until they lash out. Then she knocks her victims down, saying, 'Look what you've done to yourself, you clumsy!' Lots of the patients have bruises on their faces, but no one's been to check on us; I haven't seen the matron or Dr Bull since I arrived on the Fifth.

So far I've been lucky. As long as I stay on my bed out of the way no one pays any attention to me. But all the time, inside, I'm terrified. Not of being hit. The most fearful thing is seeing in the other patients what I might become if I give up, if I let myself sink into despair. I've tried to make myself believe I won't be here forever. I have vivid, troubled dreams, often about escaping: I climb over the gate, or disguise myself as an attendant, or – best of all – glide through the walls like a ghost . . .

But then I wake up and I'm still here and the long day drags on – so many hours to fill with only my own thoughts for company. If I let it, my mind runs wild, ideas and feelings whirling round till I feel dizzy. I've tried to control it by concentrating on something clear and calm. I recall mathematical formulae, I recite the symptoms of diseases and medical procedures, the discipline of it help-ing me to keep hold of a sense of myself. I am still me. I am Louisa Cosgrove.

But I can't keep it up.

Even if I'm moved to a better gallery, I'm still going to be imprisoned. Tom won't sign my release. I won't get another chance to escape. If I did, where could I go? What could I do? I've no money now, I'd be destitute.

I'll never see Mamma again. I'll never know if Grace is happy . . .

Every day I feel myself sinking lower, as if I'm sliding slowly into a dark sea, knowing I'm going to drown . . .

There is a way out, of course. If I still had my glass sliver . . .

Could I do it though? I don't know whether I have the courage. But if I had the means . . .

That would give me a kind of freedom, knowing I could choose.

Sometimes, if I shut my eyes and relax, I can slip away . . .

I'm in my room at home. I'm pleased with myself because I've just translated a difficult piece of Xenophon and Papa calls up the stairs, 'Lou, are you coming?'

I run down and there in the street is the gig and the whiskery horse, who rolls his eyes at being kept waiting. But Papa speaks to him and calms him and then he trots off docilely, taking us on our visits. I enjoy the breeze and the jingle of the horse's harness as Papa tells me who we are going to see.

We're nearly at the church and I hear the bell ringing,

the slow single notes of the death knell. I climb down from the carriage and watch as men with blank faces lift the coffin on to their shoulders. I look for Papa but he's not there. I follow the coffin through the churchyard and watch as it is lowered into the black hole. Then the men start shovelling earth into the hole, spadeful after spadeful. But however much earth they throw into the hole, they can't stop the terrible smell . . .

It's the smell that brings me back.

Papa is dead and I am here. But I still keep my eyes closed. For a little while longer, I can try to pretend.

Something touches my hand. Instantly I open my eyes, afraid of Scratton.

No, I'm still dreaming. Someone in a yellow dress is sitting on my bed. A yellow dress like butter, like sunshine.

I close my eyes, open them again. The vision is still here.

'Miss?'

My mind is playing tricks. 'Eliza?'

'Yes, Miss, it's me.'

I gaze at her face, that familiar freckled face.

'There now, there's no need to cry. Here.' She holds something out.

It's this small cambric square that convinces me it isn't a dream.

'Keep it. I've plenty more.'

I dab at my eyes with the handkerchief which smells of soap, of almonds, Eliza's smell.

When at last I look at her, I see the shock in her eyes. I

227

suddenly realize how I must appear to her, how *I* must smell. I'm not aware of it because I'm used to it.

When did I last wash properly? Every morning, we're allowed to go to the washroom, if we want, but it's a damp, dark place with cockroaches scuttling across the floor. There's no soap and only one grimy, frayed towel between us. I've given up trying to be clean.

Now, ashamed, I bury my face in my hands.

'What's wrong?'

'I – I hate you seeing me like this.' I sense her sitting down on the bed next to me. 'Don't. You'll spoil your dress.'

'It doesn't matter. Don't upset yourself, Miss.'

And then I feel her arm around me. The hug only lasts a minute, but I can still feel the comfort of it even after she lets go.

I look into her blue eyes. 'I didn't expect to see you.'

'I wanted to know how you were, like. Sorry I couldn't come sooner. I couldn't see you, you know, in Solitary.' She seems embarrassed at mentioning it.

Scratton isn't here this afternoon and none of the other attendants are taking any notice of us, but I still lower my voice. 'You heard what happened?'

'Yes.' The way she says it makes me think she knows everything. She gives me a wry look. 'That were a neat trick with the chloral. Martha were right riled about it. And copping Weeks! That were a good one.'

I smile briefly. 'But it didn't work, did it?'

She smiles back, rueful and sympathetic.

It dawns on me – she doesn't mind that I tried to escape;

she doesn't disapprove! And coming to see how I am. How kind she is. She'll tell me the truth, I'm sure.

But it takes me a minute or two to screw myself up to ask the question. 'Is Beatrice – Miss Hill –' I swallow – 'is she dead?' My voice wobbles on the word.

'Dead? Why no, Miss.'

I let out the breath I didn't know I was holding. 'I thought – when I went to her room and it was locked, I thought—'

'She'd been moved – to another gallery.'

She's avoiding my eye. There's more to this but I don't know what questions to ask.

'Is she safe?'

'She's safe, right enough.' She has a strange expression on her face, as if she's swallowed sour milk. For a moment she seems to be struggling with herself, then she bursts out, 'I know she were your friend, Miss, but I can't forgive her for what she's done to you.'

I go cold. 'What do you mean?'

Eliza shakes her head. Something too awful to tell me.

My thoughts scatter. What did Beatrice do? Then they settle on something so obvious I can't believe I didn't see it before. '*Beatrice* told Weeks about my plan?'

She nods.

The noise in the gallery recedes and I seem to be suspended in a white empty space. This is what it must feel like to have a limb amputated. Feeling nothing at the first cut, because of the shock.

Eliza is peering at me, looking worried. 'I'm sorry. I weren't going to say.'

I seize hold of a straw. 'Perhaps Weeks is lying?'

Eliza shakes her head. 'I were there.'

'But Beatrice didn't mean to tell? It slipped out by accident or – or Weeks tormented her, until she was forced to confess?'

I can see the truth in her face.

'Weeks didn't lay a finger on her. She just blabbed it all.'

I can't believe it. *Beatrice*. I thought we were friends. I thought you trusted me.

My heart twists as I remember the moment I stood outside, under the stars, when I was so close to freedom.

'Did you know I made it to the door, actually got outside?'

Eliza nods.

'I couldn't believe how easy it was.'

She looks at me meaningfully and suddenly I understand this too. 'Weeks made it easy for me? The keys where I could get them, my clothes on top of the pile, the door left open?'

'Yes.'

It all makes sense now.

Eliza seems distressed. 'I wanted to warn you, but I didn't get the chance. Soon as the canary sang, I were out of there, like a shot.'

'What do you mean?'

'Weeks got it out of Miss Hill that I'd let you visit her. That were the end of the Second for me. Alice has got my place now.'

I stare at her, dismayed. This is my fault. 'Oh, Eliza, I'm sorry.'

She shrugs. 'I knew the rules. It's not so bad in the Fourth.'

'You're still here, then? In the asylum? I thought – your dress . . .'

She smiles. 'It's my afternoon off.'

She's given up her afternoon off to come and see me. And after I've made things worse for her.

'Is the Fourth like this?'

Eliza surveys the room. 'Oh, no, Miss. Not like this. The patients are quieter than here, much quieter.'

I've overheard Scratton talking to another attendant about the different galleries: *At least here there's some- thing going on. With the dead-heads, you might as well be dead yourself.*

Poor Eliza. Stuck in a place like that.

'I'm sorry, Miss.' Eliza stands up. 'I'd better be going now. They'll be expecting me at home.'

I don't want her to go.

'Is there anything I can get you?'

She'll come again, if I can think of something! 'I – I don't know.'

She looks at my hair and raises her eyebrows comically. 'Wouldn't you like a comb?'

'A comb?'

She presses my hand. 'Don't give up hope, Miss. I'll bring you a comb, and some soap and stuff. You'll feel better if you wash.'

231

I think it will take more than a wash to make me feel better.

'And Miss, you should try to eat more. I know the food's disgusting, but you should try to build yourself up a bit.'

I nod, but her mentioning the food has given me an idea. 'Do you still use Fowler's Solution for your hands?'

She looks surprised. 'Yes, I do.' She holds out her hands for my inspection. 'I think they're a mite better, don't you?'

'Yes, they are.' I try to look as innocent as I can. 'Could you get me some Fowler's? I will try to eat more, but the food here gives me indigestion . . .' I can feel myself going red at the lie.

But Eliza doesn't seem to notice. 'I'll bring you some, soon as I can.'

I watch her threading her way down the room, a patch of sunshine passing through the grey. She turns at the door to give me a wave and then she's gone.

It seems much darker in the gallery now. Was she really here or did I dream it? I stare towards the door, willing her to reappear. Of course, nothing happens – only the noisy whirl carrying on as usual.

I don't want to be shut up in my head again. I don't want to think about Beatrice. If I had the Fowler's Solution now, I'd only have to swallow it all down and the arsenic in it would quickly do its deadly business. That would be the end of this misery.

The thought makes me clench my hand and I find I'm

still holding the small square of cambric. I wipe my eyes, breathing in its smell, Eliza's smell. And I think, It's true – she *was* here!

I've looked out for Eliza every day, even though I've known it's too soon – she won't have another afternoon off yet. As time passes, I've begun to believe she won't come again. Why would she? I'm not anything to her, just as I wasn't anything to Beatrice – I realize that now.

At first I felt bitter, wondering why I gave up my chance of freedom for someone who betrayed me. But now I believe it was my fault. I was too impulsive. It was a reckless plan, I see that now. Me playing the hero, rescuing the princess. But not for love – for pity.

I don't have any idea why Beatrice wouldn't want to run away from here. But then, really I don't know her at all.

And perhaps I pitied her more, because she reminded me of Grace . . .

Grace. I haven't thought of her for such a long time!

All that emotion . . . It seems a long time ago now, like a half-remembered dream – my life then, what I wanted – all a dream . . .

I feel tired today and despondent.

Scratton is scolding the woman next to me for destroying another pillow; her voice jangles my nerves. I didn't have a good night – my sleep was disturbed by the others' noise: someone screaming, another singing, someone else shouting out obscenities. I would take my chloral now, but

no one brings any – perhaps they think it would be wasted
on us.

Suddenly Scratton barks, 'Eliza Shaw, what are you
doing here?'

I look up and here is Eliza in her yellow dress, looking
calm and unruffled. My heart lifts as if the sun has come
out.

'It's my day off. I can do what I like.'

'Hobnobbing with the patients. You'll catch it, if
Matron finds out.' Scratton's eyes gleam with malice.

Eliza darts back, 'How will she find out? Unless you
tell her?'

'Sharp, ain't you! Mind you don't cut yourself.'
Scratton goes off, grumbling to herself.

'These are for you.' Eliza hands me a bunch of violets
in a jam jar.

I stare at them in wonder. Such a delicate purple . . . I
believe they signify faithfulness. And Eliza is being such a
faithful friend to me. I smile at her. 'They're beautiful.'

'I thought they'd be nice to look at while they last. A
touch of spring to cheer you up. Not much of a vase, like,
but in here . . .'

'Good idea.' I put the flowers on the shelf above my
bed. Against the grimy wall, they glow with colour. 'What
month is it now?'

'March.'

'Oh!' My heart contracts.

'Is it the flowers? Was I wrong to bring them?'

'No. I'm glad to have them. But I hadn't realized I'd
been here so long.'

235

'I brought you these.' She unwraps the bundle she's carrying; soap, tooth powder, toothbrush, comb and hairpins tumble on to the bed. 'And here's a towel. Oh, and the Fowler's Solution.' She fetches a small bottle out of her bag and passes it to me.

I feel like a traitor. If she knew what I wanted it for . . .

There's a little awkwardness then, as if neither of us knows what to say next. I realize I'm still clutching the bottle of Fowler's and I lay it aside. I don't want to think about that now; I want to think about something cheerful. 'Tell me about your family – and your home.'

Her eyebrows rise in amused surprise but she settles herself on the bed. 'Well . . . I don't rightly know where to begin.'

'Where do you live?'

'Smalcote. It's about two mile from here.'

'Is it nice?'

Eliza lets out a short laugh. 'It's just a row of cottages and the farm. And a right muddy lane. There's nine of us altogether, with Mother and Father, but we're not all at home. My sister, Florrie, she's in service, and our Charlie, he lives in at the farm. My little sister, Annie, well, she's not so little now – she's quick, quicker than me. She can write beautiful and –' she gives me an embarrassed smile – 'she's teaching me how to read, Miss. I'm not right good at it yet, but I'm getting there.'

'Good for you!'

She starts to laugh.

'What is it?'

'My brother Joe were in trouble the other week at school. He's a right scallywag.'

'What did he do?'

'Oh, Miss, I couldn't say it to you.'

'Tell me.'

'Well, teacher's reading from the Bible and she comes to the part about Joshua blowing down the walls with trumpets, you know? And Joe, he lets rip with a great raspberry!' She bursts out giggling and it makes me laugh too.

It's so lovely to have a conversation, to talk about ordinary things. Such a relief after being shut up with my own thoughts. I can feel my whole body relaxing.

'Look at you enjoying yerselves! Pair of spoonies, ain't you!' Scratton's voice cuts through our merriment.

I instantly move away from Eliza, my cheeks burning.

Scratton is surveying us from the end of the bed, arms akimbo, her face twisted in a sneer. Then she goes off, laughing in an unpleasant way.

'Take no notice,' Eliza says in an undertone. 'I caught her nicking – stealing stuff from the stores. That's instant dismissal, if they find out. She's just angry I've got something on her.' She sounds fierce. Then her expression changes. She looks round as if to see whether anyone's near and then leans towards me, her face so serious, I wonder what's coming.

'I've been thinking . . .' She stops then goes on in a rush, 'I wondered – I wondered if you knew why you're here.'

I hesitate and immediately she says, 'Sorry. I should keep me snout out. It's none of my business.'

237

'No. I don't have any idea. Mr Sneed wouldn't tell me what it said about me in my papers. I think my brother Tom's behind it all, but I don't know why.' Just saying it makes my lip tremble and I can feel tears pricking my eyes.

'Don't go upsetting yourself.' Eliza chews her lip, looking thoughtful. 'What's he like, this brother of yours?'

I tell her about Tom and me – what it was like when we were growing up, and more recently.

'Sounds to me like he's jealous cos you're cleverer than him.'

'But I'm not!'

'Sure?'

I think about it – Tom failing his exams, Papa saying he'd rather have me helping him than Tom. Maybe she's right. And then I remember what Tom said when I saw him in London – how jealous he was of Papa spending time with me.

'But he wouldn't do this just because he was jealous, would he?'

Eliza shrugs. 'Folk do things for all sorts of reasons. I've heard some terrible stories since I came to this place. A lady put here because her husband were tired of her, and a poor lass jilted . . .' She shakes her head. 'Anyway, tell me about your family. What are the rest of them like?'

Hesitantly at first, but then with increasing confidence, I describe my parents – dearest Papa, poor anxious Mamma . . .

Eliza doesn't interrupt or comment; she just listens, her head tilted slightly, her blue eyes fixed on mine.

Encouraged by her attention I find myself telling her what happened in the months before I came to the asylum. I tell her everything – nearly everything.

I only falter twice.

When I talk about Papa's illness, I can't go on; the tears block my throat. Eliza sits quietly and waits, and after a while I can continue.

I tell her about the terrible time after Papa died. Everything up to that last visit to Carr Head. That's when I falter again.

I tell her, briefly, about my aunt and uncle, and Grace – I go hot when I mention her, but Eliza doesn't seem to notice – but I skip over what happened and rush on to the plan for me to go to the Woodvilles'. And even though I feel stirred up by it all, and some things are very hard to talk about, I feel a kind of relief in sharing it.

I finish with, 'What I can't understand is why no one's written. I'm sure Mamma must miss me, whatever she said to Tom. I know I miss her.'

'Perhaps she has.'

'What do you mean?'

'They keep the letters sometimes – don't let the patients have them.'

'No!'

'S'true.'

'That's so *wicked*. How can they treat people like that?'

Eliza shrugs. 'Well, they do. But maybe the rest of your family don't know you're here. Have you thought of that?'

'I don't know what to think.'

'Maybe they all believe you're at these Woodvilles' and

your brother has told them some tale to explain why they haven't heard from you.'

I stare at her. Could Tom be capable of that? Why not? If he can put me in here, he's capable of anything . . .

I'm still thinking these bitter thoughts when Eliza shifts uneasily. 'There's something I didn't tell you before. About Miss Hill.'

'Oh?'

'She told Weeks she were frightened that if you took her away, her ma wouldn't know where she were and wouldn't be able to find her.'

I suddenly see Beatrice's face, her big violet eyes brimming with tears. I should have done more to reassure her. But perhaps when I burst in with my wild scheme, she thought I was just another mad patient.

'There's something else.' She threads her fingers together. Unthreads them.

'What?'

'I didn't want to tell you, but I can't lie to you. That gallery she's been moved to – it's where they put the incurables. The quiet ones.'

'But she was getting better, wasn't she?'

Eliza looks down at her lap.

'Eliza?'

She sighs. 'After she told Weeks about your plan, I don't know, maybe she felt guilty. Or maybe she realized what a fool she'd been. Alice told me that soon after I left she went funny, like she was having a fit, shaking and crying and carrying on. She wouldn't stop. They sent for Dr Bull and he had her transferred.'

We fall silent. Despite everything, I can't help feeling sorry. I sigh. 'The things she said – about her baby – did you believe her? I know I did at the time but now I'm not so sure.'

'I didn't at first. Because that's what everyone said, Weeks, the doctors – they all said she were having delusions. But the more I saw her . . . and the way she were with that doll . . .'

'Mmm. I'm surprised they didn't examine her when she arrived. They'd have soon found the truth of it.'

Eliza gives me a look. 'I've heard that Miss Hill's stepfather gave the asylum a great deal of money.'

Of course. With a 'generous donation', that man ensured that anything his stepdaughter said about him would not be believed. Poor Beatrice.

Eliza stirs. 'It's time I were off, Miss.'

'Yes.'

'Is there anything else you want?'

'There is something . . .'

'What?'

'Would you – would you call me by my first name?'

She raises her eyebrows in her droll way. 'I'll try, Miss.' Her hand flies to her mouth and she giggles, an unexpected, delightful sound in this place. Then she straightens her face and looking at me, very deliberately says, 'Louisa.'

I stare at her.

'What's the matter?'

'You don't think I'm Lucy Childs. You believe me!'

'Yes.'

'Why? No one else does.'

She shrugs. 'I don't know. I just do.'

Three small words. So simple, so matter-of-fact. But making all the difference in the world.

I'm going to have to ask her. 'Do you . . .' I stop, dizzy with fear of her answer. I swallow. 'Do you think I'm mad?'

She looks at me in a considering way for so long my heart races and the palms of my hands grow moist.

'Well, anyone looking at you now would think you were a right loony . . .' Seeing my face, she laughs and is immediately serious. 'No, I don't and I never have done, right from the first time I saw you.'

'Oh.' That's all I can manage, but I feel light-headed, almost giddy with relief. Impulsively I catch her hand. 'You don't know how much it means to me . . .' I stop because Eliza's cheeks are reddening and I feel strange, as if I've said more than I meant.

For a moment we stare at each other and then Eliza says quickly, 'I'll see you then. Soon as I can.'

I've hidden the Fowler's Solution under my pillow – I don't need it now. Talking to Eliza has given me hope. I've been trying to eat more and I've taken to marching up and down the whole length of the gallery. Each day I can go further, feel stronger. And I'm looking for ways out of here . . .

The next time Eliza visits, I can see immediately that something has happened.

She looks swiftly round the room. Scratton is occupied with someone at the far end; no other attendants are near. Flopping on to the bed without any ceremony, she pulls something out of her bag and thrusts it into my hand. 'It's part of your papers. I got Alice to copy them, when she were cleaning the office.'

I stare at her, my heart jumping in my chest.

'Go on then. Read it!'

I unfold the grubby piece of paper and scan the pencilled words written in a round, childish hand.

'What do you think? I had a look but I couldn't make much sense of it.'

'Listen.' My throat is as dry as a rusk. Clearing it and keeping my voice down, I read the words to Eliza.

1. *Facts indicating insanity observed by myself:*
    An interest in medical matters inappropriate for one of her age and sex.

A neglect of appearance and personal toilet, and wearing unsuitable clothing for a young lady of her status.

2. Other factors indicating insanity communicated to me by others:

Excessive book-reading and study leading to a weakening of the mind.

Desiring to ape men by nursing an ambition to be a doctor.

Self-assertiveness in the face of male authority.

Obstinacy and displays of temper.

Going about unchaperoned, for example, travelling to London alone in a third-class railway compartment . . .

With every word, with every line, my chest tightens and I grip the paper so hard it starts to shake. Tom! I see Tom's hand everywhere in this. But the words come to a stop. There's no signature. The thing I most need to see.

I go to speak, but Eliza gets there first. I've never seen her look so angry. 'It's all wrong. You shouldn't be in here. Sounds to me like they're accusing you of being mad, just cos you weren't quiet and obedient, like a good little girl. Pah!'

I smile at her wryly and nod at the paper. 'Is this all you have?'

'That's all Alice had time for. She heard someone coming.'

'Do you think she'd . . .'

But Eliza is shaking her head. 'It were hard enough getting her to do this much.'

She grimaces and I wonder what it took. I can't see Alice doing anything out of the goodness of her heart.

Eliza adds, 'She did mention she'd had a look at the signatures on this bit, but she couldn't make it out – it started with a K, she thought.'

Dr Kneale! That day he came when I was wearing that old dress to do the cleaning . . .

'The other certificate was signed by Wood-somebody.'

Mr Woodville! Of course. So I was never meant to go to his mother's . . .

No wonder he kept looking at me – Tom's mad sister . . . At the thought of how Mamma and I had both misread his interest, I can't help it – I start to laugh, a laugh that quickly turns to tears.

'Miss? Louisa? Are you all right?'

I wipe my eyes. 'I still don't understand about the name. This is all about me, so why isn't it my name?'

Eliza shrugs. 'Maybe the doctors were in on it. Who-ever asked them to certify you, like, got them to write a different name.'

Tom! My heart begins to beat like a drum. 'It must be my brother then. It can't be anyone else. He was writing to Dr Kneale about me, and Woodville's his friend. There'll be another paper in my file signed "Thomas Childs".'

Remembering what Beatrice said, I add bitterly, 'And he's the only person who can sign me out of here.'

I pass the paper back to her. 'You'd better destroy that.'

She takes it, then bending her head nearer mine, she whispers, 'Maybe I could help you escape.'

I scan her face, a wild hope dancing inside me. 'Would you? Do you think it's possible?'

A vision flashes into my mind of the two of us running through the park, along the drive and out of the gates, out, out into the world. But then reality breaks in.

'What if they found out? What about your job?'

'I don't care. I don't want to work here any more – there's too much unhappiness and people not treated right.'

My heart lurches, and I swallow hard. 'So you're going away?'

She gives me a little smile. 'I can't stay here forever.'

And neither can I. Especially if she's not here. 'You'll need a reference,' I remind her. 'If they find out you've helped me to escape—'

Her face falls. 'They won't find out.' But she doesn't sound confident.

'They caught me last time!'

'But that was because Miss Hill . . .' She breaks off, her blue eyes clouding over. 'I've something to tell you.'

I feel alarmed. She looks so anxious. What could it be? 'Yes?'

'I've been to see her . . . She's quite comfortable . . . but she's not there any more, like she's gone so far into herself she can't get back.' Eliza shakes her head. 'Poor girl.'

I look at her with surprise. 'You feel sorry for her? When she lost you your place?'

'Yes, I do. She's such a poor scrap. And it were my own fault. I knew I were taking a risk.'

'Why did you?'

She plays with a frill on her dress. 'At first I felt sorry for Miss Hill, being on her own, like. And I felt sorry for you. It seemed like it were helping you to see each other. It seemed to be doing you good.'

She becomes intent on her frill, pleating it between her fingers, smoothing it again.

'Eliza? What is it?'

At last she looks at me. 'I thought you were sweet on her.'

I stare at her for a moment, not believing I heard right. Then I have to look away, my blood racing. I can't think of a single thing to say.

Eliza chews her lip, her eyes anxious. 'I'm sorry. I've spoken out of turn.'

I turn back to her. 'No. *No.*'

There's an awkward silence and then abruptly, she stands up. 'I'd better be off.'

She's embarrassed now and probably thinks she's offended me. But I'm not offended at all. I feel as if I'm floating, light and free.

I hasten to assure her, '*I* felt sorry for Beatrice too, you know. I wanted to rescue her. That's all.'

'Oh.' Her eyes clear, becoming as blue as a summer sky. More silence as I look at her and she looks at me.

Then she says softly, 'I'll get you out of here, Louisa. Somehow.'

There's something in her tone that makes me look at her

hard, and she's looking at me and in that moment something happens, I don't know what, as if a spark leaps between us and my heart falters and then goes on faster than before. I want to say something without having the least idea of what it might be. The silence stretches and we go on looking at one another.

She is the first to break it. 'I nearly forgot.' Fumbling in her bag, she pulls something out and gives it to me. It's an orange.

I hold it cupped in my hands. The colour is so vivid it hurts my eyes. And the smell . . . I close my eyes and breathe it in.

'It's not just for sniffing – you make sure you eat it. There's more where that came from.'

I open my eyes. 'Thank you.'

'Is there anything you want next time?'

Automatically, in a kind of dream, I reply, 'No. I don't need anything, thank you.'

Even after she's gone, I go on feeling happy for hours. I sit in a daze, holding my orange, but I'm not thinking of it, I'm thinking of Eliza, her expressions, the things she said. Especially that one thing. *I thought you were sweet on her.* She said it so simply. As if it were the most natural thing in the world. As if it were *all right*.

At last, with a sigh, I turn my attention to the orange and for a long time I just look at it, savouring its colour, enjoying the weight of it in my hand, the anticipation. Finally, I start to peel it, digging into it with my nail, releasing the sharp sweetness, the sticky juice.

I'm just about to put the first segment into my mouth when I see that my neighbour has suspended her blanket-shredding and is watching me. On an impulse, I offer the piece of orange to her, but she rears back with a squawk of alarm. She utters a word which sounds like 'pisspallet' and then she starts on her blanket again. So I have the segment, and it's delicious.

Very slowly, bit by bit, I eat the orange, enjoying every mouthful. And all the time, it's as if Eliza is still with me, buoying me up.

I can't believe it! Eliza was here only two days ago and here she is again! I see her coming in at the door and Scratton, who's dealing with a screaming patient, puts out a hand as if to detain her. Eliza ignores them both and comes rapidly down the gallery. I'm grinning like an idiot and then I see her face and I go cold.

'What is it? What's happened?'

'I've been suspended.'

'What? What does that mean?'

'I've been taken off the gallery for now. I'm to go to my room and wait there until Mr Sneed sends for me. I had to tell you, in case—' She doesn't finish the sentence.

In case. In case she's forbidden to see me again, in case she's dismissed . . .

All the possibilities are bleak. And they all mean the same thing – I won't see her again. And there will be no escape.

'Oh, Eliza.' I can't say any more. My throat is blocked and something is clawing at my chest. I seize her hand and press it to my face.

'I must go.'

'I know.' But I can't let go of her hand. I search her face, taking in all the familiar details, committing them to memory.

She puts her face even closer to mine; I can feel her

breath hot on my ear. 'If you can get to the Infirmary, you might be able to get out.'

'Out? How?'

But it's too late. Scratton is at the bedside, with a twisted smile on her face. 'I don't think you're supposed to be here, Miss Shaw.' She gives the name a mocking emphasis.

Eliza straightens up. She draws in her breath. She gives me one last agonized look then she walks away from me, down the gallery to the door, and she's gone.

Scratton leers down at me, but I turn my back on her and curl myself into a tight ball.

This has all happened so quickly I can hardly take it in.

I can still see Eliza's face, feel the pressure of her fingers on mine. It's as if someone has plunged a knife into my heart and I can't do anything, I just have to endure the pain.

After a long while I come back to myself and try to think.

I must somehow get myself taken to the Infirmary, like Eliza said. It's a separate building across the park. Maybe it's easier to escape from. But how do I get to it?

Could I contrive to break an arm or leg? But that would make running away difficult. Or could I feign an illness?

My mind goes round in circles until I can bear it no longer. In frustration I thump my pillow – and feel something hard under my fist.

I feel a great leap inside.

I don't know whether I have the courage to do it.

If I misjudge it, I'll kill myself . . . and now I don't want to die. But if I don't try, what's the alternative? Without Eliza, I won't survive, I'll end up like Beatrice, in a living death.

This is the only way out I can think of.

I make myself eat as much as I can for supper, draining the bowl of greasy stew, cramming my mouth with bread until my stomach feels tight and uncomfortable.

All night I hardly sleep. If I do doze off, I wake suddenly again, my heart thudding – is it time?

I've decided early in the morning would be best. It's the likeliest time for a doctor to be on the premises. I'm hoping he'll recognize the symptoms and know what to do . . .

And now grey light filters in through the windows. Soon the attendants will arrive, filling the room with their noisy chatter. Now there's no more space for thought, for fear – now it *is* time.

With trembling fingers, I uncork the bottle of Fowler's Solution, Eliza's gift to me. *Wish me luck*, I say to her in my head, and then I swallow down what I hope is about five drachms of the liquid.

At first I feel nothing, just a metallic taste in my mouth.

Perhaps I haven't taken enough. Should I take a few more drops, just to make sure?

I make myself wait, to give it time to work its way into my system. After a while, I feel pins and needles in my hands and a pain in my head, and my heart starts beating rapidly. I push the bottle of Fowler's Solution inside my dress, feeling its cold glass against my skin.

I want them to find it, but not yet. I want them to think

253

this is something like gastric influenza, something contagious. I'm relying on their fear, their ignorance.

Now I'm feeling nauseous, my head is starting to spin. I have to lie down . . . My hands and face feel clammy, my throat is dry, darkness keeps coming and going at the edge of my vision. Griping pain is building in my stomach – I know I'm going to vomit at any moment and as much as I want this to happen, my body resists it – my teeth clench involuntarily in an effort to prevent it. But then my insides surge and heave, I can't stop it; with spasm after shuddering spasm, the contents of my stomach spew on to my pillow.

I come back to myself to find my cheek is resting in the yellow stinking mess, but I can't raise my head, I'm too weak and shaken, my eyes swimming with tears.

Come and find me. Please come and find me.

But no one comes. It's all been in vain, I'm going to die . . .

I've done it. I'm still alive and I'm in the Infirmary!

I was very lucky. They found me just in time, Dr Bull said.

He's a better doctor than I thought. It didn't take him long to discover the bottle of Fowler's Solution and then – the stomach pump . . .

All I want now is to lie here in this quiet ward, swallowing the prescribed doses of rice milk and egg white. But it won't do. Although I still feel weak and wretched from the effects of the poison, I'm better. Any day now I'll be sent back to the main building and I'll have missed my chance.

The trouble is, I don't know what Eliza meant. I don't know how to escape from here.

The ward is on the ground floor, but the windows are barred. The door isn't locked, perhaps in case of emergencies, and when I first discovered this, I felt a surge of hope. But I heard Dr Bull tell the nurses that I was to be closely watched and so far they've been vigilant, by day and night.

The other patients lie quietly: one elderly woman has pneumonia and looks to be very near the end, while another has had surgery and is too weak to move. If I were to try to leave the ward, I have little to fear from them. But how am I to do it?

Oh, Eliza, where are you? Have they let you back yet?

No use thinking of it. I must concentrate and be ready to seize the opportunity if it presents itself . . .

I jerk awake, my heart thudding. A commotion out in the corridor – voices, and someone screaming, as if in agony. Blinking to clear my sight, I see them sweep into the ward – two men carrying a stretcher with a body on it – a woman writhing in pain – and a young nurse with a lantern, calling out in agitation.

Sleepily I watch the ward nurse direct the men to transfer the patient to an empty bed at the end of the ward and then dismiss them. Two other nurses look in at the door but they too are dispatched. The ward nurse seems to have the situation in hand.

After swiftly surveying the patient, whose screams have subsided into a low moaning, she hands the younger one a key. 'Fetch dressings and brandy from the store.'

The girl scurries off, lantern swinging wildly, while the ward nurse moves her lamp to the patient's bedside. It's hard to see what's going on – the nurse has her back to me, but her shadow looms on the wall and I have the impression she is cutting at something, perhaps the patient's clothing.

The young nurse returns with her arms full, and together they minister to the patient. I overhear snatches of their conversation. It appears that the woman knocked over a lamp and her nightgown caught fire. An attendant extinguished the flames by rolling her in a blanket but she has extensive burns.

Suddenly I am alert. This could be my chance! It could

256

take them some time to dress the burns and they're both fully occupied, their backs towards me.

Moving slowly and quietly, I slide one of my pillows under the bedclothes, to make it look as if the bed is still occupied. Holding my breath, I make for the door, expecting them to call after me, but nothing happens.

Out in the corridor, I pause for a second. Which way should I go?

Off to the left the corridor is in darkness, but in the other direction there is a light. I speed towards it as quietly as I can, passing what seems to be another ward on the right, with a low light showing, voices murmuring. My heart is in my mouth. At any moment I expect a nurse to appear.

The passage opens out into a vestibule and here is the front door. I seize the knob and turn it, but nothing happens. *It's locked.*

I blink back tears of disappointment. No time for that. There must be a way out somewhere.

I daren't go back past the ward. Instead I cross the vestibule into another corridor. I try the nearest door and it opens. But it's a cupboard, with shelves stacked with linen and blankets. I seize one of these and move on. At any moment they will discover my empty bed.

I try every handle as I pass. All locked. But then I come to another door that opens. Peering in, I see that the gas light has been left on low, and I can make out a small room with a single bed in it. My heart jumps when I see that the bed is occupied, and I'm just about to retreat when the patient stirs.

'Water . . . please.'

It's a croak, hardly audible, but there is something familiar about it . . .

I should go – now, before she sees me and raises the alarm. I haven't time for this.

But I can't stop myself, I have to know. I go closer to the bed.

I was right. It's Weeks. But how changed!

She is tossing about, muttering incoherently, as though in the grip of delirium. She's obviously not aware of me, but nevertheless when she turns her head my way, I start back, my hand at my throat. For her face is covered in blisters, weeping pus.

Smallpox.

She is clearly in the final stages of the disease and just for a second I can't help thinking, Serves her right.

But then her parched lips open and she croaks again. 'Water . . .'

There is no water, and I'm sorry. This end is too horrible, even for my old enemy.

A noise in the distance jolts me back to reality. What am I doing? I must hurry.

Out in the corridor once more I see light spilling from an open door further along. I approach cautiously, then breathe with relief when I discover that the room is empty. It must be the store – the young nurse's lantern is on the table, illuminating shelves of labelled jars and bottles, a cupboard of apothecary's equipment. And suddenly I have an idea. But I must be quick.

I scan the shelves. The jars are in alphabetical order, as

they should be. I quickly find the one marked *Sal Nitri* –
saltpetre. Just along is a jar marked *Sacch* – sugar, ready
ground. My eye races round the items in the glass-fronted
cupboard, and then with a great leap of excitement, I see
what I'm looking for – an old-fashioned iron mortar, quite
narrow and deep. Hurriedly I fill the mortar with saltpetre
and sugar, stirring it together. The quantities might not be
right – it might not work. But if it does, it will buy me
some time. Now all I need are some matches.

I look on the shelves, pull out drawers, feeling more
and more frantic. I'm making too much noise, this is
taking too long. I look round one more time and then I see
it – a box of lucifers, left on the table next to the lantern.

Snatching them up, I seize my blanket and the mortar
and hurry from the room. It would be too dangerous
here – I don't want to cause a fire and injure anyone if I can
help it. I'm heading away from the vestibule when I hear
the sound I've been dreading – a bell ringing, running feet.
They're after me!

I set the mortar down on the stone floor of the passage.
Ideally I need a fuse, but there's no time to make one. With
trembling fingers, I thrust half a dozen lucifers head down
into the powder and light the ends. The sticks catch fire
with a satisfying flare and within seconds, the passageway
fills with thick black smoke.

I run on, into the back part of the building, where the
gas lamps are turned down, trying door handles without
any hope. And then one yields and I almost fall into the
dark space that opens up in front of me. In a breath, I'm
inside the room and have the door shut.

My heart's racing. I look about me wildly. In the dim light from the window I see a lavatory, a sink, and then my eyes come back to the window.

It isn't barred.

It's some distance off the ground – a fixed sheet of glass with a narrow casement above. But can I get through it? I climb on to the lavatory seat, clutching my blanket. I lay it on the window ledge and by hauling myself up with the help of the pipe running from the cistern, I manage to get one knee on the ledge and then the other.

My perch is so narrow I'm afraid I'll topple backwards into the room. I reach up, seize the window catch and release it. With a push the window opens and night air cools my face. Still hanging on to the pipes, I get one foot on the ledge and haul myself upright. Reaching down, wobbling precariously, I untangle the blanket from around my feet, throw it through the window and try to follow.

My head fits through easily, but my shoulders wedge themselves in the gap. Tears of frustration spring into my eyes.

Clenching my teeth, I twist my body. With a desperate corkscrew movement that wrenches my back, I get first one shoulder and then the other through. For a moment I hang there, half in and half out of the window, the transom bar cutting into my waist. I can see the ground about six feet below me. Then I push off with my feet and tumble out.

Pain sears through my right shoulder, my teeth jar together and for a moment I lie winded, shocked by the impact. But fear galvanizes me. I could be discovered at any moment. I feel about for the blanket.

The sky is clouded, but there's enough light for me to see. I seem to be at the back of the Infirmary, near the kitchen; I can smell rotting food, stale odours of cooking. I'm in a walled yard, with the dark humps of sheds around the perimeter. I can feel gritty cinders underfoot. There's a door in the wall and I try it, expecting it to be locked, but the latch lifts and it swings open easily. I see the park stretching in front of me. Which way should I go?

Away to the right I can see the lights of the main building shining. Not in that direction, certainly. Not so far away, probably at the front of the Infirmary, I can hear a lot of noise, shouting, bells ringing. They'll be evacuating the patients and bringing a fire-hose cart.

To the left, not far off, a dark line marks the boundary of the park. And then with an intake of breath I see that the wall round the back yard of the Infirmary joins directly to the perimeter wall. It should be easy to get over.

Retreating into the yard, I look about for something to help me climb the wall. There are some wooden crates piled near the back door. Trying not to make a noise, I carry two of them to what looks like a coal bunker. I stack one on top of the other and scramble on to the sloping roof of the bunker without too much difficulty, then I stop. From here, with a stretch, I should be able to reach the top of the wall and it's a mere four yards or so to the perimeter. But the wall is narrow. Dare I do it?

Taking a deep breath I climb up, hampered by the blanket. Standing up, I almost lose my balance, my arms

261

flail wildly . . . then I regain control. It's a long way down. Don't look. Gingerly I inch my way along, one step at a time, horribly aware that anyone looking from the windows will instantly see me. A voice in my head is saying, *Hurry, hurry*. But I daren't hurry: instead I concentrate on where I'm putting my feet.

At last my hands clasp the rough bricks of the perimeter wall. For a moment I cling to it, trembling with relief . . . then I'm over it and with another wrench of my shoulder, I drop down the other side. My right leg buckles under the pain of the impact, but this time at least I land on my feet. I wrap the blanket round me. I feel safer now, a shadow among other shadows.

And here I am, outside the asylum. Free. A voice starts singing in my head: *I've done it, Eliza. I'm out.*

Luckily it's a fairly mild night, but even so I'm shivering, perhaps more from excitement and fear than the shock of being outside in the fresh air. I take a deep breath, smelling damp earth and leaf-mould.

What now?

I must try to find Eliza's village, I suppose. Small-something, wasn't it? But what shall I do when I get there? I don't know where she lives. If I find her cottage, she might not be there. And if she is, will she be pleased to see me? What will she say to her family? They'll hardly welcome an escaped lunatic.

Stop worrying. One step at a time. But I must hurry. How long before they send someone after me?

I set off hobbling down the lane, stumbling in the ruts, wincing as sharp stones dig into my bare feet. I can see more than I expected. But the trees at the side of the lane, threatening silhouettes, are looming at me; the ground seems to be rising and falling, causing me to stagger. I've never been out at night before, certainly not by myself in the countryside. It gives me a strange, lonely feeling. I tell myself there's nothing to be afraid of, but I still jump at every rustle in the undergrowth.

A ghostly shape detaches itself from the darkness, glides in front of me and I stop dead, my hand at my throat. Only a barn owl. But it's a long time before the rapid patter of my heart slows down.

263

It seems so far. My feet are cut and bruised, my legs don't want to do this any more. I come to a crossroads. Which way? A signpost glimmers, half buried in the hedgerow. I have to strain to read it: SMALCOTE, 3 MILES. That's Eliza's village! But the finger points back the way I have come.

I could weep. It's too far. Everything hurts: my feet, my shoulder, my knee. I just want to give up, sink down into sleep. They can discover me by the roadside, take me back. I'm too weary to care.

Don't give up. I jump. I know the voice is in my head, but it's just as if Eliza has spoken to me. Gritting my teeth, I turn and begin to trudge back the way I have come.

Eventually I reach the asylum wall. At the end of the lane a signpost tells me I have to turn left, past the main gate. I am certain there will be men out in the lane looking for me, dogs rushing snarling from the shadows. Wearily I drag myself on, resigned now to failure.

But, miraculously, none of this happens. By the lodge I shrink into the hedge in case someone is looking out. There are lights at the windows, and I can hear voices in the distance, but nobody shouts after me. When I have gone a good way beyond the wall, I let out my breath.

On and on. I move in a dream, one foot in front of the other, again and again. I feel faint now. I mustn't faint. But I've no strength left. I come to a straggle of cottages. Is this Smalcote? Even if it isn't, I can't go any further. But I can't sleep here by the roadside. I must find somewhere.

At the back of the first cottage there are dark shapes of outbuildings. Holding my breath, I tiptoe past the cottage and make for them. At every step I expect furious barking, but everything remains silent. The first shed seems to be a henhouse, shut up for the night. Then something that must be the privy. Beside it, a ramshackle construction, from which a strong smell emerges. A pigsty.

Enter the pen. Slip-slide in the mud. Careful, careful. Here's the door. No lock. Take a deep breath, push open the door, stoop under the roof. A shadow detaches itself from the darkness and lumbers forward. Stand still, keep your fingers out of the way. The pig snuffles at my night-gown, pushing me so firmly I nearly fall over. It chews at the material then with an *ouff* it flops on to its bed.

Straw. Too exhausted to think . . . I sleep.

I am back in the Fifth Gallery and an attendant is prodding me. I groan. I don't want to get up yet – my whole body aches, my shoulder throbs . . .

I open my eyes. The pig is nudging me. As soon as I move out of the way, it goes and stands with its snout pressing against the door. Someone may come to feed it soon. I mustn't be found here.

With a painful effort, I rise, wincing as I put my feet down on the floor. Picking up the blanket, I squeeze past the pig and open the door a crack. Nothing stirs in the garden but dawn is already well over the horizon. Slipping out, I shut the door behind me quickly and crouch in the pen. What shall I do? I daren't go past the cottage now. Someone might be up.

I creep through the gate and scramble round the back of the sty. I wait a moment, but no one shouts. From here it's a short step to the boundary – a bank, a sparse hedge of hawthorn trees. But to reach it means crossing open ground and I might be seen from the neighbouring cottages. I haven't any choice though. I can't stay where I am.

I make a dash for it and scramble through the hedge, twigs scratching my face. On the other side I crouch down in a ditch edging the field. What now? From here I have a good view of the backs of the cottages. I can also see the lane. If this is Smalcote and Eliza passes there or comes into the garden, I might see her. But she may still be at Wildthorn . . .

Don't think about it. Keep hoping.

I huddle in the ditch, wincing with spasms of cramp. I daren't move too much in case I draw attention to myself and I don't want to lose sight of the lane. My mind drifts . . .

Every now and then a noise rouses me – a woman comes to feed the pig and let the hens out, I hear children's voices, the sounds of the cottagers going about their business . . . but none of them is Eliza. Each time I hear a noise, I shrink down, holding my breath . . .

The sun has come out with a brightness that dazzles me. The sky is too blue, overwhelming. I'm tormented by thirst now. My head aches, my tongue feels swollen in my mouth. I shake myself, stretch my eyes, but my lids keep closing . . .

The sound of hoofs jerks me awake, my heart pounding. Spying out from my hiding place, I watch the lane. Two horses appear. My muscles tense. I know the riders – the lodge-keeper from Wildthorn and one of the servants, a burly man. They must be searching for me.

I flatten myself to the ground, not daring to raise my head to look. The hoofbeats stop, I hear voices. I shut my eyes, expecting at any moment to hear a shout, feel a rough hand on my arm . . .

I hear a wonderful sound – the clop of the hoofs moving off. But then I realize – the cottagers will know about me. They'll come looking for me. I must get away from here now. Now.

267

I drag myself to my knees and start crawling along the ditch. One yard. Another. My vision blurs, my head swims with dizziness. A few more inches . . . but suddenly my arms and legs fold under me, my cheek hits the ground. I can't move.

I will be found, I know it. After all my effort, I will be found.

Tears of frustration trickle down my face.

Somewhere a voice calls. 'Joe! It's dinnertime.' A pause and then the voice again, nearer now. 'Joe, are you there?'

With an effort, I lift my head. My crawling has brought me to the back of a different cottage. Coming down the path is a girl with corn-coloured hair.

Eliza.

I blink, look again. Not Eliza. A younger girl.

I try to call out, croak feebly. Clenching my teeth, I pull myself to my knees. I manage to raise my arm and wave it.

A shocked face in a gap in the hedge. Round blue eyes staring at me. Then the gap is empty and I hear running footsteps, an urgent voice calling, 'Mother! Come quick!'

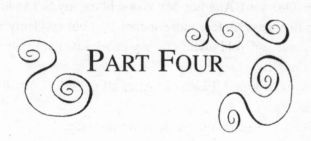

PART FOUR

I'm lying on something soft, and I half open my eyes and see a brown curtain hanging beside me. My eyelids close, I drift . . . and then I hear a slight noise, smell a dear, familiar smell. Eliza is here. Everything is all right. I sleep again.

I drift in and out of sleep, and when I open my eyes, Eliza is here again. She brings warm water and a cloth and washes me, avoiding my injuries. Her hands on my bare skin are skilful, soothing, and I don't want her to stop. Once, she lifts her head and catches my eye. I feel a sudden heat in my face and I'm glad when she bows her head again.

Another time she brings me soup and feeds it to me, the savoury taste fanning out over my tongue, like a blessing. All I have to do is lie here, which is just as well because my body doesn't want to move . . .

At some point in this floating, timeless dream, I have a thought, like a sudden stab of toothache. Eliza is at home all the time, not at Wildthorn. I fumble for the words to ask her why.

'I've been dismissed.' She says it lightly, but immediately I'm full of guilt.

'Because of me!'

She doesn't answer, busies herself tidying my covers.

'Tell me.'

'They thought I'd helped you to escape.'

271

'But that's not fair! You didn't.'

'I would've if I could. Saved you sleeping in a pigsty.' She laughs.

But I'm not laughing. 'What if they come looking for me? Won't that make more trouble for you?'

'They've been back since you've been here and Mother sent them packing. They won't come again.'

She sounds very certain. Perhaps she's right. Perhaps they don't trouble themselves about one lunatic more or less. And there are other things to think about besides being captured. 'What will happen now?'

But she won't discuss it. 'Wait till you're better.'

After a few days, I do feel better. Well enough to sit in a chair while Eliza combs through my hair, cutting out the worst tangles, and then washes it and towels it dry. Wonderful to have clean hair at last! Well enough to dress, in clothes borrowed from Eliza, and come out from my alcove and meet some of the family.

I feel very nervous, but as Mrs Shaw, in a little flutter of fuss, waves floury hands towards the only chair, I realize she's as nervous as I am and I feel less daunted. I'm introduced to Lily, who stares at me with big eyes, and to curly-haired Arthur, who takes no notice of me at all. Then Eliza and her mother continue with their chores. I offer to help, but Mrs Shaw won't hear of it.

'You sit and rest yourself, Miss.'

'Please, call me Louisa.'

She smiles uncertainly and turns back to her mixing bowl.

Getting up seems to have exhausted me and I feel shaky. Really I'm glad just to sit and look around me.

The door is propped open, presumably to let in light and air, as it's warm with the range lit. After the drab uniformity of the Fifth Gallery, the small and sparsely furnished room seems vivid and crowded with things vying for my attention: a rag rug on the clean-swept flagstones; a collection of bright crockery on the mantelpiece; a coloured picture of the Queen cut from a magazine, now somewhat yellowed and curling at the edges; bunches of dried lavender hanging from the beams in the low ceiling.

In the doorway, the children are playing with some pegs, Lily wrapping them in bits of stuff and walking them about to entertain Arthur, while Mrs Shaw rolls out pastry at the scrubbed deal table. Out in the scullery, Eliza hums to herself as she peels potatoes.

The day passes peacefully. After dinner I take a long nap and evening brings Mr Shaw home from the fields, with Annie and Joe.

Having washed in the scullery, Eliza's father comes to greet me, his weather-beaten face turning a deeper shade of red, his blue eyes sliding shyly from mine. Annie is hugely excited to see me up – having been the one to find me, she takes a proprietorial interest in me and insists on sitting next to me at the table. After giving me one bold stare, Joe turns his attention to his ''taters' and cabbage.

The family talk as they eat – about the state of the ground, how much barley remains to be sown. I'm not part of this, but I don't mind. I feel comfortable, put at ease by their kindness, their acceptance of me. But then I catch

Eliza looking gravely at me, and I wonder what she's thinking. I hope she's not finding it awkward to have me here. Catching my eye, her face breaks into a smile. I smile back, but I feel disturbed now, uneasy.

I still have bad dreams from which I wake shivering, but every day I grow stronger.

Every day I also feel more uncomfortable.

I'm an extra mouth to feed and it's obvious that there's no money to spare. I don't like being treated as a special guest, sitting about while everyone else is busy.

One useful thing I'm allowed to do is help Eliza with her reading, but really, it's coming on so fast now she doesn't need any help. Eventually, after much insistence on my part, Mrs Shaw lets me do light jobs – darning stockings, mending torn pinafores – but she won't let me help with the real work of the household.

I know this can't go on. I'm also worried about Eliza. I'm sure something's troubling her, but I don't get a chance to speak to her privately – all activities, except for sleeping, happen in this one small room. In a way I'm glad, because until we talk about the future, everything can carry on as it is.

But one morning Mrs Shaw ladles some porridge into a bowl, and calls in to Eliza, 'I'm taking this down to Hetty. I'll see what else needs doing, while I'm there.' She explains to me, 'Hetty's a neighbour, Miss Cosgrove. Her lad came this morning to say she's poorly.'

As soon as she's gone, Eliza comes from the scullery, drying her wet hands.

For a moment there's a shyness between us. Outside in the sunshine Lily and Arthur are making mud pies and their chatter floats in through the open door.

I'm the first to speak, plunging in awkwardly. 'Is anything the matter? Only you seem – I don't know – preoccupied with something.'

Eliza's gaze shifts away. 'Oh, I've been thinking about what I'm going to do, that's all. But there's no rush.'

I clear my throat. 'You know, I'm so grateful to you and your family for what you've done for me. I don't know how I'm ever going to thank you.'

It sounds all wrong – stiff and formal. At Wildthorn we talked easily. What's changed?

'That's all right. We're glad to help you.'

'But listen, Eliza. We must talk about what *I'm* going to do.'

She spreads a worn cloth on the table. 'Wait till you're right better.'

'You keep saying that. But I am better and we can't keep putting it off. I've been here nearly three weeks now . . .'

Ignoring me, she sets the lamp on the cloth and fetches some rags. Removing the glass chimney, she starts to clean off the soot.

'Are you tired of it here?' Her voice is low, muffled.

'No!'

'Only I wondered if you were missing your books . . . and clever talk, like.'

'Not at all.' How can I tell her how much I don't want to go?

A silence falls as she rubs away at the glass and I watch her. I remember something I've been meaning to ask her.

'Did you know Weeks was in the Infirmary? I saw her when I was looking for a way out.'

'I heard the others talking about it. Joking that no one would be able to escape from there now, if she were there. That's what gave me the idea . . .'

I smile wryly. What would Weeks think if she knew that, in a roundabout way, she'd helped me to escape . . .

Eliza goes on, 'No one knew why she were there. They were keeping it hushed up, like.'

'It looked like smallpox to me.'

Eliza raises her eyebrows and I add hastily, 'Don't worry, I didn't get too close. She was pretty far gone. I don't think she'll have pulled through.'

'That's a pity. She were a nasty piece of work, but still . . .'

'Mmm.'

Eliza fetches a lantern.

'Shall I do that, while you do something else?'

'No. Mother will be cross if I let you.'

'Look, this is what I mean. I can't go on sitting about, like some fine lady, while your family feeds me. Especially as you're not working.'

'There's no need to fret about that. Father's paid steady, like, at the moment and Charlie and Florrie, they send most of what they get.'

'But I'm not contributing anything.'

She doesn't answer.

'I've been thinking. The best thing to do is to write to Aunt Phyllis.'

Her hand freezes in mid-motion, and she looks at me in some alarm. 'I wouldn't do that.'

'Why not?'

'It's just that . . .' She puts down the lantern and rag. Her expression makes my heart start beating faster. What's she going to say?

'I'm sorry, I haven't been straight with you.'

'What do you mean?'

'When I told you I'd been dismissed for helping you get out of there, that weren't the real reason – well, not the whole of it, anyhow.'

Of course! She was suspended *before* I escaped. Why hadn't I remembered that? 'So why? For coming to visit me?'

Gnawing her lip, she shakes her head. Then she says, 'You wanted to know what the signature was on your papers, so I thought I'd have a go.'

'You were caught!'

She nods. 'With the papers in my hand – I couldn't find the right place to put them back in the drawer.'

My stomach lurches. 'You saw it? The signature?'

'Yes – and it weren't Thomas Childs –' She swallows.

For a moment, I can't breathe. I stare at her, paralysed. I manage to say, 'Who?'

She grips the table. 'I knew I was going to have to tell you, but I kept putting it off.' Eliza fixes her eyes on mine. 'It were your aunt, Phyllis Illing-something.'

'Illingworth.' As I say the name, a terrible pain spreads

277

through my chest, so bad I don't think I can bear it. *Aunt Phyllis?*

Everything solid is falling away from me, leaving me trembling, giddy. I keep trying to breathe, but the air is too thick . . . I can't draw it into my lungs . . .

Finally I manage it and the world stops spinning. I just keep thinking, Why? Why has she done this?

And then it comes to me: the only possible explanation. Grace must have told her what I did. Grace told her and she was so appalled, she wanted me locked away. She wanted to keep Grace safe from me.

A vision of Aunt Phyllis's drawing room presents itself to me: flowers everywhere, painted, embroidered. And me sitting there like a serpent in her Eden.

Eliza breaks into my thoughts. 'Why would she do such a thing? Have you any idea?'

I close my eyes. I want to tell her, more than anything in the world. But how can I?

I open my eyes and there she is, looking at me so sympathetically, her blue eyes as honest as the day.

I can't hold back. Taking a deep breath, I tell her what happened at Carr Head . . .

'Louisa, my dear.'

I fell into my aunt's arms, tears spilling down my face. After a long hug, I wiped my eyes and she said, 'Let me look at you.'

We hadn't seen each other since Papa's funeral.

'Are you well? You look so pale.'

'Yes. Of course I am.' I tried to smile.

Aunt Phyllis clearly wasn't convinced. 'Come and sit by me and tell me how you've been. How is your mother? And have you heard from Tom?'

I longed to pour everything out to her, all my loneliness and grief and disappointment . . . but I thought of Mamma, and I couldn't. It seemed disloyal, but also, my aunt would want to know why I hadn't let her know all this in my letters. I couldn't tell her about Mamma's hostility towards her.

'Lou?' My aunt was waiting.

I said something stilted about Mamma still feeling Papa's loss deeply. Tom was – Tom was well. Of course Aunt Phyllis wasn't satisfied with my replies, I could tell. But she said, 'We'll talk more later. While you're here, you must have a lovely holiday.'

'Thank you. I'm sure I will.' Then – all I cared about: 'Where's Grace?'

Aunt Phyllis smiled. 'She'll be down in a moment. Come and see what changes I've made in the house.'

*

We were in the conservatory admiring the passion flowers when I heard Grace's light step.

She took my hand, exclaiming, 'How cold you are, Lou! And on such a hot day too.' Before I could speak, she laid her face against mine. It was a brief embrace but when she drew away, my cheek burned.

'I'll leave you two to talk,' said Aunt Phyllis. 'The men will be home soon.'

The men. William! Remembering Tom's ridiculous idea about me and William, I went hot again.

As we sat down, it came to me that we were sitting in the very seats we had sat in earlier in the year when she had drawn my portrait. That picture . . . It was creased from my constant looking at it, not because I wanted to see myself, but because Grace had drawn it.

'Do you remember?'

Grace looked enquiring.

'We sat here in April and you drew my portrait.'

'Did I? Such a lot has happened since then.'

'Yes, it has.'

She was instantly contrite. Leaving her chair, she knelt in front of me. Taking both my hands in hers, she said, 'Oh, Lou, how dreadful of me to be thinking only of myself.' She looked up at me. 'Has it been really awful without poor Uncle Edward?'

'I'm all right.' I couldn't tell her the truth.

'I hope so, truly. And I'm sorry you aren't going to be my bridesmaid now, but I do understand.'

'It's not long now, is it?'

Grace launched into details of the revised wedding preparations, the trip to Europe that was to follow, the new house in

280

London. Her animation brought a flush to her face and I was glad I hadn't burdened her with my woes. I didn't want to make her unhappy – and she was happy, I could see that.

Eventually she stood up. 'It must be time for tea. We've been having it in the garden, it's still so fine.' She went to the garden door and looked out. 'Yes, it's there. And so is Charles, of course.'

I had the sensation of falling. 'Charles?'

She laughed back at me from the doorway. 'Yes, he's always first. He can't resist cake.'

I peered over Grace's shoulder. Charles was sitting at the tea table, napkin already in his lap, looking hopefully towards the house.

'I didn't know Charles was here.'

She gave a little laugh. 'Yes, poor dear. He's bored to death with all the wedding talk. Come and say hello.'

She stepped outside but I hung back.

'I'd like a wash before tea. I'll come in a minute.'

I watched as Grace ran across the lawn. She sat down next to Charles and their heads moved together as they spoke.

I turned away.

What had I been thinking of? I'd imagined the two of us, Grace and I, walking together, riding perhaps, talking . . .

Now, here was Charles. Seeing him again reminded me of the stark reality: Grace really was going to be married, her heart belonged to someone else.

She would never love me in the way that I loved her. There was no room in her life for me – except as her cousin of whom she had been fond, whom she would be glad to see now and

 281

then, but wouldn't miss, not really, in the intervals between meeting.

My poor, silly dreams shrivelled, leaving behind a hollow, aching space.

I found the guest room Aunt Phyllis said I was to sleep in, where my things were already laid out on the bed. It was a spacious, well-appointed room. But it wasn't Grace's bedroom.

After I'd washed, avoiding the mirror, I walked down the stairs, along the passage to the back door, across the gravel, to the lawn.

There they all were, gathered in the autumn sunshine as if for a family portrait: Uncle Bertram, Aunt Phyllis, Maud, Charles, Grace and William.

Maud raised her arm and waved and I moved towards them, greeted everyone, sat down, accepted tea, declined cake, answered questions about Mamma and Tom – but I did all these things mechanically as if someone else were moving my limbs and opening my mouth. I felt as if I were behind glass, existing in a world cut off from theirs.

At dinner I sat between William and Maud. Thankfully, Maud chattered on and didn't seem to notice my monosyllabic replies. As for William, he scarcely spoke to me, apart from paying polite attention to my needs.

'Would you like more wine, Louisa?'

I tried to adopt the same careless tone. 'Yes, please.'

He filled my glass again, then turned away to talk to Uncle Bertram.

The wine was red, like rubies . . . or blood. I swallowed some, finding it more enjoyable now, liking the warmth that was

spreading through my body, the loosening sensation in my shoulders. The more I drank, the more my spirits rose.

A fleeting thought of Tom went through my mind and I smiled wryly to myself. William wasn't in the least bit interested in me, as I knew he wouldn't be. And I had no desire to try and charm him, even if I knew how.

Giving Maud minimal attention, I was able to watch Grace secretly. She was engrossed in conversation with her mother; the words 'tulle', 'corsage', 'nosegays' drifted towards me, through the hum of talk.

In the candlelight she glowed, as if her skin shared the luminescence of the flames. I couldn't stop looking at her, though looking made my heart ache.

I gulped some more wine. I was beginning to feel lightheaded, a not unpleasant sensation.

Suddenly my attention was caught by something Uncle Bertram was saying about a law recently passed in Parliament: '. . . letting women register for medical training! Pshaw! Whatever next?'

My heart sped up.

Uncle Bertram carried on, 'They'll be wanting to be lawyers next, eh, Charles? What do you think of all this nonsense?'

I held my breath. Charles picked up his glass of wine, and appeared to consider it carefully before replying, 'I'm with Maudsley on this one. You know what he says – a girl who is educated beyond what is necessary for her role as wife and mother cannot possibly reach the perfect ideal of womanhood.'

I turned my eyes towards Grace to see whether she was as shocked as I was. She was obviously listening, but appeared to be unconcerned. A pulse began to beat in my head. It wasn't just

 283

what Charles was saying but the way he was talking. What a cold fish he was. How could Grace want to marry him?

Uncle Bertram shook his head. 'He's right. These women – they hardly deserve the name! They're a disgrace to their sex! Aping men!'

'I quite agree.' Charles smiled, and I think it was that that did it. It was such a smug, self-satisfied smile.

Leaping to my feet, I shouted, 'How can you say such stupid things! Elizabeth Garrett Anderson is married, with children! And there are other brave, clever women who have struggled against all the odds to be doctors and proved themselves the equal of any man. They're not a disgrace to their sex but a fine example!'

The silence was absolute. Everyone was looking at me. I found I was trembling and I clutched the edge of the table for support.

Red in the face, Uncle Bertram said, 'Hoity toity, Miss! That's no way to speak to your elders and betters. Show some respect.'

'But if the elders don't know better, why should they be respected?'

My heart was beating wildly. I was out of control, I knew, and I felt I might say anything. It was a glorious feeling.

Aunt Phyllis was behind me, her hand on my shoulder. 'Louisa, dear, I don't think you're quite yourself. Wouldn't you like to retire?'

I shook off her hand. 'But I *am* myself, can't you see? This is who I am. This is what I believe. And I tell you something . . .'

I paused and looked round the table – at Maud, who looked shocked but delighted; at William, who looked embarrassed; at Uncle Bertram, who was scarlet with apoplexy; at Charles, whose features – oh, joy! – were bulging as if he'd swallowed a frog. And then I looked at Grace, who had turned pale, and I looked at her the longest . . .

'I want to be a doctor and it doesn't matter what my brother or any of you say, somehow, I don't know how, I will do it.'

With my back straight, proceeding in as stately a manner as I could, I left the room.

I couldn't go to my bedroom; I couldn't possibly lie still, let alone sleep. Lighting a candle from those standing ready in the hall, I took it into the conservatory and set it down. Then I strode about, grateful for the cold air that cooled my hot face, glad to be alone amongst the shadowy silhouettes of fronds and leaves.

My elation didn't last long. All too soon it was replaced by anxiety. What had I done? What would Aunt Phyllis think of me? Surely I'd be sent home in disgrace. But even as these thoughts nagged at me, there was still part of me that wasn't sorry. I had spoken the truth, which we were always being told was the right thing to do.

I heard footsteps and turning, found Grace hovering in the doorway. I was relieved to see her. I dreaded facing anyone else, especially Uncle Bertram.

'Lou? Are you all right?'

'Yes. I think so.' I swallowed. 'Is your father still angry?'

She came closer. 'I'm afraid he is. But Mamma is calming him down. Don't worry. He'll get over it.'

I wasn't so sure, but I was comforted by the fact that she, at least, didn't seem upset, even though it was Charles who had provoked me most. But perhaps she didn't realize that.

 285

'Shall we sit down?' She seemed nervous, as if she thought I might suddenly erupt again.

When I settled on a chair, she relaxed visibly. 'I didn't know – about you wanting to be a doctor. You never said.'

'No. I was going to tell you, the last time I was here, but then – I was called home . . .' I trailed off.

She nodded sympathetically. 'So how long have you had this ambition?'

I told her how I so wanted to go to the London School of Medicine for Women. She listened, nodding now and then encouragingly. It felt so good to be talking to someone who seemed to understand, someone who seemed to be on my side.

'Couldn't you? Study, I mean.'

I told her about Tom's opposition – how I needed his approval and, more, how getting the money depended on his support.

'I could speak to Mamma, if you like. She might help you.'

I smiled bitterly. 'I don't think so. She wasn't very happy about the idea before and now I've upset your father . . .'

'Don't worry about that. Papa has a temper, but he'll come round if Mamma persuades him.'

'Why would she?'

'She might, if I speak to her.' Grace smiled. 'She can't help indulging me.'

I looked at her, with a dawning sense of hope. 'Would you?'

'Yes, of course. And, Lou –' she suddenly clapped her hands together – 'I've had such a capital idea! When we come back from our travels, if you come to study in London, you must stay with us.'

For a moment I was tempted. It was like a dream come true.

But I told myself not to be stupid. I wouldn't just be living with Grace, but with Charles too, and the thought of seeing her with him every day was unbearable. Apart from the small matter of Charles having to agree to the idea . . .

Seeing my hesitation, she asked, 'Wouldn't you like that?'

'I don't think Charles would.'

'Oh, he'll be delighted, I'm sure. Besides, he's already warned me that when we return from Europe, I can't expect to see so much of him. He's an important man, you know, on all sorts of committees . . . he'll hardly notice you're there.'

I wondered whether Grace anticipated being lonely, and wanted me to stay for some company. I had a sudden vision of her life – long periods alone and then Charles coming home . . .

'Are you sure about this?'

'Yes! It would be lovely to have you.'

'I mean your marriage. Are you sure about it?'

She gave a surprised laugh, but was frowning too. 'Whatever do you mean?'

In the candlelight she looked so beautiful, and suddenly I couldn't bear it. Flinging myself on my knees in front of her, I grasped both her hands in mine.

'Please, don't do it. Please don't give yourself to that man. He's not worthy of you. He won't make you happy.' She stiffened and tried to withdraw her hands, but I hung on. 'No, listen to me. You heard what he said tonight. I know you're excited about having your own home and everything, but what if, after a while, you want something else, something more? He won't allow it, will he? You know he won't.'

Gently she pulled her hands away and this time I let go.

Her look was bemused. 'It's sweet of you to worry about me,

Lou, but really, you don't know Charles as I do. When you get to know him better – and I do so want you two to be friends – you'll see what a dear he is.'

I could have said more, much more, but just then she raised her head and broke into a brilliant smile. I looked over my shoulder and my heart jumped.

Charles was standing in the door of the conservatory. How long had he been there? How much had he heard?

Ignoring me, he said, 'Ah, there you are, my dear. I've been looking for you. They want you to play.' He seemed unperturbed. Perhaps he'd only arrived just that second.

Grace sprang up immediately and went to him. 'Are you coming, Lou?'

Had she forgotten my outburst at dinner. 'No. I have a headache. I think I'll go to bed now.'

'Goodnight then.' Grace blew me a little kiss.

Charles inclined his head coolly. He hadn't forgotten.

Alone in the bedroom, the rituals of undressing and brushing out my hair failed to calm me; the events of the evening kept coming back to me. I opened the window and leaned on the sill, hoping the cool night air would soothe me. The moon was almost full, the sky pricked with stars. Some way off, a shrill shriek was suddenly cut short and I guessed an owl had found its prey.

I could hear the sound of the piano floating up from the drawing room, and then Grace's voice, singing that familiar lovely song: *I dreamed that I dwelt in marble halls.*

As I listened, I thought, bitterly, how appropriate. *I dreamed that suitors sought my hand . . .*

When she was near the end, I had to close the window. I couldn't bear it. But the words went on in my head:

I also dreamed which charmed me most
That you loved me still the same
That you loved me still the same . . .

I felt desolate, overcome with weariness. Slipping into bed, I blew out the candle and shut my eyes. I couldn't stop thinking of Grace. I'd tried to save her from what seemed to me a dreadful fate, but I'd failed. I felt a sadness as painful as when Papa died, a sadness that seeped into my very bones.

To distract myself, I stared at the inside of my shut lids, as I'd done as a child, and there they were . . . shoals of tiny, glittering fish swimming in an ink-dark river. And I found I could still do the trick of slipping out of my body and merging with them, flowing on and on in an endless stream, that carried me away . . .

. . . Ahead the light grew brighter and brighter until in its heart I saw a figure. I came nearer and it was Grace, wearing a white dress with a circlet of pearls round her red-gold hair. I moved towards her and she held out her arms to me, smiling . . . As we embraced, I closed my eyes and held on tight . . . tight . . . but then with a horrible sense of chill, I felt Grace shrinking, dwindling in my arms, her ribs pressing into my flesh . . . I opened my eyes . . . She lay in my arms, her eyes shut, her face white. I touched her thin cheek and it was as cold as marble. A voice said, 'Let her go, Louisa. Lay her in her grave.'

I came to in darkness, my heart pounding, my face wet with tears. I didn't know where I was.

'Mamma?'

No answer.

Trembling, I felt for the candlestick, and knocked something with my arm that fell with a crash. I got out of bed and fumbled around. Where was the candle? I caught my finger on something sharp, the stab of pain bringing tears to my eyes. I gave up my search and sat huddled with my arms wrapped round my knees.

'Lou? What's the matter?'

I lifted my head. Grace stood silhouetted in the doorway.

At the sight of her, I went weak with relief. 'You're all right,' I sighed.

She shut the door and setting down her own candle beside the bed, she crouched beside me.

'I broke the candlestick.'

'It doesn't matter.' She put her arm round me and I quivered at her touch.

'You're cold. Get into bed.'

She helped me in, pulling up the covers, and then sat beside me, a warm weight against my legs.

'I was on my way to bed and I heard the crash.' She smoothed my wild hair from my face.

'Is it Uncle Edward? Is that what's making you unhappy?' Her voice was soft and low, full of concern. In the candlelight her hair shone like copper.

She was alive and so beautiful I ached to hold her. But I knew I couldn't, I mustn't. She mustn't know of my feelings that were so wrong. The longing to tell her, and the knowledge I couldn't, formed a choking lump in my throat, a spreading pain around my heart.

'Poor Lou.' Her gaze dropped and her expression changed. 'You're bleeding.'

I looked down and saw a red stain on the white sheet. I sucked my finger.

'Let me see.' She took my hand and bent her head over it, examining it. Her face was very close to mine. I could smell her perfume, see the hollow at her throat, feel her warm breath on my palm.

I didn't mean to . . . but I had only to move my face an inch or two and my mouth found hers. Her soft lips were a surprise and my heartbeat quickened. A slow fuse lit inside me, the heat spreading from the pit of my stomach, until my whole body was suffused with it . . .

But then I realized that Grace wasn't responding but had turned to stone, my hand still gripped in hers.

I drew back and saw in her eyes such a look of shock and embarrassment, I had to look away.

After a long silence, I felt her weight shift.

'I—'

'Don't,' she said, in a strange voice. 'Don't say anything. And Lou, I won't say anything either, I promise. Not to anyone.'

I heard the swish of her dress, the door click open and close again. She had gone.

I was overcome with an agony of shame. I screwed up my face and tried to shut out the memory, but still her expression haunted me.

What had I done?

For a moment I pretended that it had been part of my nightmare, that it hadn't happened. But when I opened my eyes, there was her candle burning beside me, and on the floor the broken fragments of mine.

 291

I pinched out the flame, wanting to hide my guilt in darkness. But it wouldn't leave me. Over and over again I relived that moment. Sleep was impossible. Fumbling for the matches I relit the candle, then I paced up and down.

I don't know how long I continued, but walking had a calming effect and after a while I was able to think. I would have to leave Carr Head. I couldn't face Grace again. Or Aunt Phyllis. But surely Grace wouldn't tell her? She promised she wouldn't. But they were close, like sisters. And even if she didn't, my face might betray me. Aunt Phyllis would know what I had done. I imagined going down to breakfast, the family gathered there. They would look at me and they would all know.

I would have to leave early in the morning before anyone was up. But how would I get home? I would have to walk. Then there was my bag. Should I leave it behind?

I stopped pacing. This wild rush of thought was achieving nothing. Taking a deep breath, I tried to pull myself together.

First I must dress. Then pack. My bag wasn't heavy; I could manage it if I stopped for rests and perhaps, when I reached the main road, a wagon might come along and I could beg a lift.

My decision made, I felt somewhat steadier. I went about my tasks methodically and when I was ready, I sat down to wait for dawn.

Then I had another thought. My disappearance would cause alarm. Possibly search parties would be sent out to look for me. I'd have to leave a note. But what could I say?

After a false start or two I wrote:

I am sorry to have left so suddenly without saying goodbye. It

was kind of you to invite me but on reflection I realize Mamma needs me at home. I am making my own way there as I do not want to put you to any trouble.

Louisa

I addressed the note to Aunt Phyllis and left it propped up on the writing table.

By now the sky had turned from black to grey. It was time to be off.

I turned the doorknob slowly, in case it clicked. There was no one about in the hallway. Closing the door quietly behind me, I made for the stairs. I descended cautiously, afraid of creaking steps, but I reached the lobby undetected. I'd decided to leave by the garden door rather than attempt the bolts at the front. Before I could reach it, the door of Uncle's study opened, and I came face to face with a maid.

She gasped and dropped her ash bucket with a loud clatter. 'Oh, Miss, you gave me such a fright!'

'Sorry – I'm sorry.' I tried to move past her but the passage was narrow.

She looked at me with open curiosity. 'Are you not well, Miss?'

'Yes – that is, no . . .' I hardly knew what I was saying. Surely that noise would have roused someone. At any moment they might appear. 'Please, let me pass.'

She moved aside then, but her eye fell on my bag. 'You're leaving?'

'Yes. I've been called away suddenly.' An absurd thing to say. Why was I explaining myself at all?

 293

I moved on, but she hurried after me. 'Please, Miss, let me call the master and he'll get James to bring the carriage for you.'

'No!'

She recoiled as if I'd slapped her.

I softened my tone. 'There's no need to disturb the master.'

Fumbling in my purse, I drew out a sixpence, and pushed it into her hand. 'Here, take this. Please don't call anyone. I'm sorry I frightened you. But everything's all right, really it is.'

I moved away from her then, found the garden door, turned the key and I was out in the fresh morning air. My footsteps on the gravel sounded thunderous to my ears but no face appeared at the windows.

I hastened down the driveway and out into the road, like a murderer escaping from the scene of the crime.

My voice falters into silence. I can't look at Eliza.

'I see.' Her tone isn't at all what I expected. I look at her now, and her face, if anything, is – sad?

'You don't seem . . . shocked.'

'Why should I be shocked?'

'But –' I feel wrong-footed, as if I expected a step that wasn't there – 'but what I did was *wrong*.' And in case she misunderstands me and thinks I'm talking about shouting at my uncle, I add, 'I mean, kissing Grace like that.' I feel myself blush.

'No it weren't. You were just showing your feelings. That's not a crime.'

Again I have that extraordinary floating feeling. I stare at Eliza. I can't believe how calm she is . . . as if she hasn't just said the most unexpected thing in the world. She's just sitting there, looking at me, as if she *understands*.

I clear my throat. 'So you don't think that's why my aunt had me admitted to Wildthorn? That Grace told her?'

She shrugs. 'I don't know.' She stands up and starts gathering up the dirty rags. 'I know one thing though.'

'What?'

'You can't go there, to your aunt's, can you?'

For the rest of the day, I find it hard to focus because I keep coming back to the one impossible thing: not Tom, but Aunt Phyllis.

295

But Tom signed that letter and presumably asked the doctors to sign the certificates. Tom *and* Aunt Phyllis. Does Mamma know? Is she in on it too? And Grace?

After the numbness of the first shock wears off, I feel utterly wretched. I keep asking myself, Why? I keep picturing Grace telling her mother what I did.

It isn't a crime. Eliza. If only I could believe her. And she was just as direct about Beatrice. *I thought you were sweet on her.*

I look up from darning Lily's stocking to find Eliza's eyes on me, as she wields the flat iron. She smiles, but not with her usual sunniness. Again I have the feeling that she's sad about something. Perhaps she's sorry on my account.

The reality of my predicament is dawning on me. Sure that Grace wouldn't break her promise, I've been counting on Aunt Phyllis . . .

What on earth am I going to do now?

Luckily, in the morning Mrs Shaw goes off to visit her neighbour again.

As soon as Eliza comes in from feeding the hens, I say, 'I've been thinking and I know what I must do. I must find work of some kind, perhaps in a shop or a clerk in an office . . .'

Saying it, I feel sick. The last thing I want to do is leave here. It's the only place in the world where I feel safe. But I can't go on taking from the Shaws. From now on, I'll have to support myself. I'll have to learn to survive alone.

I've only the haziest notion of what such work might

involve, but I can't think of anything else. On my own, penniless, with my family against me, what choice do I have?

'A shop or an office? There's nothing like that round here. I reckon you'd have to go to London for work like that.' Her tone is doleful.

'Yes, that's what I thought.' I pause and then, feeling very awkward, I go on, 'I hate to ask, when you've all done so much for me already but—'

'You'll need some money, for the fare and lodgings . . .' She's still speaking in that same flat voice, and I feel dreadful. I've asked too much.

'No,' I say hastily. 'Really, I'm sure I'll be able to beg a lift from some farmer going to market . . .'

At that she smiles, at last. 'You're so fond of those hogs, you want to ride with them, do you? Don't be daft. I'll ask Mother – she'll have a bit of egg money set by.'

I can't help giving her a hug. 'Oh, Eliza, I'll pay her back as soon as I can, I promise.'

Letting go, I notice she's gone red, but before I can ask if she's all right, Eliza puts her finger to her mouth in a hushing gesture. Then I hear it too – the sound of wheels in the lane. We look at one another with wide eyes.

'Quick,' she says. 'Upstairs.'

I scramble up the steep wooden stairs and, opening a door, I find myself in a small bedroom tucked into the roof space. There's no cupboard to hide in or drawers to crouch behind – the whole space is filled with an iron bedstead pushed under the slope of the ceiling. Crawling under it, I press myself against the wall, trying not to cough as I breathe in dust. I strain to catch what's happening down-stairs.

I can hear Eliza's voice but can't tell who she is speaking to. Is it the lodge-keeper? Or Mr Sneed himself come in a carriage to carry me back?

I grip the leg of the bed with both hands. If they've come for me, I won't make it easy for them.

Hearing footsteps on the stairs, I freeze. The door opens and Eliza's boots stop near my head, then her face appears, upside down. 'It's someone for you.' I can hear the strangeness in her voice.

Struggling out from my hiding place, I whisper, 'Who is it?' but she's already on her way downstairs.

I follow her slowly, my thoughts in turmoil. Has Eliza betrayed me? Is that why she's been so awkward?

I step into the kitchen, my eyes following Eliza as she slips out of the door. Then I hear a small sound, a sigh or an exhalation. A figure rises from a chair.

'Lou?'

The last voice I expected to hear.

Grace, here in the Shaws' kitchen! A vision in pale blue-grey silk that shimmers like opals, her flounced skirts draped in elegant curves.

I instantly feel self-conscious: I'm wearing a dress borrowed from Eliza, its hem a good six inches above the floor, and an old pair of Charlie's boots.

Remembering the last time I saw her, I blush, but I also feel wary. Why is she here? Has she come to take me back to Wildthorn?

'Lou!'

She steps forward as if to embrace me, but I back away. Her face falls. 'What's the matter?'

I can't speak. There's too much to say, too much to ask.

Alarmed, she says, 'Lou? Are you all right? You know who I am, don't you?'

She thinks I'm mad. Swallowing hard, I manage to say, 'Hello, Grace,' and her face relaxes a little.

I glance through the doorway. Down the garden, Eliza is cutting rhubarb. The sight of her steadies me. 'Are you by yourself?'

'Yes. I left Mamma at Wildthorn Hall, sorting things out.'

At the mention of my aunt, a tremor goes through me, but Grace doesn't seem to notice.

At least on her own she can't make me go back there.

'We were hoping to get some information about you

299

here. I didn't count on actually finding you!' She gazes at me. 'You look well. From what they told us at the hospital, I was afraid . . .' She breaks off, shaking her head.

'How did you find me?'

'I'll tell you.' She takes the chair and I perch on a stool.

Grace keeps looking at me, shaking her head, as if she can't get over seeing me. 'I had no idea, you know. I thought you were with that family . . .'

'The Woodvilles?'

'Yes. I wrote to you from Europe, but of course I didn't expect a reply, because we were never in one place for long. And when we got back, there was such a lot to do – sorting the house out . . . Lou, I'm so sorry I didn't realize sooner . . . that I didn't start asking questions—'

'But you didn't know.' It makes me feel better that she didn't.

'No! Not until I saw your photograph!'

'My photograph?'

'Yes, in an exhibition. Charles is always being invited to charity events – you know, people wanting donations. Such a lucky chance I went to this one! It was organized by the superintendent of Wildthorn Hall.'

'Mr Sneed!'

'That's right. He was giving lectures on phrenology and to illustrate them there was a display of photographs of patients.'

The photographs. So that was what Mr Sneed was up to. Roberts was right.

'At first I wasn't sure . . . but there was something about

300

it that drew me . . . and the more I looked, the more I was certain it was you. Charles . . .'

She breaks off, and for a second her mouth presses into a thin line. 'Charles said it was nonsense. But I insisted that he find out the name. Of course when Mr Sneed said "Lucy Childs", Charles said, "There, what did I tell you?" But I wasn't convinced. It preyed on my mind. Later, without telling Charles, I went back and persuaded Mr Sneed to sell me the photograph. The next time we visited Carr Head, I showed Mamma and —'

I put out my hand to stop her. 'I know.'

'You know?'

'That your mother signed the papers to put me in Wildthorn.'

'Oh.' There's a pause. 'Lou, I . . .' She falls silent, watching me anxiously.

I burst out, 'Why, Grace? Why did she do it? Why did you tell her about me? You promised you wouldn't.'

She frowns, clearly puzzled.

I can feel myself going red again. 'You know, when I broke the candlestick . . .'

Her face clears. 'Oh, that! No, of course I haven't said anything to anyone. I just thought you were upset about your papa.'

'Then why did your mother do it?'

'I think she'd better tell you herself. I'm sorry, Lou. I was hoping you didn't know —'

'So you could keep it from me?'

'No. *No!* I only meant – if you knew – it's complicated . . .' She takes a deep breath. 'You must be terribly hurt, and I wanted to spare you that . . . and until you know everything . . .' She trails off, looking stricken.

I feel torn. I want to believe her, to trust her, but what if, really, she is on her mother's side?

I try to sound cooler than I feel. 'You were telling me about the photograph.'

'Oh, yes. When I showed it to Mamma, I could tell she knew something. I pestered her until I found out what had happened and where you were, then I insisted we come and get you . . .' She looks at me, her eyes wide. 'It was a terrible shock when you weren't at the hospital and no one knew what had happened to you.'

'How did you find out I was here?'

'The superintendent, Mr Sneed, said he believed Eliza Shaw knew something about it.' Grace pauses, crinkling her forehead. 'What I don't understand is why he hadn't followed it up himself.'

'Someone did come, but – well, he didn't try very hard. I expect eventually he was going to write to your mother and tell her I'd died.'

Grace's eyes widen. 'No, really? Would he do such a dreadful thing?'

I shrug. 'Eliza says it's happened before. They go on taking the money as long as they can.'

'That's awful.' Grace shakes her head. 'He was certainly very flustered when Mamma and I turned up. I think he's frightened Mamma will make a fuss and ruin him.'

'I don't expect she will.' I smile sourly.

'Oh, Lou – I can imagine how you must be feeling, but why don't you come with me now and speak to Mamma?'

'I'm not going to set foot in that place again.'

'No, of course not. We've booked a room at the village inn. Mamma will be there now, waiting for me.'

'She'll want me to go back to Wildthorn Hall.'

'Of course she won't. She signed your release papers. I saw her do it. She was taking your box to the inn.'

Her look is imploring. But I don't know what to believe.

'You don't think I'm mad, then?'

'No. *No!* Please, Lou, I promise you'll be quite safe.' She stands up. 'So, will you come?'

I won't find out the truth unless I speak to my aunt, so I suppose I have no choice. But everything's happening too fast. Am I really going *now*?

'I must see Eliza before I go.'

'Of course. I'll wait in the carriage.'

I look out into the garden, into the sunshine. 'I can go outside now?'

'Yes.' She smiles. 'You're free to do as you like.'

On the threshold, I hesitate. I take a step forward and light strikes me in the face, like a blow, making my eyes water.

Lily and Arthur look up from their play, curious, and I try to smile, but I feel light-headed, strange.

I make my way unsteadily down the cinder path between beds of sprouting seedlings. Eliza is coming towards me, carrying a bundle of rhubarb. She stops in the middle of the path, her face expressionless, watching me, waiting.

'I'm going with my cousin, to see my aunt. She's at the inn in the village.'

When she doesn't say anything, I go on, 'Grace won't tell me why her mother signed those papers. She wants me to speak to her myself.'

Her eyes never leave my face.

There's so much I want to say. That I've no idea what will happen now . . . that I feel afraid . . . that I wish – I wish she could come with me . . .

'Eliza, I've got to go, but I won't be long.'

Her head lifts a fraction. 'You'll come back, then?'

Her look is one of disbelief – that and something else, some hidden feeling.

'Yes, of course.' Whatever's going to happen, I want Eliza to know. I want to share it with her.

While I've been shut inside, the world has turned green, that fresh lovely green that comes at the very beginning of summer. All along the hedgerow, the may trees are clothed in a froth of white blossom.

For a moment my heart lifts, but then apprehension about what lies ahead closes in on me again. Grace and I are silent, as if, by unspoken agreement, everything is held in suspense until I have found out what Aunt Phyllis has to say.

We reach a turning in the lane and suddenly, up ahead, I see the familiar wall of the asylum. My stomach lurches. This is a trick! Grace is taking me back!

'Stop! Stop the carriage!'

Alarmed, Grace cries, 'Driver, will you stop, please.'

As soon as we come to a standstill, I scramble down.

'Lou, what it is? What's the matter?'

Trembling, feeling as though all the blood has drained from my face, I shout, 'I won't! I won't go back in there!'

The driver stares at me over his shoulder and I know what he's thinking. I must look and sound just like a lunatic. But I don't care. I fix my eyes on Grace, who looks hurt.

'Lou! How could you think I would do that to you? This is the way to the village. Please get back in.'

Mutinous, I stay where I am.

I can see Grace doesn't know what to do. Then she asks, 'Is there another way back, driver?'

He frowns. 'There is . . . but 'twill be a fair old ride round through the forest. Three mile more, I reckon.'

'It doesn't matter. Please take us that way.'

I stay where I am while he turns the carriage with difficulty in the narrow lane. Only then do I climb back in.

'Thank you,' I say to Grace.

Another carriage is drawn up outside the inn and as we enter we pass a couple going out. The woman stares at me before hurrying after her husband, but I ignore her, just as I ignore the whispers of the porters carrying out bags and boxes. I cross the lobby and follow Grace up the stairs to the first-floor front room, steeling myself for the encounter with Aunt Phyllis.

Grace opens the door, saying, 'Look who's here, Mamma.'

At our sudden entrance, my aunt drops her hairbrush with a clatter and turns pale.

Perhaps she's shocked at my appearance. I must look exactly like the mad niece she wants locked up.

I have an impression of beams, faded rose chintz, a smell of dust overlaid with beeswax polish, but my attention is fixed on my aunt.

For a moment no one says anything. There's a painful knot in my chest, but I am determined not to be the first to speak, not to show any weakness.

After a second, she seems to recover herself. 'Lou, so Grace found you!' She takes a step forward.

I don't say a word.

'Will you not speak to me?'

I keep watching her. She's smiling, but it's an anxious smile and her eyes are wary. In my head Eliza's voice says, *Folk do things for all sorts of reasons* . . . but she did sign the papers.

As if she can read my thought, Grace says quietly, 'Mamma, Louisa knows that you had her committed to Wildthorn Hall.'

'Oh!' My aunt sinks on to a low chair, one hand at her throat.

At the word 'committed' something breaks in my chest. 'Why? Why did you send me to that terrible place?'

For a moment she seems unable to speak and then she says in a low voice, 'Was it really so terrible?'

'Yes, it was. They . . .' I break off. I can't begin to tell her what it was like. But of course, she knows – she *chose* it. I'm almost crying now, a hot pain burning my chest. 'Why did you do it?'

She lets her hand drop. 'I meant it for the best.'

Her eyes slide towards Grace, who has sat down on the ottoman at the foot of the bed, and I catch my breath.

She *does* know! And that's why she had me locked up.

I glance at my cousin.

Her expression is grave, but there's no sign of guilt for betraying me. In fact, she pats the ottoman, inviting me to sit down, but I won't, not yet. Standing, I feel less trapped. I have the vague notion that, if necessary, I could run away and hide somewhere until I could get back to Smalcote.

307

I wait, watching my aunt, who speaks, at last. 'It was after your last visit to us . . .'

I knew it. I keep my face smooth, but something starts to flutter in my chest.

'Charles came to me and—'

'Charles!' Not Grace then, but Charles. But how would he have known unless Grace told him? My eyes flick towards her, but she is staring down at her lap.

'He said –' my aunt appears to be labouring under some distress – 'he said he believed you were suffering from moral insanity.'

'I thought he was a lawyer, not a doctor!' I look at Grace accusingly. 'You didn't tell me about this.'

Grace looks shamefaced. 'No, I'm sorry. I . . .' She breaks off, looking away. It strikes me for the first time that she looks different – as if somehow the light has gone from her. With a sigh, she says, 'Charles has a great interest in the subject and has read widely – especially some German papers, I think.'

Rather than defend him, she sounds almost apologetic.

'Of course, at first I thought it was nonsense,' says Aunt Phyllis. 'But when he explained more, I began to be persuaded.'

My mouth has gone dry but I manage to say, 'May I know what he said?'

Her hand flits nervously to her mouth. 'Oh, I don't think you want to hear all that, do you?'

'I think I have a right to know.'

She presses her mouth into a line. She's not going to tell

me. But then Grace says, 'I think you should tell her, Mamma.'

My aunt sighs. 'Very well. But Lou, please won't you sit down?'

Reluctantly I pull out the chair by the writing desk and perch on its hard seat. At least I'm still near the door.

Aunt Phyllis hesitates and then begins, 'You have to admit that you're not like most girls—'

'And that makes me insane?'

My aunt presses her hands together. I have the feeling that she's choosing her words carefully. 'Charles felt that your extraordinary desire to be a doctor was a clear indication of your condition.'

'Because it showed a want of proper feminine delicacy, I suppose!' I can feel myself beginning to tremble with anger.

'That was part of it, yes.'

'What else?'

'Lou, dear . . .' My aunt's expression is pleading, but I won't relent.

'Tell me!'

'Well . . . not wanting to be married – I never could understand that myself, Lou. And your determination . . . being set on a course that your brother was so against . . . your attitude to authority . . . Charles was shocked by your outburst at dinner. I must say I was too, Lou. Such a loss of control! But I was prepared to excuse you on the grounds that you were still grieving for your papa . . . But then the way you left us, without a word to anyone . . .'

Those so-called 'symptoms' in my admission papers,

that I thought originated with Tom . . . as much as she is trying to blame it on Charles, some of it was her! And still she hasn't admitted what I am sure lies at the bottom of it all.

I brace myself. 'Was there more?'

Grace shakes her head at me almost imperceptibly at the same moment as her mother says, 'No, that was all.'

I look down at my hands and find that I'm clenching them so tightly, my knuckles have turned white.

I uncurl my fingers, make myself breathe.

All this time I've carried this guilty secret. Now it seems, if my aunt is telling the truth, it wasn't my behaviour towards Grace that condemned me . . .

Knowing this doesn't make me feel any better. That I could have understood, but *this*?

I raise my eyes and look her in the face.

'Let me get this clear. Because I refuse to conform to the role expected of me, because I long to lead an independent life and be of service to others . . . that makes me mad? I know that many doctors, many people in the world would think so, but how could *you*?'

My aunt ducks her head. 'I – I didn't know what to think. But Charles was so sure. He said that, left untreated, your malady could only get worse. That there was a good chance that your behaviour would bring disgrace to the family. He thought you should be admitted to an institution where you would receive appropriate medical help . . .'

'And Tom? I suppose he fell in very readily with your plan?' I say bitterly.

'No, Lou, he didn't.'

310

I'm taken aback. I'd imagined Tom and my aunt concocting the scheme together.

'So the false name, that wasn't his idea?'

'No. It was Charles's idea. He persuaded Bertram that it would safeguard the family's reputation. At first Tom was unwilling to agree to it. He wanted you to be helped, but he didn't like not being open with you.'

'How did you change his mind?'

'Oh, Lou. What's to be gained from raking over all this?'

'Tell me.'

'Your uncle was giving Tom an allowance.'

It takes me about a second to work it out. 'I suppose the allowance would have stopped if Tom hadn't agreed?'

My aunt nods, shamefaced.

Lost for words, I stare at her. I can't believe it . . . that Tom had me shut up, for *money* . . . that they would have stooped so low . . .

Eventually I say quietly, 'I thought you loved me. Whatever Charles said, how could you do it?'

My aunt shifts uncomfortably.

'Tell her, Mamma.'

Something in Grace's tone causes a shiver to run down my back.

'Tell me what?'

My aunt looks as if she would rather be anywhere else but here.

'Charles said . . .' She stops and seems to gather herself for a moment. 'He said that, if we didn't commit you to an asylum, he would break off his engagement to Grace.'

The silence is absolute.

My aunt and my cousin are looking at me, but I can't move or speak. A hand is squeezing my heart.

It's Grace who speaks first. 'Lou, I'm sorry . . . so, so sorry.' She looks ashen-faced.

'You knew?'

'No.'

Aunt Phyllis, then, on her own, her decision.

I can hardly bear to look at her, but I make myself do it.

'You sacrificed me for Grace's sake.'

My aunt lifts her chin in the gesture I know so well, that I have seen Papa make, that I make myself when I am convinced I am right. 'Any mother would have done the same!'

A bitter thought flashes through my mind: *Not my mother, for me.* But I dismiss it. It's irrelevant. What matters now is my aunt, the cold anger I feel.

Perhaps she senses it. At any rate, she says in a softer tone, as if to explain herself, 'I did think you were ill. And I couldn't bear to see my darling unhappy.'

I can't sit still any longer.

As I stand up, my aunt starts in her chair as if she thinks I'm going to attack her.

I'm not. I never want to touch her again. But she has to see what she has done to me.

Pacing up and down, I fling out, 'You didn't care that *I* was wretched.'

'I didn't know.'

'You never came to see me to find out.' I spit the words at her.

She puts out her hands in a helpless gesture. 'We were told it was best not to. Mr Sneed said that visits from family upset the patients and interfered with their recovery.'

'And you believed him?' I swing round to face her. I'm aware of Grace watching me tensely.

'Why would I not? He seemed an experienced doctor – he came with the highest recommendations.'

'From whom?'

'An associate of Bertram. Mr Sneed is his brother-in-law.'

I might have known.

'I worried about you, of course I did. I sent money so you could go out for carriage rides or have nice treats, like fruit or flowers in your room.'

With a cry, I strike the mantelpiece. 'Aunt, none of that happened. Someone must have kept your money.'

'But—'

'That was the kind of place it was. Your respected Mr Sneed probably had no idea what was going on because he didn't trouble himself to find out. Just as you didn't.'

My aunt is on her feet now. 'But I didn't just take it all on trust. Before I made up my mind, I went to look at Wildthorn Hall and was shown round. It seemed a decent sort of place.'

'That's because they only show you what they want you to see. What galleries did you visit?'

'I don't know. It was a ward upstairs, very spacious, with a library and a pleasant sitting room. I spoke to some of the ladies there and they seemed quite content.'

A great wave of anguish floods over me. 'Aunt, that

was the First Gallery, the best ward, the only ward like it! You should have asked to see the cell where I was tied down on a filthy mattress for weeks and fed nothing but bread and water, or the ward where there was nothing to do but sit on my bed day after day and watch the other patients being hit or smearing the walls with their own excrement!'

I'm shaking now and can't stop crying.

There is a long silence.

When I finally raise my head, I see that Grace's face is wet, too. She murmurs, 'I had no idea . . . Oh, Lou, I'm so, so sorry . . .'

Then she says, 'Mamma?' in a quite different tone.

Aunt Phyllis bridles. 'I'm sorry too, of course. Especially as it was all for nothing . . .'

I wonder what she means, but before I can ask Grace leaps in, 'We're all upset. Perhaps we've said enough for now.' She looks at her mother meaningfully.

My aunt hesitates. 'Yes, of course, you're right.' She turns to me. 'Really, Lou, I never meant for you to suffer.'

I don't know whether I believe her. I don't know what I think or feel.

Sighing, she goes across to the looking-glass and makes some small adjustments to her hair. Then she turns and says, 'Lou, I'm forgetting myself. Will you take some refreshment?'

The perfect hostess! As if I'd just come for a nice visit!

'That's a good idea,' Grace says hurriedly. 'Why don't you go and ask for some tea, Mamma. And would you like something to eat, Lou?'

I shake my head. Eating is the last thing I want to do.

As soon as my aunt has gone, I collapse on to the low chair and shut my eyes.

There is still so much I don't know. For instance, was Mamma involved?

But right now, I don't care.

I want to go back to Smalcote. I want Eliza to help me think about what it all means and what I should do.

But Aunt Phyllis isn't just going to go away and leave me. She will have plans for me. And I feel so worn out, I don't know whether I have the strength to fight her.

After a while I open my eyes to find Grace watching me. We exchange rueful smiles.

'How are you now, Lou?'

'I'm not sure . . .' I pause. 'Charles hasn't managed to persuade *you* that I'm mad. Do you think he really believes it himself?'

She looks thoughtful. 'I don't know. I think he does, or at least he's convinced himself that he does. He quoted all sorts of learned references . . . But, since I've found out about it all, I've wondered whether he overheard what you said in the conservatory that night at Carr Head.'

'Mmm, I wondered that, too.'

'When I wanted you to come and live with us, he wouldn't hear of it. He said he wanted me all to himself, but of course, now, I wonder . . . What if he was afraid you'd influence me, somehow turn me against him, and that's at the bottom of it? I don't know.'

Sighing, she looks down at her lap. 'It was our first quarrel.'

Guiltily I realize I haven't thought about what all this means for her. She seems to be on my side . . . How does she feel about Charles now? What has he said about her coming to rescue me?

She raises her head and says quietly, 'I should have listened to you.'

I've never heard her sound so – so old, so world-weary. 'Grace—'

But at that moment the door opens and Aunt Phyllis appears with a serving-maid carrying a tray. After the girl has gone, my aunt busies herself, pouring and stirring, offering me a biscuit, which I refuse.

A strained silence follows, during which we occupy ourselves with our tea. Eventually, with a feigned bright look, Aunt Phyllis says, 'Lou, you'll be happy to set off early tomorrow morning?'

I put down my cup. This is it. Probably she's planning to take me to some other institution where she'll make sure I'm well treated . . .

At the thought of it, a kind of horror rises in my throat, but I try to keep my voice steady. 'I'm not going anywhere with you.'

She flinches as if I've hit her. 'But—'

'I won't go to another asylum. I won't be shut up again.'

'But I'm not taking you to another asylum! We're going home.'

'Home?'

'Yes. To Carr Head.'

'No!' I don't trust her.

My aunt sighs, and my cousin gives me a pleading look, but I won't give in, not even for Grace.

There's an awkward silence.

Finally I say, 'When did you decide I wasn't mad?'

Aunt Phyllis sighs. 'When Grace saw your photograph, she spoke so fiercely on your behalf . . .'

317

Grace nods. 'I pointed out to Mamma that what you wanted was quite natural. You were following in Uncle Edward's footsteps and he'd encouraged you . . .'

'Dear Edward . . .' My aunt shakes her head. 'You're so like him, Lou. He never would do what anyone thought he should.'

For a moment I almost soften, but then she says, 'But bringing you up in an unconventional way was perhaps not altogether to your benefit.'

I bridle immediately. How dare she criticize Papa? And what would he say if he knew what she'd done? 'I'd be quite happy, if only other people would let me do as I want!'

'But, my dear—'

Grace intervenes. 'Remember, Mamma, I told you lots of girls nowadays are looking for a new sort of life. In London I've come across several independent young women, making their own way in the world . . .'

I'm sure Charles doesn't like *that*. But I hold my tongue.

'Yes, you did.' My aunt frowns, as if the idea is distasteful to her too. 'Anyway, Lou, you see, Grace wants – we *both* want – you to stay with us. You will come, won't you? A little holiday at Carr Head first and then your mother will be glad to see you.'

Mamma . . .

'Does Mamma know where I've been?'

My aunt is clearly startled by this abrupt question. 'No . . . no, she doesn't.'

'Why not?'

She reddens. 'Tom and I thought it best not to worry her. She thinks you're still at the Woodvilles'.'

I stare at her, astonished, thinking rapidly. I'm glad about Mamma, but . . . 'Surely, after a while, she would have wondered why she hadn't heard from me – why I wasn't visiting her? What were you going to say then?'

Her flush deepens and she looks down at her lap.

There's a long silence.

My mouth has gone dry. What could she say? Apart from telling the truth. Surely she wouldn't have told Mamma I was *dead*, would she?

Grace is the first to break the silence. 'Let's be thankful it hasn't come to that. Let's not think about it any more.'

But I can't shake it off so easily. 'You lied to Mamma, and would have gone on telling lies.'

My aunt shifts uneasily in her chair. 'Remember, I did think you were ill and needed help . . . I should have told your mamma, of course. She had every right to know. But . . .' She gives me a pleading look. 'Amelia has never really liked me and since Edward died . . . I thought that if I came to her and said that you needed treatment, she would have resented my interference. It seemed best to involve Tom, rather than try to persuade her.'

Grace slips from her seat and kneeling beside me, she takes my hand. 'Lou, dear, I'm sorry. All this must be very painful for you. Why don't we stop talking about it for now? If you come home with us, we can say more then, if you wish.'

My aunt stands up. 'Yes, that's a good idea. Don't you think so?'

I look from one to the other. I have only one clear thought in my mind.

'I want to go back to Eliza now, please.'

Feeling numb, I gaze at the trees sliding past.

My locket – with Papa's hair in it – is hanging safely round my neck, but my mourning ring's too big now. It's strange to be wearing my black silk frock. That, too, is looser on me, but that's not the reason it feels unfamiliar. It's as if the frock belongs to another girl, a girl who isn't me any more.

But who am I now? I don't know.

I can feel Aunt Phyllis watching me. I can't shake off the feeling that my rescue is all my cousin's doing, that really my aunt's opposed to it.

I wish Grace had come with us – I'd feel safer – but she said she needed to rest.

'Is Grace quite well, Aunt?'

'Yes.' She looks puzzled. 'Why do you ask?'

'She seems – different – and needing to rest . . .'

Her face clears and, with a glance at the driver, she lowers her voice. 'She's expecting a child.'

'Oh!' I have to struggle a moment to frame an appropriate response. 'That's . . . lovely. You must all be delighted.'

My aunt doesn't look very delighted. 'Yes, of course, but in the circumstances . . .'

'What circumstances?'

'Grace didn't say?'

She whispers that Grace has separated from Charles 'temporarily' and is living at Carr Head.

'Because of me?'

She sighs. 'All this has obviously had a great effect on her feelings for Charles, but sadly, even before this, things were not . . . not as they should be.'

Nodding at the driver's back, Aunt Phyllis conveys that she doesn't want to discuss this now and we lapse into silence.

This news sets my thoughts whirling. I was right, then. It has not been the happy marriage Grace anticipated. Surely she must be better off without that awful man. But it must be so difficult for her. Poor Grace. And with a child to think about now . . .

A thought occurs to me. If Grace's marriage were still perfectly happy, would Aunt Phyllis have released me from Wildthorn?

I give her a hard look, wondering.

Perhaps she senses my gaze. 'What is it, Lou?'

'Nothing.'

Mrs Shaw must have seen us arrive because she's waiting in the doorway, Lily and Arthur clinging to her skirts and staring at my aunt.

For a moment there's an awkward silence. Then Aunt Phyllis looks at me and I remember how these things are done.

'Mrs Shaw, this is my aunt, Mrs Illingworth.'

Eliza's mother gives a kind of half-curtsy, her face red

and flustered. 'You're welcome, Ma'am, I'm sure. Won't you come in and have some tea?'

Inviting us to sit down, Mrs Shaw bustles about, setting out her best blue and white china. More tea . . . but clearly Mrs Shaw would be hurt if we refused.

Aunt Phyllis draws Lily into conversation and the little girl soon forgets her shyness. From his stool in the furthest corner of the room, Arthur fixes the visitor with a solemn gaze.

'Where's Eliza?' I ask.

'She's feeding the pig.' Mrs Shaw looks up from the range. 'Shall Lily fetch her for you?'

'No, I'll go myself.'

She's down by the ramshackle pigsty. Hearing my step on the path, she looks up.

At the sight of her, something slides in my chest.

With her hair awry, a smudge on her cheek, clutching the old pail in one hand, she looks simply . . . herself. And I am so glad to see her.

Setting the pail down, she raises her eyes to me, her face a troubled question mark.

Quickly I tell her the gist of what I've learned. '. . . And now my aunt is waiting in your house, and she wants me to go back with her.'

Glancing at the cottage, Eliza touches my elbow and signals that we should walk down to the end of the garden. Here, hidden from view by the pigsty, we stand, side by side, gazing over a field of barley. It's still green, but the ears are showing.

I turn over in my mind what my options are. Really, it seems as if I've no choice . . .

'I think I will go back, you know.'

'Yes.' Eliza's tone is hollow. She starts to pick at a piece of tar on the fence post. 'Soon as I saw her – your cousin – I knew you would.'

'No, not to Carr Head with them! I couldn't bear to stay with Aunt Phyllis. I'd better go home. I want to see Mamma and Mary . . .' I pull a face. 'I don't want to see Tom. I never want to see him again.'

There's a silence then. Eliza goes on picking at the tar, while I contemplate the future that's unexpectedly presented itself to me.

Eventually, with a sigh, I say, 'You know, Eliza, I'm not sure I can go back to my old life, looking after the house and Mamma. I think I'd feel even more trapped than I did before. It would be almost as bad as being shut up in Wildthorn!'

Eliza looks sideways at me and I correct myself. 'No, it wouldn't be as bad as that, of course. But it would be bad enough.'

We stare out at the barley.

I know I have to go, but I don't want to, not yet.

Eliza says, 'Maybe there's a way you could be a doctor, like you want.'

I look at her, considering. 'I don't know. I've been wrong about so many things . . . what if I'm wrong about that, too?'

'You'd be good! Better than Sneed and Bull and that lot. You'd help people.'

'You think so?'

'Yes, I do.'

I smile at her briefly. 'But I can't see how it's possible. Mamma won't agree to it and even if I defy her, it's expensive to train. I can't ask Aunt Phyllis for the money now . . .'

At the thought of it, of what she did, I feel overcome again. 'I've never hated anyone before, but I hate her, you know, Eliza.'

'I'm not surprised.'

'Anyway, never mind her, what about you? What are you going to do?'

She becomes intent on the piece of tar again. 'Oh, I'll try to get something, I suppose.' Her voice is flat, colourless.

'But you haven't got a reference, have you?'

She shrugs. 'It don't matter. Not everyone's that particular about references.'

Something's wrong. I can tell from her voice, from the way she won't look at me.

'Eliza? What is it?'

'Nothing.'

'Tell me.'

She turns her head then and her look sears me.

'D'you think any of that matters to me now? You – you're the only thing I care about. I know you can't stay here, you've got to go. But I'm afraid you'll not think of me. I'm afraid you'll go back to your old life and forget me and I'll never see you again.' Her face crumples and she starts to sob.

I'm stunned. I've never seen her cry before.

I put my arms round her. 'Eliza, don't . . . don't . . .'

As she leans against me, crying, letting me hold her, I close my eyes, breathing in her warmth, her familiar almond scent, and my thoughts fly like birds.

Eliza cares for me, very much . . . I never thought, never expected, that anyone would . . . and I . . . with a rushing sense of wonder, I discover . . . I care for her very much too, and this, standing here together, holding her close, this feels . . . *right*.

After a moment she lifts her face and it's as if I'm seeing it for the first time – her fair eyelashes, the cluster of freckles over her nose, her mouth . . .

Without my quite knowing how it's happened, we're kissing. Her lips are dry and warm and I feel shy at first, tentative . . . and then I can't help myself . . . I melt into her soft, moist mouth, taste honey. My bones are turning to liquid, I feel breathless, dizzy with longing . . . and, floating into my head, with absolute certainty, comes the knowledge – this, this is who I am, this is what I want.

After what seems hours, but can really only be a minute or two, Eliza pulls away.

Her face is flushed, her breathing as rapid as mine, but her eyes are wide, anxious, and she says, 'I'm sorry, I shouldn't 'a done that.'

'Why not?'

'Because . . . your cousin . . .'

'Grace?'

'Yes. You said her marriage might be over and—'

I seize her hand, as if I'm drowning and she is the only

person who can save me. 'Eliza, listen, what I felt for Grace, it was . . . it was like a dream . . .'

As I say it I know it's true. My feelings for Grace – I realize now they weren't about Grace herself, but about an image of her I had in my head . . . When I think about it, really I don't know her all that well. I've never felt I could share my innermost thoughts and feelings with her, not as I can with Eliza. And as for those feelings I had for her . . . they've gone. It's as if, while I was in Wildthorn, they just leaked away . . .

'It's over now. But this –'I shake her hand fiercely – 'this is real.' I kiss her hand, press it against my cheek. 'I don't want to leave you, ever.'

Her eyes fill with tears again. 'I never thought . . .' She stops, swallows. 'I never thought you'd care for me as I care for you. I thought, if it weren't your cousin, you'd find someone else, someone like you . . .'

'Liza!' Lily's shrill voice is suddenly close and we hastily break apart.

The little girl comes skipping round the pigsty, announcing in a high sing-song voice, 'Mother-says-your-tea's-stone-cold-and-that-lady-wants-to-go.'

She comes to a halt and eyes us curiously.

'Tell them we're coming now.' As Lily still lingers, Eliza gives her a little push. 'Go on.'

As soon as we're alone, I say urgently, 'What shall I do? I'll have to go, won't I?'

She nods, looking as wretched as I feel.

I'm thinking rapidly, desperately . . . hopelessly. 'I

327

don't know what will happen. I don't know what we can do, but I'll come back, and we'll think of something.'

She stares at me, mute, and the look in her eyes makes me feel as if my heart is being torn from my chest.

'I'll think of you. Every minute of every day. And I'll come back, I promise.'

Then I turn my back on her and walk up the path to the cottage, and it's the hardest thing I've ever done.

'Miss Louisa!' Mary positively beams as she opens the door to me.

Her cry brings Mamma into the hall. At the sight of her tremulous smile, I feel happy and sad all at the same time. After a moment's hesitation, she hugs me and I hug her back. I'm overwhelmed. I can't remember her ever showing me such affection.

I sent a telegram to warn them of my arrival, but of course Mamma thinks I've come from the Woodvilles'. She asks anxiously, 'Is anything wrong that you've come away so suddenly?'

'No, Mamma, not at all.' I don't want to blurt everything out at once. I want to find out how she is, first.

In the parlour, I'm introduced to her companion, Mrs Grey, a pleasant-faced woman – a widow, I guess, as she's wearing the slate-grey silk of half-mourning. Tactfully she withdraws after a while, leaving us alone.

I try to fend Mamma off but it's no good. She asks so many questions, in the end I have to tell her where I've been for the last eight months, trying to keep my account brief and sparing her the worst details. When it comes to Eliza, I just refer to her 'kindness' and hope my face isn't giving too much away.

I can't avoid telling Mamma that Aunt Phyllis was responsible. Mamma's shocked, of course, but not as much as I was. As if it just confirms the low opinion she has of her sister-in-law . . .

The worst thing is telling her about Tom.

She turns pale and stares at me. 'Are you sure? Tom did that?'

I feel very sorry for her. It must be so hard for her to accept the truth about her 'darling boy'.

When I tell her about Uncle Bertram's allowance, she just shakes her head.

'You don't seem very surprised, Mamma.'

'Oh, my dear, your brother and money . . .' She sighs. 'Ever since he went away to London . . . he doesn't often write, as you know, but he always asks for more. I don't know what he does with it all.'

I know, but of course I don't tell her.

'It's not as if we didn't give him a generous allowance, and then of course, when Edward died . . .' She trails off.

'Yes?' I prompt her.

'Why, he left Tom all that money.'

A stab of jealousy takes my breath away. Papa left Tom money? I'm desperate to know more about this. How much money? Why didn't Tom tell me? But Mamma is obviously lost in her thoughts. It doesn't seem the best moment to press her.

She sighs again. 'But to think that he would do that to you. And all that business with the Woodvilles. What an elaborate pretence. I wrote to you there, you know.'

'Tom must have made some arrangement with them. Didn't you wonder when you didn't receive a reply?'

'I was saddened, but I thought . . . we parted on such bad terms . . .'

Remembering how I refused to speak to her, I feel ashamed. 'I'm sorry for that, Mamma, but what you said hurt me.'

'What I said?'

I frown. 'Yes, you complained to Tom that I'd been neglecting you. I thought it was – unfair.'

Putting her hand to her forehead, she says, 'My dear, I never said that. I was grateful to you for looking after me so well when I was afraid I was a burden to you.'

I stare at her. Another of Tom's lies! How could he let me misjudge Mamma and think so badly of her? And all along she was grateful . . .

Looking at her worn face, I'm moved to a new, unexpected tenderness. Perhaps I've always misjudged her. Perhaps she knows how hard it can be if you're not as others expect you to be. Maybe what I took as criticism was her doing her best for me . . .

She regards me sadly. 'I wasn't surprised when Tom said you were weary of it and wanted to go away.'

I feel even more ashamed. That, at least, was true. But when I was desperate, I turned to her. I want her to know that.

'I did write to you from Wildthorn Hall. I wanted you to come and rescue me. I wanted to come home.'

'Did you?' A fleeting smile lights up her face, but then the shadow returns. 'I never received your letter.'

'Tom must have intercepted it.'

'No doubt.' She lapses into silence, looking drawn, and

right now I can't think of anything to distract her from her sorrowful thoughts.

After the Shaws' cottage, our house seems stuffy, too full of *things*. I've tried to take up my old activities again, but I can't seem to get interested in them. I prefer to go out, finding it incredible still that I'm free to open the door and leave, that no one tries to stop me. I take long walks, thinking of Eliza and wondering what she's doing. When I'm in, I wander round the house or spend hours gazing out of the window, and all the time there's a pain round my heart that won't go away.

I keep having nightmares, one in particular. I'm back in the Fifth, unable to move or cry out, knowing that I'll never see Eliza again . . . and I wake, trembling, with Scratton's laughter ringing in my ears.

At least Mamma seems better than she used to, less anxious, though not a day goes by without her saying, 'I still can't believe it of Tom.'

As we go about our chores or sit in the parlour together with Mrs Grey, I often catch her gazing at me. Once or twice, completely unexpectedly, she's put her hand to my face in a loving gesture. Perhaps in my absence she's come to miss me. Whatever the reason, I'm touched by her affection, and I think how glad Papa would be to know that we are closer.

But gratifying as this is, as the days slip by I keep wondering what will happen now.

Will Mrs Grey go, now I'm back? Will I just take up my life again and not see Eliza?

The thought is unbearable.

My mood is not helped by a le been home a while.

It's from Grace, from an address initial pleasantries she writes:

After much, much thought, I have Charles, as you see from the address. *is possible, we live separate lives, but in the es of the world, we are together as man and wife. I know you have every reason to feel hostility towards Charles, but I hope you will understand that I felt I had to do this for the sake of my unborn child.*

Overcome, I stop reading. My first reaction is protest – she mustn't do this, she mustn't bind herself to a loveless marriage – but then, as I think about it, I can see that it is just what she would do – put her child first, before her own happiness . . . Oh, Grace . . . I feel so sorry for her . . .

I resume reading.

I am resolved not to communicate with Mamma, now or in the future. You may imagine that I did not come to this decision without much heart-searching. But when I saw you and heard the truth about Wildthorn Hall, when I realized what Mamma had done to you – it was so wrong of her and, even though she did it for my sake, it changed the way I feel about her. I can't find it in my heart to forgive her.

333

down, shocked. I didn't expect this. It

unt Phyllis's heart to be estranged from Grace.

good, she deserves to suffer . . . but it will break

Grace's heart too . . . poor, poor Grace! *She* doesn't deserve all this . . .

I go about my tasks in sombre mood. When I was locked up in Wildthorn, I thought if only I could escape, I would be happy. How wrong I was.

One morning, bracing myself, I go into Papa's study.

It's just the same! His chair by the hearth, his desk with the silver ink stand, his tobacco jar, everything as it was, as if he's just gone out on some calls and will be back soon.

I sit down at the desk, briefly touching the head of one of the owls on Papa's pipe-rack. 'What shall I do?' I ask it. It stares back, mute.

Leaning my elbows on the blotter, I rest my head in my hands. If only Papa were here now, if only I could talk to him.

The pain of missing him, of missing Eliza, shifts up into my throat and tears slide down my face.

Some time later, the door opens and Mamma looks in.

I turn my face away, brushing it with my hand so she won't see I've been crying.

She hesitates in the doorway and then comes in.

More in control of myself now, I wave at the room. 'You haven't changed it.'

'No, I couldn't, I . . .' She falls silent.

I can't say any more either, but I hope she can see that I understand.

With a little gesture as if she's dispelling the memories, she says, 'How are you, Louisa?'

Her eyes are full of concern, and I think: I haven't got Papa's support any more, but Mamma is here, and perhaps, now that we seem to be getting on better, I could talk to her . . .

'Mamma . . .' I pause, not knowing how to put it, then I decide to tell the truth. 'I'm not very happy.'

She puts her hand on my arm. 'I thought not. Is it Tom?'

'He *has* caused me great pain, and Aunt Phyllis . . .'

At the mention of that name, Mamma's face tightens.

I go on hastily, 'But what's making me most unhappy now is what I shall do with my life.'

And Eliza, my heart cries, but of course I don't say it.

'The thing is, Mamma . . .' I swallow. 'I don't think it's enough for me to stay here at home with you.'

Immediately I wish I hadn't said it. I feel terrible. 'Oh, Mamma, I'm sorry.'

She doesn't say anything, but goes to sit in Papa's armchair and the longer she's silent, the worse I feel. 'Mamma, I—'

'Louisa, there's something I have to tell you.' Mamma's eyes are dark, intent. 'I know that you want to be a doctor.'

I gape at her. 'You know?'

'Yes. Your father told me, before he died.' She looks down at the arm of the chair and strokes it gently once or twice.

'You never said!'

335

'I've thought about it often, and I'm sorry now that I didn't.' She looks up. 'I wanted to honour Edward's wish, of course I did, but I thought, if I waited . . . I hoped you'd change your mind.'

I don't really need to ask her why, I can guess. All the old reasons why women can't be doctors . . .

'When I thought I would never get married . . .' She hesitates. 'I don't want you to suffer as I did. I had such joy in my relationship with your father. I want you to have the same.'

I'm touched. This isn't what I expected her to say. For a moment I'm tempted to tell her, *Mamma, I think I've found the possibility of this joy*, but I stop myself. To announce that I've fallen in love with another girl . . . I can just imagine her face.

'Mamma, I could have such a relationship and a fulfilling career. Other women do.'

She nods in acknowledgement of this, but I can see she's not easy with the idea. 'But for a woman, the greatest satisfaction she can have in life is to devote herself to her husband and children.'

There's nothing I can say to this. Mamma and I will never see eye to eye on this subject.

She gazes at me seriously. 'So you haven't changed your mind? About being a doctor?'

I look at the worn couch where Papa used to examine his patients, at his Gladstone bag still sitting by the desk. If I were to open it, I'm sure I should find it packed ready with medicines and pills. The shelves are barer since Tom raided them, but he's left behind Papa's endoscope and head mirror, a box of syringes . . .

All at once I remember it – the acute excitement I used to experience when I set off with Papa on his rounds, my satisfaction when 'we' – really Papa – helped patients and I could see that they felt better . . .

I know what my answer is.

'No, Mamma, I haven't changed my mind.'

She nods again as if this doesn't surprise her. 'In that case, that's what you'd better do.'

My mouth falls open. I manage to splutter, 'What do you mean?'

'I mean that you'd better do what your father wanted and set about your medical training.' Mamma smiles and I guess my stupefied expression must look comical.

'But . . . how?'

'By applying to the London School of Medicine for Women. Isn't that where you want to go?'

I stare at her. She means it. She really means it. 'But how can I pay for it? It's expensive, Mamma.'

'Your father left money to both of you, for when you are twenty-one.'

I can hardly believe my ears. 'Papa left us money? Why didn't you tell us?'

Mamma looks down at the chair arm again. 'I was afraid it would have a bad effect on you both, that it might encourage you to be idle . . .'

I see. It's just like Mamma not to want to spoil us and just like Papa to indulge us . . . 'But Tom has had his?'

'Yes, and I'm afraid it hasn't been good for him.'

I don't care about Tom. If he wants to waste Papa's gift, that's up to him. For me, it opens up a world of possibility . . .

Mamma is watching me. 'So what do you think?'

'It's a long time until I'm twenty-one.'

She nods her head unhappily. 'I thought that's what you'd say.' She sighs then says with a half-smile, 'If you're really sure that this is what you want, I think I can support you until then.'

'Mamma!' I leap across the room and hug her.

In a tone of mock-severity, she says, 'You'll have to pay me back, mind.'

'Of course!' And I hug her again. Then, too excited to sit still, I walk about the room, thinking aloud. 'I wonder if it's too late to apply for this autumn. If not, I shall have to work hard to be ready for the preliminary exams. I've forgotten all I knew! Mamma, do you think I could do it?'

'It is soon. Could you not wait?'

'I'd rather not! It might take me a long time to qualify. The sooner I can start the better!'

Mamma shakes her head. 'I wish you didn't have to go so far. You're very young to be living in London.'

'After what I've been through, Mamma, I think I'll cope.'

Her face darkens and I wish I hadn't reminded her. 'You will keep in touch, won't you? And come home sometimes?'

'Of course I will, Mamma.' Perching on the footstool, I take her hand. 'Are you worried about Tom?'

She nods. 'He hasn't been home for such a long time.

338

And he hasn't answered my letters.' Her eyes fill with tears.

Tom! All my anger with him flares up again. How can he do this to Mamma! I expect he's enjoying himself too much to think of her. He's so selfish . . .

As I think this, it comes to me that I want to see him. For Mamma's sake, yes, but I also need to see him on my own account. He must understand what he did to me – his sister – and all for *money* . . .

'Listen, Mamma, if I write to the School of Medicine and they want to see me, I could visit Tom . . .'

Mamma looks uncertain. 'Would you? Could you bring yourself to see him?'

I have a sudden joyful realization. While I'm in the south I can go and see Eliza! I can tell her my news and who knows, maybe . . . maybe . . .

'Oh, yes, Mamma, I could.'

O n my way to Tom's lodgings, I can't help thinking about the last time I was here.

I was nervous then, worrying about what Tom would say, and now I don't care. In fact I'm looking forward to seeing his face when I tell him that this morning I was accepted into the School of Medicine! He won't like it, but what does that matter? He's forfeited the right to have any say in what I do with my life and I don't need his approval now.

I just hope I can keep calm.

When I think about what he did – letting me suffer all that, just so he could go on gambling – I want to hurt him as badly as he hurt me.

Arriving at the door, I see more of the brown paint has flaked off, but otherwise it looks just the same. I press the bell.

'Yis?' It's the same scrawny girl in the grubby mob-cap.

'I'm here to see Mr Cosgrove.'

She narrows her eyes suspiciously.

'I'm his sister.'

'Oh, yis? You'd better come in.'

As I follow her up the staircase, stepping carefully to avoid a broken tread, I brace myself for what I might find.

I notice the smell first. I could be back at Wildthorn – that unmistakable smell of unwashed bodies in an airless room. There's another smell that's also familiar, but I can't identify it.

It's hard to make anything out, the window is so caked with grime. When my eyes adjust to the dimness, I find I'm in a cramped room whose walls and sloping ceiling are black with soot and dirt. There's little furniture: a rickety table and a wooden chair; a small cupboard, where candle stubs sit in a pool of hardened wax. Near the window is what I take to be a heap of rags, but then it shifts and sighs.

As I kneel by the makeshift bed, a quiver of shock runs through me.

Tom's eyes are shut, he's breathing heavily. His face is thinner than when I last saw him – almost gaunt. He's unshaven and his skin has an unhealthy yellow tinge. That smell I couldn't place is stronger here, and I now know what it is – opium.

Choking back a cry, I force myself to remain calm.

Oblivious to his squalid surroundings and the wretched state he's in, Tom smiles, as if he's having a wonderful dream.

I sit back on my heels and watch my brother sleeping, a sick feeling in my throat. How could he have let himself sink so low?

After a while his eyelids flicker and open.

His gaze focuses on me, and at once he starts up from the bed, a look of horror on his face, and cries, 'Don't come near me! Stay away!'

Shivering, he presses himself against the wall, hiding his face in his arms.

Alarmed, I say, tentatively, 'Tom?'

341

Keeping his face buried, he exclaims, 'I didn't mean to do it! Don't hurt me!'

I lay my hand on his shoulder. 'Tom, it's me . . . Lou.'

As if my touch has woken him properly, he lifts his head, blinking, and a look of astonishment fills his face. 'Lou, is it really you? Here?'

'Yes.'

'But I thought . . .' He shakes his head, as if he's trying to clear it. 'Just now I thought . . . I thought you were a ghost, come to get revenge.' He shudders.

'No, Tom, I'm not a ghost,' I say drily.

His face creases with perplexity. 'But I don't understand. How is it that you're here and not in the asylum?'

'No thanks to you!' As if the word 'asylum' has triggered it, the anger I have buried rises into my throat, its bitter taste threatening to choke me. 'Tom, how could you do it? Let me be sent to that dreadful place? You read my letter to Mamma, you knew what it was like . . . How could you be so wicked?'

Struggling for control, I glare at him. Then I add quietly, 'And just for a measly allowance . . . I know about it, Tom. Aunt Phyllis told me.'

He hangs his head, says nothing.

'Tom?'

I can hardly hear him. 'It wasn't just for the allowance. I wouldn't do that to you, Lou.'

'What then?'

'I thought – I thought, if you were certified mad, I'd get your inheritance!'

His face crumples and he cries out, 'Oh, Lou, I'm sorry.

I shouldn't have done it, I know I shouldn't. It was a terrible thing to do to you. But I was desperate.'

He collapses into sobs, his shoulders heaving.

I'm stunned. The inheritance. Of course. That makes more sense. Opium is expensive. And I wonder if he's still gambling. All that money he had from Grandfather and Papa, just thrown away . . .

I look at him, my brother.

He's always patronized me. At times in my life, he's infuriated me. And he's just admitted to the cruellest thing a brother could do to his sister.

This is the moment to say, *Yes, it was a terrible thing and I'll never forgive you and I'm glad you're suffering!*

When we were children, I wouldn't have hesitated. But I do now. I'm trying to hold on to my anger, but I can feel it slipping away, and something else taking its place, something that feels like pity. I wanted him to be punished for what he did to me, but nothing I could imagine was as bad as this.

Would it make me feel better to hurt him further?

An image of Papa comes into my head. Not saying anything. Just watching. Waiting for my reaction . . .

And I say, 'Never mind that now. I'm here, as you see, safe and sound.' He raises his wet face.

'Mamma's really worried about you, did you know?'

He groans, pushing his hands through his hair so it sticks up even more. 'I know, I know. I should have written, but . . .'

'I'm surprised you didn't. Since you could obviously do with some more money.' I can't resist that gibe.

At least he has the grace to look ashamed.

What am I going to do? I can't possibly take him home in this state, even if he'd come. It would break Mamma's heart. I will have to think of something.

'Listen, Tom. I'm going now, but I'll look in again in the morning. If I send out for some food, will you try to eat?'

He looks at me despairingly. 'I haven't any money.'

'I have some.' Safe in my waistband again, thanks to Mamma.

His face brightens. 'Can you lend me some?'

'No.'

He looks crestfallen.

'Tom, you know it's no good. If I give you money, you'll only waste it.'

He looks at me imploringly, but I harden my heart. 'I'll see you tomorrow.'

On the way out I speak to the maid, giving her money to fetch some food of a light, nourishing kind. I don't know whether I can trust her, but there's no alternative. I tell her I'll be back in the morning, so she knows I'll be checking up on her. I'll call in on my way to the station, to see how Tom is. But he'll have to manage on his own for one more day.

Nothing is going to stop me seeing Eliza and telling her my plan.

Lily and Arthur are in the lane watching for the carriage. As I walk down the path they run ahead, calling out excitedly, and Mrs Shaw comes out to meet me, drying her hands on her apron, Eliza following behind.

At the sight of her, my heart turns over. Her face has more of a tan than when I last saw her – it makes her eyes look bluer than ever, and in the sunshine, they seem to dance. It's hard to drag my eyes away and attend to Mrs Shaw, and Lily, who tugs at my sleeve, chattering on. Arthur, suddenly shy, puts his finger in his mouth and tries to hide behind his big sister.

I'm touched by Mrs Shaw welcoming me in and fussing over me, as if I'm part of the family, insisting I have a cup of tea and hear all the news. But as the minutes tick by, I fidget more and more. I asked the coachman to return at five. What if I don't get a chance to speak to Eliza alone?

Just when I'm thinking I can bear it no longer, Eliza says, 'Mother!' and looks pointedly at the clock.

'Bless you.' Mrs Shaw pats my arm. 'Here am I letting my tongue run away with me. As it's such a fine day, Eliza thought you might like to take a walk. Is that right?'

I leap up at once. 'Oh, yes. That would be lovely.'

'I want to come,' Lily pipes up.

'Me too! Me too!' shouts Arthur, jumping up and down.

Eliza exchanges a look with her mother and Mrs Shaw

says, 'You can go another time. I need you to help me pick the gooseberries.'

As soon as we're out in the lane, we turn to one another and grin. But I'm surprised at how nervous I am. I've spent so many hours dreaming about this, imagining rushing into Eliza's arms, but now I feel shy. I can't help wondering whether Eliza really cares for me as I care for her. Now she's had time to think about it, does she still feel the same?

We walk along, a decorous distance apart, giving each other sideways glances, as if each is waiting for the other to speak.

In the end I ask what she's been doing.

'I've been helping with the hay-making.'

'So you've not found yourself a new position yet?'

'No.'

'Oh.' This is what I'd hoped to hear, but I can't talk about that until I've told her my news and it seems difficult to start.

We walk in silence again. This is silly. We've so little time.

Eliza indicates a path into the forest and we turn on to it. The shade is a relief after the hot lane and the fallen beech leaves are soft underfoot. Soon, the path opens out into a sun-dappled glade. Eliza stops, her finger to her lips. 'Can you hear it?'

I listen . . . and then I hear it – a clear *tap tap* somewhere over to our left.

'A woodpecker!'

'Yes, only we call it a woodsprite.'

'That's nice.'

We smile at one another and I have to go on looking into her eyes and she's looking into mine and there it is again, that spark leaping between us . . .

'Eliza, I—'

But before I can say any more, her arms are round me and mine are round her, our noses bumping as our mouths come together, and I feel light-headed and shivery with joy because it's all right, it's still all right.

Breathless, we finally break apart, but we can't stop looking at one another.

'I thought you might not . . .' Eliza trails off.

'So did I.'

We both start laughing. Then she puts out her hand and I take it and we walk on, disturbing blue butterflies and small copper ones who settle further ahead then flutter up again as we approach.

Now I feel I can tell her all about going to medical school. '. . . But I don't know if I'll be ready for the exam – it's only five weeks off and I've forgotten everything!'

'You'll do it.'

She's pleased for me, I think, but I sense something in her, some shadow, though all she says is, 'What about your brother? He won't be pleased.'

'Oh, Eliza!' In the excitement of seeing her, I'd forgotten about Tom. I tell her what's happened.

'He sounds in a bad way.'

'He is and I don't know what to do. After what he did

to me, I thought I'd be glad to see him suffer, but, oh, Eliza, I don't want him to die!'

She squeezes my hand.

'I spent the whole train journey thinking about it – no, that's not true actually – I spent most of it thinking of you, but I did think about him a bit and I had one idea, but I'm not sure . . .'

I stop and face her. 'I feel it's partly Uncle Bertram's fault, and Aunt Phyllis's . . . for involving Tom . . . for giving him the means to harm himself . . . So I thought, what if I write to them and tell them what's happened? Perhaps they could persuade Tom to go and stay at Carr Head and perhaps there, under medical supervision, he could recover. What do you think?'

Eliza puts her head on one side, considering. 'Your mother wouldn't like that, would she? 'Specially after what they did to you.'

'No, she wouldn't, that's true. But that's another thing – I don't know what to tell her. If I say he's not well, she'll want to rush down to London . . . and she mustn't see him like that.'

'Do you want to know what I think?'

'Of course.'

'I think you should tell your mother the truth.'

'I couldn't! She'd never get over it.'

'But you said yourself she was better now. And look at how she's coped with finding out about you.'

'It's not the same, though. This is her beloved Tom, remember!'

'That's the point. Think how she'd feel if she found out

about him later . . . when it might be too late. I think you should tell her. And then it's for her to decide what's to be done.'

I stare at her, turning it over in my mind. Finally I say, 'I think you're right. I'll write to her tonight and, until I hear from her, I'll stay in London so I can keep an eye on Tom.' I feel relieved at having come to a decision.

We resume our walk, arriving before long at a pond, where white water lilies float amongst the flat green pads.

'I used to call them cups and saucers, when I were little,' Eliza observes, stopping to look at them. I notice how the sun has brought out the freckles on her nose even more, how her hair has glints in it of pure gold.

'I wish I'd known you then. What were you like?'

'Pretty much the same as I am now, I reckon. A bit dafter.'

'You're the least daft person I know.'

I put my arms round her and hold her and it's good, just standing like this, holding, breathing in the smell of her skin. I can feel her breath hot on my neck, my mouth is close to her ear and without knowing that I'm going to say it, I find myself asking, 'Have you loved other girls before?' and my heart starts beating quickly.

'Yes,' she says simply.

I feel a stab of jealousy, which is not fair of me, because after all I did think I loved Grace. I pull away a little so I can see her face.

She looks up at me, her eyes solemn. 'But none that loved me back.'

'Really?'

She nods.

My heart leaps. 'Oh, Eliza . . .' I draw her close again.

Eventually Eliza stirs. 'We should be getting back now, else you'll miss your train.'

'You sound as if you want me to go,' I say teasingly.

'Course not!' She sounds hurt and, to my horror, I see tears in her eyes.

'I was only joking!'

'I know.' She dashes the tears away with her hand. 'Don't take any notice. I told you I were daft.'

I suddenly realize all I've been talking about is myself. 'Eliza, I'm sorry, I've been rattling on . . . how are you, really? How have you been?'

'There isn't time—'

'There is! I'll catch the next train, if necessary . . . the carriage can wait. Tell me . . . I want to know.'

She hesitates.

'Please.'

'Well, it's been funny, like, because part of me kept hoping that you and me . . . somehow it'd work out . . . and that's why I've been putting off getting a place . . . but part of me . . .' She stops, shamefaced. 'I – I've been trying to forget you, that's the truth of it.'

I stare at her, aghast. 'Forget me! Why?'

'Because I didn't think you'd come back.'

'But I promised I would!'

'I didn't know if you meant it, and I thought . . . I thought once you were back home, you'd have second thoughts, like, because after all . . . I'm not a lady like you—'

'*I'm* not a lady! I hate all that!'

'You know what I mean. To toffs like your family, I'm a nobody.'

'We're not toffs!'

'That's what your aunt and cousin looked like to me.'

'Oh, they're much grander than us . . . but anyway, none of that's important!' I seize her hand and shake it, I want her to believe me so much. 'What matters is us, you and me, and how we feel about one another! I love you, truly I do!'

She looks at our two clasped hands, and then she searches my face.

As if she's satisfied with what she sees there, she puts her other hand on top of mine and squeezes it. 'Right.'

'Is that all you can say? "Right"?'

She looks up at me solemnly. 'It's enough, I reckon, don't you?' In the sunshine, her eyes are very blue.

I nod. 'I reckon it is.'

All around us the quiet forest stretches, beech, oak and hornbeam, ancient trees, and I think of other lovers who must have found shelter here, away from the gaze of the world.

'Look, Eliza.'

Behind us is a wild rose in full bloom, its delicate pink flowers trembling slightly, as if, another kind of butterfly, they have just alighted. Breathing in the lovely perfume, I go to pick one, and my thumb brushes against a thorn.

I remember my first day at Wildthorn, how I stood looking through the gate, longing to escape . . .

'Do you realize something? If Aunt Phyllis hadn't sent

351

me to Wildthorn, we'd never have met each other . . . Perhaps I should be thanking her, instead of hating her.'

Eliza smiles. 'That's true enough.'

I offer her the rose and she takes it, and then we are kissing again, a long lingering kiss . . .

With a sigh, I say, 'I must go. But, listen, it won't be long before I see you again.'

She frowns.

'Eliza! I mean it!'

'But . . . what about your studying? . . . And then you'll be off to London . . .'

Now is the moment to ask her, and now I feel sure of her answer. 'Look, I don't want to leave you, but I must, for now. But when I go to London, will you come with me?'

Her eyes widen. 'Come with you?'

'Yes. I'll be sharing a house with other women from the college and you could live with us too.'

'You mean, like a servant?'

'No! Not a servant! Don't be silly!'

'What then?'

I don't know what word to use. 'My – my companion.' I add hastily, 'I don't mean like a paid companion, I mean . . . as my true companion, my equal.'

Eliza's eyes are round, staring at me.

Minutes pass and the trees sigh, as a breeze ruffles their leaves.

Then she says, 'I'm sorry.'

My heart drops to a place I never knew existed.

She's very earnest, very clear. 'That's daft, that is. I

can't live with you as your equal. Those other women in your house, they won't like it. And other folk – what will they think?'

I must say something but my throat has closed up and a drumming in my ears almost drowns out what she's saying, but I hear it clearly, and every word is like a dart piercing the most tender part of me.

She says, 'I won't come to London with you. I can't live with you like that.'

And she's saying more but now I can't hear her because everything at the edge of my vision, the pond, the lilies, the wild rose, the forest, is blurring and all I can see is Eliza getting smaller and smaller and smaller . . .

EPILOGUE

The house is unusually quiet for a Saturday afternoon.

Pausing in the middle of writing my letter, I leave my chair to look out of the window, down at the street where nothing is happening, except a cat licking something in the gutter. I look at the bedroom windows of the houses opposite, at the cloud-filled sky. Then I return to my table.

Papa's pipe-rack, brought down with me to London, rises above the litter of textbooks and papers; I like having the three wise owls watch over me as I study.

Patting one on the head, I pick up my pen with a sigh.

I'm struggling to think what to say to Grace. I've told her all the family news, including the fact that Mamma is glad to have Tom home, although I think she's having a hard time with him. I've told her how much I'm enjoying the classes in Pharmacy and Anatomy, though the Chemistry's more difficult than I expected.

I could tell her that I've been wondering about specializing in mental diseases . . .

For a moment I indulge myself in my favourite daydream, the one where I take charge of a hospital like Wildthorn, only not like Wildthorn, because I see to it that the patients are cared for properly . . .

I won't tell her that I'm thinking of going back there to visit Beatrice – I want to see for myself how she is, find out whether I can do anything for her. But Grace doesn't know Beatrice.

This isn't getting my letter written. When I think of Grace trapped in that house with Charles and baby Richard, I don't think my hopes for the future are going to cheer her up, though she won't begrudge me my happiness, I'm sure.

She is still estranged from her mother and I can't help feeling sorry for my aunt now. Her efforts to secure Grace's happiness have driven her daughter away . . . she is cut off from her grandson . . . and what is left to her?

The door opens and the maid's face appears.

'Nearly finished.'

She comes in and waits a respectful distance away from the table while I add to my letter, telling my cousin that I hope we can somehow meet soon. I send her all my love and sign the letter.

With a sigh, I put it aside and turn to the maid.

'Where is everyone?'

'Miss Gaskin's out to tea and Miss Lloyd and Miss Summers have gone to the British Museum.'

I can't help it – all thoughts of Grace fly from my mind. 'We've over an hour then.'

I look at the maid and she looks at me. Her face is solemn but her eyes are laughing.

We pull our clothes off as fast as we can. The last thing to come off is her housemaid's cap, releasing a tumble of corn-coloured hair.

358

When Eliza turns towards me my breath catches in my throat.

I'm always amazed by her beauty: her creamy white skin, with its faint freckles like a dusting of gold. The first time I saw her naked I was dazzled; I didn't want to take my clothes off because I felt so ugly. But she undid my buttons one by one, and her eyes and her mouth and her hands said *You are beautiful too*, and now I almost believe her.

As we climb on to my narrow bed, the springs creak, making us giggle. And we kiss, gently at first, my hands moving over the smooth warm curves of her body, her hands hot on my skin. But then our mouths become fierce, urgent, hungry, and soon we are dancing, my love and I, dancing together in a rhythm that's easy, sweet and easy . . .

Afterwards, we lie quietly, my arm round Eliza, as she rests with her head on my shoulder, her hair spread like a yellow scarf across my chest.

In a minute I know Eliza will stir and yawn like a cat, showing the pink inside of her mouth. She'll put on her demure dress, her white collar and cuffs, and quench her hair with her cap. Then she'll go and put the kettle on. And when the others return, she'll bring the tea tray into the parlour and they won't have the least idea of what is between us.

Sometimes I can't bear it. I hate pretending all the time, when the others are around . . . the way she stands there, saying *Yes, Miss, No, Miss*. I want to seize her hand and tell them the truth and never mind the consequences.

But Eliza's so stubborn. She won't hear of it. She says that this is the way things are, the way they have to be. But I'm stubborn too, and I'm determined that one day we'll live together openly, as equals, in a home of our own.

In the meantime, we have this.

She opens her eyes and smiles at me and I smile back. The clouds in the window shift and a stripe of pale wintry sunshine falls across our tangled bodies, linking them with its golden band. And I rest my cheek on her head, knowing that, sometimes, this is enough . . . more than enough.

Acknowledgements

I am indebted to many people for their help with my research, in particular Dr Brian Bowering, Dr Alex Contini, Dr Hywel Evans, Professor John Hannavy, Dr Paul Skett and Dr Peter Wothers for their assistance with details of science, medicine and photography.

Thanks to the Writers' Pool and the Royal Literary Fund. I was privileged to be mentored in the early stages of this novel by Julia Darling, sadly missed, and the brilliant Jill Dawson.

Many other people have helped me, including fellow writers and long-suffering friends. I don't have the space to thank them all; they know who they are, and how much I owe them.

A selected list of titles available from
Young Picador

correct at the time of going to press.
reserve the right to show new retail
order than those previously advertised.

Julia Bell
Dirty Work   978-0-330-44571-9   £5.99

Julie Burchill
Sweet   978-0-330-45371-4   £6.99

Lian Hearn
Across the Nightingale Floor   978-0-330-41528-6   £6.99

Jaclyn Moriarty
Becoming Bindy Mackenzie   978-0-330-43885-8   £5.99

Suzanne Phillips
Miss America   978-0-330-44228-2   £5.99

All Pan Macmillan titles can be ordered from our website,
www.panmacmillan.com, or from your local bookshop and
are also available by post from:

Bookpost, PO Box 29, Douglas, Isle of Man IM99 1BQ

Credit cards accepted. For details:
Telephone: 01624 677237
Fax: 01624 670923
Email: bookshop@enterprise.net
www.bookpost.co.uk

Free postage and packing in the United Kingdom